Her Elysium

Also by Emmy Engberts

As Skylar Heart
Hunter/Shattered
Blaze/Unraveled

As Rosa Swann
Mated to the Alpha Serial
The Baby Pact Trilogy
Second Chance Mates Serial
Making a Family Serial
Omegas' Destined Alpha Serial

Her Elysium

Flowers and Keyboards 1

Emmy Engberts

© 5 Times Chaos / Easily Distracted Media
ISBN 97890825832 5 0
NUR 285

20180614IS

This lovely story takes place in the Netherlands. Groningen is a real city, the city I was born in, and have returned to after my studies. The things that happen within this story are fictional, though.
I have chosen to write this story in British English, although there are some elements of American in it as Dutch people grow up with a lot of American TV and we do use some American loan words. Some of these have been kept in place.

1

Fleur

MMORPG = Massive Multiplayer Online Role Playing Game = A world where you can be who you want and don't have to be yourself. Levelling up doesn't happen by year, but by gaining experiences. If I really lived in a world like that, I wouldn't be sixteen, I'd be level thirty by now.

As soon as I walk through the front door, I step out of my favourite high heeled boots and put them to the side. Then I make my way to the kitchen. The house is quiet, but I'm sure Mum is at home. And, sure enough, she's standing in the doorway to the living room waiting for me, her hands on her hips.

"Fleur..." Uh-oh, I don't like that voice.

"Yes?" I turn to the fridge. It's Friday, weekend, time to get ready to game all evening. And you need snacks and drinks for that.

"Can you look my way?" Because, of course.

I turn, in one hand a bag of chips I've just snatched from the counter. "Yes?"

"Don't forget you have to work tomorrow. And we're having dinner at six." She sighs, apparently whatever she was going to say wasn't that important after seeing me like this.

"I know." She acts like I don't know I have to work tomorrow. I've only been the shop assistant at the flower shop since last winter, it's just three more weeks until summer break, I'm pretty sure I remember that I have to work on Saturdays. "Anything else?" Because she's not leaving the kitchen yet, still staring my way.

"Are you going out with Hannah and Sydney tonight?" She dawdles.

"Why?"

"I ran into Hannah's mum at the shops today. She said you never go out with them on Fridays anymore. I thought you said there wasn't anything to do on Fridays and that's why you stay at home all the time." Oh, great. *That* little lie...

"Hannah and Sydney know Friday evenings are for videogames. I go out with them on Saturdays." I turn to the fridge and pull out a bottle of some all-natural fizzy drink, lemon flavour this week. I'm not exactly sure what Mum thinks is so good about these 'all-natural' drinks, they're still sugary and fizzy, which is all I really want from them anyway, but the 'all-natural' on the bottle probably makes her feel better about letting me drink it on the weekends.

"You and your videogames... When are you going to do something social? Like meeting your friends?"

Do I really have to have this argument every other week? "I'm going out with them tomorrow. You don't want me drunk twice every weekend, do you?" The words slip out. They popped into my mind and seemed to instantly transport to my tongue, I didn't mean to speak them.

"What?" I know how to push Mum's buttons though. "What do you mean, *drunk*? You're not drinking alcohol when you're going out, are you?"

Me? I can barely keep myself from laughing. No, alcohol and I aren't friends, even if I'm technically still two years too young to drink it. "I'm not. But that doesn't mean the other girls aren't."

I take my loot upstairs as I hear Mum frantically move through the house. She's going to be obsessed with the idea of me or Hannah and Sydney drinking alcohol for a while. Good. Not that they drink, at least, not when I'm around or when we're out to parties. But getting my control-obsessed Mum scared about the idea gives me some time to myself and will probably keep her off my back for another week.

I dump the chips and the bottle of fizzy on the bed. 'All-natural' fizzy because Mum realised that I don't sleep for days if I have caffeine and sugar at my disposal... Something about me starting to hallucinate last winter when the whole family was around for Christmas dinner... I don't really remember it, I was so into Destruction of Elysium that I kind of forgot to sleep for a few days, and then the Christmas dinner... Well... Ehm... That didn't really end well, my parents sent me to bed after I started talking nonsense to people. DoE had a special Christmas event and I had to catch up a lot of game content to complete it before it ended.

Not that I hadn't pulled a couple of all-nighters before... My parents just never caught me at it.

After that, my parents insisted that I'd get a job to pay for my computer and my videogames myself, especially the subscription games. They probably thought that if I had something to do on the weekends that I wouldn't be able to play as much. But that kind of backfired. Because of the job I was able to afford to upgrade my computer with a better video card and to add an extra monitor to my setup. And now that I'm making and spending my own money... They can't complain. Well, they can, but they can't stop me. I'm pretty sure that wasn't exactly their plan.

I boot my computer and change into my comfortable clothes, just an old T-shirt and some leggings, then I pull my hair up into a sloppy ponytail and slide into my chair. Ah, just me and my computer for the next couple of hours. At least... until six, I guess, but it's only just past two now, so that's long enough.

I pop *Netflix* onto the second screen and then start Destruction of Elysium. Multitasking is one of my greatest skills. I can keep up to date on all sorts of TV series and still get all my gear and level up in videogames. This is probably the biggest advantage of having two screens, being able to do two things at the same time.

Sure, I could just keep a walkthrough of the game on the other screen, but I prefer something to watch, it makes me less likely to get distracted from the game, no matter how weird that sounds. I semi-distract myself from the game so that I won't really be distracted from the game. It makes sense in my head, I promise.

I log onto DoE and select my character, then I click on the most recent show I've been binge-watching, *Pretty Little Liars*, on the other screen. It's one of the few shows I've been meaning to watch but never got around to. And now the show is finished, it seems the perfect moment to actually watch everything in one go. That way at least I won't forget too many of the clues, I hope.

As the show starts to play, I click around in-game. The first couple of minutes usually consist of making sure I collect all the money I made selling things on the market place and then checking the quests I'm working on. But, as has been the case a lot lately, being at the maximum level and mostly only playing endgame content, the normal quests just aren't that interesting anymore and all the quests for epic gear require me to do a lot of dungeons and raids, two things that always take up a lot of time.

I click on the button for the group finder and select some dungeons. Then I sit back and wait, opening the bag of chips as I watch *Pretty Little Liars*.

The class I'm currently playing is a healer. I love being a healer in *Elysium*, even if it happened by accident. I just clicked around when I was creating my character, choosing a race that seemed cool and a class that seemed very cute to match it. It wasn't until a few levels into playing that I realised I wasn't doing a lot of damage, but I was getting quite a lot of healing spells...

My character, *BelleFleur*, is a forest-creature-person. Not a normal elf, but more of a wood elf or a dryad, I don't really know the real name for it. The race is humanoid, but my character's hair is green and literally covered in flowers, which apparently grow there on their own, as they don't wither and I don't think she has to water them. Her skin is green-ish, although she has almost a rose-pink kind of blush on her cheeks, and her gear, especially as a healer, is all designed to look like flowers or to look like they've been made out of flowers, things like that.

She's a combination of cute and in a way a little kick-ass too. I liked it so much when I made her that I didn't really pay attention to what her class description actually was.

A screen pops up to notify me that I can now join a group going into the 'Minotaurs' Labyrinth'. That's fast. Though, I guess there aren't many healers online at this time of day.

I accept the invitation and am immediately transported into the dungeon. I've done this dungeon a couple of times now, it's one of the final dungeons from when the game was just released, and I'm still waiting on some gear drops from the final boss, Asterion. But, with the drop rates of these things... it could take me another fifty run-throughs before I get all of them.

A green message pops up in the chat screen at the bottom.

AlexTheDestroyer: We're doing a speed run. Can you handle that?

I shrug.

BelleFleur: Sure.

It's not like I don't have the skills, it's just that some people are better at doing those things than others. You need a very focused group to do a speed run or we'll just pull too many creatures at the same time for the damage classes to kill off and we'll get hacked to death.

AlexTheDestroyer: Cool. Let's go.

As soon as the message appears, the tank starts running into the first room of the dungeon. A tank is a class who pulls all the mobs or enemy creatures to them, away from the others. That way they're protecting all the other players who are a little more squishy. Mostly because those classes don't wear plated armour, like the healers or damage dealers. The rest of us follow him quickly.

I take a deep breath, moving my fingers over the keys smoothly, reminding myself of each skill that is connected to each key; 'base heal', 'heal over time', 'strong heal', 'dispel debuff', 'group heal' and 'group heal with heal over time'. Just one run over them makes me feel like I can handle anything the game throws at me.

The tank is pretty good, he pulls the mobs from the first two rooms of the dungeon to him as he moves them to the best location to kill them off. And the damage classes seem to be able to kill the creatures in the right order for smooth progression, making this very efficient.

I make sure to heal the tank the most and I rarely have to heal any of the rest of us, a sign that we all probably know this dungeon like the back of our hands. I'm even able to get in some attacks on the mobs myself between the heals. Then the tank moves on and pulls the next couple of rooms.

I'm a little surprised at the ease of this run. It's like the tank just knows how to run this with me, even though I'm pretty sure I've not played with him before.

Then we're at the first boss of the dungeon, a satyr.

> **AlexTheDestroyer:** You know what you need to do?

The message pops up on my screen again.

> **BelleFleur:** Yes. Don't worry. Just don't go stand in the
> shiny stuff.

I can't help the comment, but I've run this dungeon often enough by now, there's a rhythm to it that's easy enough to pick up on.

> **AlexTheDestroyer:** Go!

The tank runs towards the boss and pulls him to one side of the room as the rest of us position ourselves in different corners, ready to sidestep and avoid any big attacks that the boss will throw at us.

I quickly switch between screens to put the TV series on pause, I don't need that distraction during a boss battle. Then, as I switch back, I'm right in time to heal the tank and step out of the way of a beam attack from the satyr.

As I focus on all the shiny things on the screen and on our own health bars, the boss is down before I even realise it. *Wow.*

> **AlexTheDestroyer:** Healer, you're good.
> **BelleFleur:** You're just making it easy on me.

I click on the chest that has appeared at the other side of the room to check for good loot, but nothing interesting pops up.

The rest of the dungeon goes by in much the same fashion. The tank pulls the mobs, the damage dealers try to kill them off as quickly as possible and I try to keep us all alive. If all the dungeons this weekend go like this, I may be able to upgrade two parts of my gear before the end of the weekend, finally allowing me to join in with the latest raids.

Dungeons like this have only one party at a time, so five players at most, but raids can be up to thirty players at a time. I've seen them around, but I've never been able to join in since I've not been playing long enough to have the right level of gear yet.

We all stop in front of the door to the final boss, the big Asterion, the Minotaur of legends. I take a big gulp from my bottle, a little out of breath for the speed we've been running through this.

Another message pops up, this time from one of the damage classes.

> **PathTroying:** You got any preference for location?
> **BelleFleur:** I like to stay on the right side.

This boss has a lot of huge cleaving attacks and by positioning him on the left or right side of the field we can avoid most of them.

AlexTheDestroyer: I'll pull him to the left.

We step into the final room and I throw a shield buff on us all. The damage dealers all throw their own buffs onto themselves so they do more damage and the tank waits for us all to be done.

Then he taunts the boss and runs to the left side of the room. We all make our way to the right side of the room.

And the final boss battle has started.

2
Alex

Tank = The person who voluntarily gets beaten up by creatures, especially by the big boss monsters who would kill the other players in a single swipe. I don't know what it says about my survival instincts that I'm the one who searches the mobs out, rounds them up and takes the beating while others kill them off...

I know I'm teetering on the edge now, the last third of this boss battle takes everything from all of us. The constant damage cones, the bombs scattered around the room, and I'm here, trying to keep the boss, Asterion, as far away from the other players as I can because if he turns to them for even a single moment... One of his big sweeping attacks on them will be the end of the battle for all of us. It would mean that we'd have to start all over with this boss, the last ten minutes of this battle all for nothing.

For a moment I register that my health is running very low, a sliver in angry red, low enough that a single blow could put me out, but just as I flinch, knowing that this will be the end, the health bar is full again. *Oof.*

I look across the field, trying to see the others around Asterion in front of me.

"Dude. Alex." Troy, our ranger, seems a little too relieved by this save, as he lets out a quick sound over the group voice chat.

"Focus on the battle." I can't help it, we're not done yet. Just two more attack sequences from Asterion and we'll have a moment to breathe.

I sidestep an easy frontal cone attack but am back immediately in my previous position. It's not just Troy who needs to focus, me too. I can't let my eyes off the boss or we'll lose. When Asterion prepares for his next sequence of attacks, having just thrown out room-wide damage, we get a moment to breathe and I flex my fingers.

"How are you doing?" I ask. All of us, apart from the healer we've just picked up, are in a group voice chat program, and the three damage class characters in our party, Troy, Aaron and Owen, are all part of my raiding guild.

"The healer keeps a close eye on us and she really knows how to predict where the next attacks will be." Aaron answers me, but just as he does, Asterion is back into action.

"Good." I pull Asterion back into the corner and keep him there, not letting him go, not letting him out of my sight or my range. When I check everyone's health bars I realise that the healer really does keep us all pretty well topped up, enough for almost all of us to withstand at least one attack or accidental misstep.

"You want me to use the final attack?" Owen, our mage, asks.

"Yes. Make this fast and easy, no use letting it drag on for much longer."

"Okay."

A blue circle appears around Asterion, the sign of Owen's final attack. Then there is a huge light and Asterion goes down.

Done. He's down.

I sit back, stretching my arms and fingers for a moment.

"Alex?" Troy's voice is urgent. "What did you think of the healer?"

"She's good." Okay, maybe more than just good. She's been on top of her healing the whole dungeon, apart from that short lapse in attention during the boss battle, but it didn't affect us too badly.

"Yeah. She really is." Troy's somehow excited.

"So?" What's Troy's interest in her?

"Don't let her go yet. We're going to need a healer for this evening and you know that Dylan can't run tonight."

"Ah. Right. Of course." *Crap.* I'd forgotten about that. We recently had one of the healers from the raid guild leave and the second in line is at... I don't even know, but he can't play tonight.

I reach out for the keyboard again, letting my finger fly over the keys.

> **AlexTheDestroyer:** BelleFleur?
> **BelleFleur:** Yes?
> **AlexTheDestroyer:** Ehm. Would you like to do another run with us?
> **BelleFleur:** ??
> **AlexTheDestroyer:** We'd like to try a different dungeon with you and if that goes well... We've got a raid tonight that we need a healer for.
> **BelleFleur:** Sure...
> **BelleFleur:** but my gear isn't good enough for a raid yet.

Eh? I click on her character and pull up her gear screen. She's right, she's going to need at least a few more items before she can join us. It's simple game mechanics, if the average level of your gear isn't over a certain level yet, they're not letting you in the door of the raid. "Guys. She's right. She can't yet."

"What does she need?" Owen is not only our mage but he's also one of our gear crafters, specifically one for magical classes like mages and healers.

"Two Asterion rank set items at least. Either from this dungeon or with dungeon currency." It would be too bad if we had to let her go now, she... she seems to fit right in with us, something that doesn't happen often.

I stand up, start walking around for a moment, still tethered to my computer with my headset, then I return to the keyboard.

> **AlexTheDestroyer:** How much time do you have today? We start the raid at ten.
> **BelleFleur:** Until six and then from seven or so again.

I check the clock, it's half past three now. That means we do have a couple of hours... "Guys?"

"Yeah?" Owen responds.

"Can we run her through some Titans?" Titans are only single boss events, but they're really strong, probably stronger than the boss we just did. On the other hand, they don't require thirty or forty minutes of dungeon to go through before we get to them.

"Hmmm." That's Troy again. "Probably."

> **AlexTheDestroyer:** How many titans have you done?
> **BelleFleur:** The first three.

Okay. Good enough for collecting some fast dungeon currency.

AlexTheDestroyer: We can regroup outside the dungeon
and queue to defeat a couple of them.
BelleFleur: Really?
BelleFleur: I don't want to take you from other stuff, you
don't have to do this…
AlexTheDestroyer: Two birds, one stone. You get the
gear you need and we can do a few trial runs with you
as our healer.
BelleFleur: Okay.
BelleFleur: Sounds good.
BelleFleur: See you on the outside!

BelleFleur walks to the exit of the dungeon and then disappears.

"Are you sure this is a good idea?" I may have sounded confident to BelleFleur, but she's right. Helping her now doesn't mean that she'll be ready to make tonight's raiding. Training a new healer this close to our weekly raiding night, and especially this close to the release of the next raid… I'm not sure it's the best idea.

"Do you *want* to be able to play tonight?" Troy's character also leaves the dungeon and we follow him shortly. "And, how often do none of us die in that dungeon? She's good, just, a little under-geared. Which makes it even more impressive if you ask me."

"Yeah. I guess." He's right, of course, but just the thought of having to train a new player after we just finally reached the top five in raiding guilds… I don't know. It's not the most appealing. At the same time… She is good and she seems to match my, or our, playing style really well.

When I appear in the middle of the city again, I make my way to the closest gear-repair shop. If we're going to get our butts kicked by Titans, I'm going to make sure that my gear doesn't give out on me. A purple message at the bottom of the screen pulls my attention.

> **BelleFleur:** Hi. Is the offer still good?
> **AlexTheDestroyer:** Yes.

I click on her name and invite her to our party, the guys are still in it from the previous dungeon, this way we can all queue up for the same event in the group finder at the same time.

> **BelleFleur:** Hi. Thanks for letting me join, and putting up
>   with me.
> **PathTroying:** No problem.
> **PathTroying:** Why aren't you in a guild?

Oi. I want to say something, but Troy's right, a player like her generally has a guild. Good healers usually don't wander around alone.

> **BelleFleur:** Not very interested. Just been levelling a lot,
>   not been doing a lot of content that requires a guild.

Right. Makes sense, in a way, I know that a lot of players prefer to do the levelling side solo. "Guys, I'm switching from voice chat to some music. I'll be hearing your voices enough tonight."

"Yeah. Yeah. Later." The guys laugh as I disconnect the chat. I turn on my music player and put on some Japanese electronic music, the high number of beats per minute will keep me focused.

> **AlexTheDestroyer:** Are you ready?
> **PathTroying:** Ready
> **BloodyBAaron:** Ready
> **OwenLeFay:** Ready
> **BelleFleur:** Ready

I open the group finder window and queue us for the first three Titans. Because we're a full party, the screen to transport us into the area pops up immediately and I click on the accept button. A few seconds later the load screen appears and we're in the Titan's arena.

I bounce my leg to the beat of the music, my whole body gearing up to start moving again. There is nothing like a Titan battle to get your blood pumping.

> **AlexTheDestroyer:** You know the mechanics of this one?
> **BelleFleur:** Yes.
> **AlexTheDestroyer:** Good.

I run onto the battlefield as I pull the boss with one of my taunts. The vibrations from the music go through my body, making my fingers and my muscles move to the sound of it. The high beats per minute of the song keeps my fingers tap, tap, tapping at the keys.

Around me, light effects, other things moving, it doesn't matter now, it's just me, the music and the guy I need to defeat. I get into a groove, it's almost a trance so I can focus on doing my thing, trusting that the others will do exactly the same, that they know what they're supposed to do and that they're capable of doing it.

The health bar from the Titan in front of me drops to zero faster than I expect and when I look up, I realise that we actually defeated this guy in a single go. No hiccups, no casualties. A single smooth run and we're through.

I laugh, standing up for a moment, walking around to make sure I lose some of my nervous energy. If we keep going like this, getting this new healer up to speed won't be a problem.

When I return to the computer, the others have already left and there is a message in the chat area.

> **BelleFleur:** Again?

I leave the arena and as soon as I'm back in the city, I queue us up again.

So... Wait... This may actually work? We may actually be able to run a raid with a new healer within hours of meeting her?

The next two hours go by really quickly. We're able to defeat every Titan the game throws at us. We only get wiped, all of us defeated until there wasn't anyone standing, twice. The first one was my own fault, and the second one was BelleFleur not paying attention to her own positioning for a moment because she was healing Aaron.

BelleFleur: I've gotta go. Dinner. I'll be back in an hour.

She drops out of the party immediately after that and leaves the game. I check the clock and realise it's ten past six, so she's probably in a hurry. It's not until that point that I realise I forgot to add her as a friend.

Oh, *great*, let's hope she remembers who we are...

I turn the voice chat back on for a moment, right when the guys are laughing really loudly. "What's going on?"

"Well..." Owen has a hard time not laughing so he can actually talk. "Troy was joking that the healer really has the whole flower theme down."

"Yeah? So?"

"Innocent and stuff. He..." Aaron sighs. "Never mind."

I shake my head. "You were being gross again." Really? I leave these guys alone for a moment and they do this?

"Maybe." Troy laughs.

"It's that I can actually punish you for that the next time I see you." Troy goes to the same secondary school as me. "So I'll let you get away with it this time."

"You would have appreciated the joke too." Troy tries to defend himself.

"Really?"

"Maybe." He doesn't sound so convinced anymore.

"Right. Okay, you guys go be gross. I'm getting something to eat." The guys are generally pretty good, but sometimes they forget that I'm a girl too and they make weird jokes that aren't really… girl friendly. I know it's sometimes part of boy-culture, but that doesn't mean I have to like it and I can still call them out for being idiots.

I turn the chat back off and put the headset down. Then I go down the stairs to the kitchen and look in the fridge. It seems like there is food stuff, but I don't feel like making anything.

"Alex?" Dad comes into the kitchen too. "What are you having for dinner?"

"Pizza?" I open the freezer and see that we've got enough of them.

"Sounds good. Your mum won't be back until nine, so it's just the two of us today." He turns the oven on and sits down on a chair, grabbing his tablet to read on.

My mum works a lot of long hours as a psychologist at an inpatient centre for people with autism and anxiety related problems, or something like that, and my dad teaches developmental psychology at university. And yes, they totally met at university… It's totally sappy and they're still totally in love with each other.

And me? I spend my days playing videogames and trying not to fail my biology class.

I walk to the back of the house, where our dog Yukio is trying to cool down a little on the tile floor. When he sees me he jumps up, his little legs scrambling to get to me as fast as he can.

"You want to play with the ball?" I grab his favourite ball and make my way to the back door.

As soon as I throw the ball, he's off, slipping between my leg and the door with his slim body even though there is more space on my other side.

I sit down on a couple of steps and wait as Yukio brings the ball back. Then I throw it again. My mind starts wandering back to this afternoon.

Could it be true? Did we actually find a healer who can match my crazy playing style? If so, that would be really good, right?

3
Fleur

Dungeon = An instanced zone inside a game where you defeat monsters and bosses with a group of people. You can play this with specific players or choose to use a group finder and get assigned random party mates based on their class. Some people prefer one over the other. I like playing with just random people. Though, if I could find a group of people to play with who understood my style... Maybe I could change?

I was late for dinner... Which, of course, made my mum angry. Well, I can't help that the last Titan run took a little longer than I'd expected. Not all runs always go according to plan...

But now I'm stuck putting away the dishes and refilling the dishwasher while I promised the guys in the game that I'd be back at seven. I check the clock, it's already a quarter past seven. I hurry up and put the last plates away.

I don't want to make them wait any longer, even though, during dinner I realised I hadn't actually friended any of them... We were too wrapped up in actually playing and since we were a group already, I guess we kind of forgot... And since I left the party before I shut down the game... I can't just join them again.

I'm a little stupid for someone who is supposedly smart. According to my mum that is, the smart bit, I mean.

"Fleur?" Mum is standing in the doorway again. "Can you be a little more careful? You don't need to break anything."

"Just trying to do this fast." I also try to flash her my best smile.

"Why? Are you going out?" Suddenly she's interested again.

"There's people waiting for me in Destruction of Elysium." I say it before I can stop myself and when I look back up at her, I wish I hadn't because Mum's face falls and she looks very not-amused by my reply. Why doesn't she get that I don't just have a social life offline, but also online?

"The *game?*" She sighs. "Don't you pay a little too much attention to that game? There are actual people out in the world, you know? Actual people who would like to spend time with you."

"And they can. Six nights out of every week. Friday evenings I play videogames." I put the last plates away and turn the dishwasher on.

"I think that you maybe..." She starts following me out of the kitchen but I turn around to her.

"Mum. It's *one* evening. I play online with people living all over the country and all over the world and we all like playing the same thing. We all like doing this. I'm not fighting, I'm not drinking, I'm not doing drugs. I'm not getting into trouble. What more do you want me to do?" I look at her for a moment longer and then run up the stairs to my room, taking them two at a time. It's not like we'll ever agree on this.

"Don't make it too late. You have work tomorrow," Mum calls after me.

"I know." I close my door behind me, making sure not to slam it, and start DoE again, logging on and looking around. I hope I'm not too late and that they haven't already started without me, with a different healer. That would suck, all that chat with my mother for nothing.

A private message appears in the chat box, the text purple instead of green like the party chat from before.

> **AlexTheDestroyer:** You there?
> **BelleFleur:** I'm here!
> **AlexTheDestroyer:** Yes!
> **AlexTheDestroyer:** Been sending your account a message every couple of minutes.
> **BelleFleur:** Yeah, sorry, Mum kept me busy for being late for dinner.
> **AlexTheDestroyer:** Yeah, sorry about that. Hope she didn't give you too much trouble.
> **BelleFleur:** Nothing I'm not used to.

Mum is always on me for things, she just can't seem to accept that I'm not like her. That I'm not into always going to social events and showing up everywhere. I like my dresses and cute clothes well enough, but I also like to just veg out in front of my computer and play videogames. I can do both, but they will have to happen at different times.

> **AlexTheDestroyer:** Okay. Are you ready for another run?
> **BelleFleur:** Yep.

I accept the friend request from AlexTheDestroyer and then the group invite, and suddenly I'm in with the same guys as before.

> **PathTroying:** Welcome back.
> **BelleFleur:** Thanks.

OwenLeFay: We doing more Titans?

BelleFleur: Sure, if that's okay?

AlexTheDestroyer: Should be fine. Just gotta leave a little time for BelleFleur to check out a video about the raid later and get her gear in place.

BelleFleur: You can just call me Fleur.

AlexTheDestroyer: Good. I'm Alex.

OwenLeFay: Owen.

PathTroying: Troy.

BloodyBAaron: Baron would be nice, but just Aaron for me.

I laugh. Right... Whatever.

A screen pops up and we're transported to one of the Titans, Hyperion. His arena is bright, with the sun high in the sky and we're standing in a sort of golden field. Hyperion uses a lot of fire attacks in the first half of the battle.

I want to do this well, if I can get my gear up to the right level today then I can actually do raids, even in just regular group finder settings. Although, I'm pretty sure that these guys are a little more hardcore than me. They seem to be one of those groups that actually run raids according to schedules, and I'm not sure I'm really that type of player...

I throw some buffs on the party and Alex pulls the Titan, forcing us all into action, and I do my best to not let anyone die. At first, it's going very well and I'm on top of everything, always doing the right move at the right time, but then I get distracted by my bottle of fizzy drink standing a little too close to the edge of the desk and I get us all killed.

Crap!

BelleFleur: Sorry.

PathTroying: LOL.

PathTroying: No problem. Happens to us all.

They don't seem to mind, they really don't seem to mind that I just got us wiped.

When we're all back at the starting point and we've all put up our buffs, Alex pulls the Titan again. This time the battle is a lot smoother.

The second half of the battle, the field changes and goes dark, Hyperion's night mode. This is a little more tricky as you can't see all the area of effect spells that well in this light.

Luckily, I don't make another stupid move and we finish Hyperion off easily.

A private message shows up in my chat again.

I have, but the headset is crap and old, and I don't really like doing voice chat, especially with people I barely know...

I check my currency on the character screen and realise that I really need to repair my gear, all the parts are showing with an orange or almost red overlay. I close the screen before I remember I was supposed to be checking my currency, not my gear, and open it again.

I transport out of the Titan arena and find a gear-repair shop nearest to my location. When I reach it, there is a player standing nearby with their name in green, which tells me that they're in my party, and it's Alex. I make my character wave at Alex before I repair my gear.

> **BelleFleur:** I'm ready to go again.
> **AlexTheDestroyer:** Two more, right?
> **BelleFleur:** Yep.

The Titan screen comes up again and we battle another Titan, Oceanus. I need to focus, I really need to focus this time.

It's different when you're playing with people for a longer length of time. When you're not just playing one round or maybe accidentally a few times after another, but to really keep playing with the same players, over and over again. I don't want to let them down after the good runs we've had this afternoon, especially since I still feel like it's a fluke. That these guys have just really mistaken me for someone else. That, I don't know, that it's just some weird prank and I'll wake up tomorrow morning and none of this has happened or something.

But what would be their goal? They're really helping me in the game, no matter whether they actually take me on the raid with them this evening or not. It doesn't really matter right now. So, why would they take on a noobie healer like me?

> **AlexTheDestroyer:** Final one!

It's Rhea again, she wiped us right before I had to go downstairs for dinner. Not going to let that happen this time! Nope! I stay focused, even when Owen missteps and nearly gets killed before one of the huge room-wide attacks and I have to use one of my best healing spells with the longest cooldown timer.

But I'm able to heal us through it, frantically hitting the keys on my mouse and keyboard. Rhea has a couple of insanely high damage attacks, some of which I really have to heal through when they hit Alex, and on top of that she has an attack that creates lava puddles on the floor that we need to stay out of.

I have to look all over the place, making sure I'm not in the wrong spots, making sure everyone's health is up high enough, all of that.

Then the screen changes and we've defeated her.

I sit back, taking a deep breath. *Wow*. That wasn't easy. Let's hope the raids aren't as insane as this, although... we'll also have six times as big a group to play with. More attacks, more lights, more of everything and above all, more to keep track of.

AlexTheDestroyer: You okay?
BelleFleur: Yeah.

I leave the Titan area and, after repairing my gear at the repair shop again, I go in search of the endgame gear shop for the gear that I need.

I look at the gear I'm wearing in my gear screen... It's a cute outfit, but I know that it's not going to last, not if I want to play raids. I buy a chest piece, well, a shirt really, and then boots, my final two pieces of gear that I've needed to upgrade to allow me to go queue for raids.

An envelope blinks in the top of my screen, pulling my attention to it, but I need to find a mailbox to read it. So I hunt one down. It's not too far off from the gear seller, luckily.

It's a letter from AlexTheDestroyer, with an item attached to it. 'Thanks for running with us. I thought you'd enjoy this.'

The attached item is a costume item that my race and gender can wear and it will show up instead of my gear. It's a pale yellow

32

dress with a sort of flower petal shaped skirt that changes from yellow into red at the ends. It's really cute, I've been trying to get my hands on this dress for a while. It's a rare drop from one of the earlier dungeons in the game, but even after running it for fifteen or so times, I've only ever seen it once, and I didn't win the loot roll for it and in the market place they sell it for way too much. *Wow.*

I send a private message to Alex.

> **BelleFleur:** Thanks for the dress!
> **AlexTheDestroyer:** Yeah, no problem. Had it anyway and
>   I can't wear it.

I can't imagine what a tank class like him would look like if he'd be allowed to wear an item like this. It would be... interesting. A character wearing this dress and then standing in front of one of those huge bosses, taking all the hits. Though... I guess it could be fun.

> **AlexTheDestroyer:** Do you want to go watch a
>   walkthrough of the raid? It's early, but you can ask
>   questions if you need to.
> **AlexTheDestroyer:** Also, would you like to join our guild?
>   We're a raiding guild, and it would be nice if you could
>   join us for raids as often as possible, but... You know...

I don't reply yet. It's a sweet offer, and maybe actually meeting some more people in-game would be good. Especially if we all work together as well as the small group I've been playing with.

> **AlexTheDestroyer:** Our main healer had to drop out
>   because of finals and then immediately started her
>   internship afterwards, so she hasn't been around, and
>   our secondary healer isn't always around either. Like
>   today.
> **BelleFleur:** So, I'd be what... your tertiary healer?

AlexTheDestroyer: Back-up Primary?

That makes me laugh out loud. *Right.*

Well, if he makes it sound so attractive… The idea that he may prefer me over the other healer is a little blush-inducing and I feel like he may just be flattering me. But at the same time, having a steady group to quickly do dungeons and maybe even raids with is a nice thing to look forward to.

BelleFleur: Sure. I just can't run late during the week and not at all on Saturdays, day or evening.

AlexTheDestroyer: We can work with that.

He sends me an invite and when I click on accept to join the guild, I'm suddenly surrounded by more people. The chat screen fills up with orange text from people talking about the upcoming raid and just general goofing off.

AlexTheDestroyer: Guys, we've picked up a really awesome healer today, BelleFleur. She'll be running the raid with us this evening. It's gonna be her first, so be nice!

BelleFleur: Hi all.

I don't know what else to type and people start to ask me all sorts of questions, one faster than the next and some of the guys from the party that I ran the Titans with also join in. I try to answer all the questions, which isn't easy. They range from the simple questions like how long I've been playing, to my favourite dungeons, and my favourite soundtrack from a dungeon, which I'm all perfectly fine answering, to the more personal, all of which I don't answer, because I don't like giving out personal information. I thought they may not like that, but it seems they're fine with it, luckily.

BelleFleur: I'm going to watch the raid walkthrough, I'll be back in a bit.

I minimise the game, and start the walkthrough video from someone whose walkthroughs I've used in the past.

Within seconds of it starting, I know that I'm going to be in for a very rough evening. Not just the bosses, but the positioning, the extra members, the mechanics. It's all not just one step harder than the dungeons or a Titan, it's almost three times as hard.

I thought this was going to be fun and interesting, but this seems more like it'll be a lot of me getting my butt kicked... And I kinda feel bad for the guys after all they've done for me this afternoon... They've helped me all day and I'm going to get them killed over and over again...

How was this a good idea?

4
Alex

Healer = Person who makes sure that the rest of us don't die in battle. Their primary target to heal is the tank, though they should always make sure they don't die themselves. A dead tank can be raised from the dead, a dead healer means a wipe for the whole party. Not as much fun. So I guess, target zero should be themselves and other healers, and then their primary targets would be the tanks. When a tank and a healer fit together well, when their play styles match, that's one of the best things in the world. They'd be nearly undefeatable.

I sit back in my chair as I wait for Fleur to return and the rest of the players to finally settle down so we can jump in as soon as possible.

Then a private message pops up.

> **BelleFleur:** I don't think I can do this...
> **BelleFleur:** I'm just going to get you wiped a hundred times until everyone's tired of me.

AlexTheDestroyer: We've all been in that same place, that first time when you run a raid.
AlexTheDestroyer: Don't worry about it. You'll be fine.
BelleFleur: It just seems like so much.

I laugh. Yeah, I know. And, as a tank, it's not as hard for me as it will be for her. Especially the raid we're going to run, it has a good number of healer checks, elements that will put out a huge amount of damage on the whole party that the healers will have to heal through. It's always rough, no matter how experienced the healer is.

AlexTheDestroyer: Which part are you scared of?
BelleFleur: All of it.

I laugh again. Well, at least she's honest, though I think she's totally underestimating her own skills.

AlexTheDestroyer: Well, you won't know unless you give it a try. As long as you know the mechanics you need to keep an eye on, you'll be fine.
BelleFleur: Don't hate me if I get us wiped a hundred times.
AlexTheDestroyer: We'll just start over a hundred-and-one times and get through it. We've got all evening to do this.

Most of us have anyway, and I know the other people won't mind wiping a few times because we have a new healer. It happens, that's part of the game, that's part of creating a group who play together. And having another endgame healer to work with for dungeons and raids is something we all really want. So we're willing to mess up a few times before we get a good fit.

AlexTheDestroyer: We're starting in 20 minutes, are you ready?
BelleFleur: What if I say no?
AlexTheDestroyer: You'll have 20 minutes to prepare.

I can't help but laugh at Fleur. I get her fear. Running this raid for the first time, especially with people who have already done this a good number of times, is scary, but we really have all been in that same situation. And the way I've seen her play this afternoon, I think she'll be fine. She just needs the experience of how the raid really feels to play and then gain some confidence in her skills.

BelleFleur: I'll be right back.

I turn the group voice chat on and it's already quite crowded in there. "Hi everyone. Ready to go?"

Multiple people respond with different variations on "Yes", "Definitely" and "Can we go yet?".

"We're just waiting for the last few members to come online, and I haven't heard from one of the other guild leaders yet, but they should be checking in soon." I look through the text chat in the program to see who of the other guild leaders are online yet. Tonight we're running a raid with three guilds, a large party each. A normal party is five people, but a large party is ten, so double that, and then three guilds... It's always a little chaotic the first ten minutes.

Then one of the other guild leaders comes online, messaging me though the chat program. 'We're almost ready to go. You ready there?'

'Almost.' I check in-game again, but Fleur hasn't returned yet. 'Waiting on a new healer. Hasn't run this raid yet, so may need extra support.'

'Will tell the others. Can you invite us into the chat?' The other guild leader sends me a link and we merge the two voice chats into one big group.

Time for the crazy to begin.

I take a deep breath as I step out of the way of the boss, one of the tanks from the other guild takes over from me as there are too many damage modifiers on me, which means more chance of me actually dying.

"How's she holding up?" I ask of the group, most of us are too focused to actually talk too much during a battle, so in the middle of the battle it's mostly quiet apart from some cursing.

"Holding up well. Hasn't died yet." Troy answers quickly.

"Good." And it's time for me to take my position in front of the boss again as the damage multipliers have either run out or been healed away.

We're doing well, which is no surprise for the most part, as we've run this raid so often, but it still requires a lot of focus. The mechanics are crazy, but not too bad.

Two damage dealers from one of the other guilds suddenly die and then I see both Troy and Aaron go off too.

"What happened?" I nearly step into instead of out of a huge attack from the boss.

"Sorry. Sorry." The tank who is supposed to take care of adds, additional strong creatures that spawn during the boss battle, speaks up. "My fault."

Troy and Aaron are resurrected pretty quickly, and come back into battle. Luckily, stuff doesn't go wrong again for the rest of this boss. When we're all getting ready to walk to the next boss room, I send a message to Fleur.

AlexTheDestroyer: How are you doing?
BelleFleur: Ehh...
BelleFleur: It's insane, but I think I'm holding up.
AlexTheDestroyer: I'd say. Yeah. You're doing well.
BelleFleur: It looks more insane than it really is.

"Alex!" Someone calls me through the group chat. "Get your backside to the next boss."

When I look around me on the screen, everyone else is already gone. "Whoops."

"Focus, dude. Focus," teases Troy.

"Yeah, yeah." It's not like focusing is my best skill and I just got a little distracted by talking to Fleur.

Of course, now it's two sides who will tell me to hurry up. I laugh, but then I'm in the next room and stand with the rest of our group.

One of the other tanks starts pulling the boss and I turn on some damage buffs for my tank. This boss doesn't require more than one tank, as long as the tank and healer can pull it off, so I try to get as much damage in as I can while I also try to get an angle that lets me check in on Fleur. For someone who is doing this raid for the first time, she seems to be pretty on top of everything.

Our luck, running into a healer who actually knows what she's doing and she's not part of a guild yet. With the recent changes in our line-up, this could turn into a great weekend.

W A S D

After we finish the raid, I go off the voice chat. We only got wiped once, and that was on the final boss battle. Fleur felt really responsible for it, even though we were all at fault for not being in the correct spot at the right time a few times. And with a boss with multiple mechanics which all do a lot of damage that quickly adds up to a wipe. The second time went better, everyone was in the spot they were meant to be in and such.

Even though the rest of the guild is hanging out in the group voice chat and having fun, I'm not joining them today. I'm actually going to do a couple of things for my mining skill, where you mine stone and ore, and Fleur invited me to her party, as she's doing the same.

> **BelleFleur:** I'm sooo behind on this gathering skill...
>
> **BelleFleur:** Like, it's twenty levels behind on my main class.
>
> **AlexTheDestroyer:** Well, that's not too bad, is it?

I look at my class and skill screen. I have two gathering skills and one of them hasn't even got to level twenty, but I have no crafting skill over level ten. I tend to just source that out to others in the guild, or sell my gathered items and buy crafted stuff from others in the market place.

> **BelleFleur:** It feels like school.
>
> **BelleFleur:** On track with one skill, but behind on all the rest.
>
> **AlexTheDestroyer:** You mean on track with the only one you like?
>
> **BelleFleur:** Yes.
>
> **BelleFleur:** I'm always ahead in biology

I laugh.

> **AlexTheDestroyer:** I'm always behind in that one.
>
> **AlexTheDestroyer:** I'm ahead in maths.
>
> **BelleFleur:** Maths? Wow.
>
> **BelleFleur:** I'm not that good with numbers.
>
> **AlexTheDestroyer:** For me, just when they make sense. Maths usually makes sense.
>
> **BelleFleur:** I can see that.

> **BelleFleur:** Well, help me out, please. What's the best place for me to gather herbs and stuff right now? You're the one with the numbers.
>
> **AlexTheDestroyer:** Fine, follow me.

I like talking to Fleur. She's funny, even if she may not mean it.

When we get to the location where she can gather items for her harvesting skill, I switch to my mining skill gear and start gathering around the same area. Both the harvesting and mining nodes here, spots where the gatherable items respawn, are the most profitable in the market place, so I come here often to get a little extra stuff to sell off between dungeons and levelling a few other classes and skills.

It's brain-numbing and not very exciting, but that also makes it easier to do other things on the side, like talking to Fleur.

I don't know why, I barely know who she is, but somehow, she makes me feel good.

W A S D

A loud knock on my door startles me as I look up from the game, pulling me out of a trance.

"Yeah." My voice is groggy.

"It's six in the morning." Mum opens the door a little, looking at me. "Have you played all night?"

What? I check my phone but it really is six in the morning. *Ack!* "Apparently."

"Well, luckily it's the weekend." She shakes her head. "But you may want to get some sleep."

"Thanks. Will do."

"Night." She closes the door behind her and I turn back to the game.

I should have realised how much time has passed, Fleur and I both levelled a new skill up to level fifteen, something that tends to take a good couple of hours.

A message from Fleur is waiting for me.

> **BelleFleur:** Alex?
> **BelleFleur:** You there?
> **AlexTheDestroyer:** Yeah. Sorry. Mum came in.
> **BelleFleur:** Awkward.
> **AlexTheDestroyer:** Yeah. Especially when she says it's six in the morning...
> **BelleFleur:** Don't joke.

Her messages stop for a moment.

> **BelleFleur:** Crap! I have to be at work in three hours.

I remember her saying something about not being able to play during the day on Saturdays... I guess this is why.

> **AlexTheDestroyer:** Oops?
> **BelleFleur:** Wouldn't be the first time...
> **BelleFleur:** Crap...
> **BelleFleur:** My mum's going to be furious...
> **BelleFleur:** I'm gonna go, see if I can get at least an hour and a half of sleep or something...
> **AlexTheDestroyer:** Sorry for keeping you up.
> **AlexTheDestroyer:** See you tonight?
> **BelleFleur:** Tomorrow.
> **BelleFleur:** I'm seeing friends tonight.
> **AlexTheDestroyer:** Aren't I your friend?

I know, it's a little bold, and looking at it after I've already sent it, makes me feel a little awkward, but I couldn't help myself saying it. It feels like we've got to know each other so quickly. And, yeah, I tend to say brash things when I'm tired.

> **BelleFleur:** One of those real-life friends things. Those I share the meat-space with and such.

At least she's taking it well.

> **AlexTheDestroyer:** Well, I guess meat-space can never beat the digital, right?
> **BelleFleur:** I don't know. I had fun tonight.

The little flip my stomach makes tells me I may be a little too invested in this thing we've got going on. Definitely too invested for someone I've met online in a videogame just yesterday…

> **BelleFleur:** But I really need to go now.
> **BelleFleur:** See you tomorrow.
> **AlexTheDestroyer:** See you tomorrow.

And BelleFleur logs off.

I'm glad I don't have a job, but it's still bad that I've kept Fleur up all night. Even though we both didn't mean to, it still wasn't a good idea. But I guess that's what happens when you play and have fun together. It's been a long time since I've had this much fun with someone and I hope Fleur doesn't get into too much trouble...

Crap. Now I feel bad for her. And I guess I should really go to bed too...

Although, I have a feeling that sleep may not happen any time soon.

Just a hunch, you know.

5
Fleur

Guild = Group of people you play a game together with more closely. You often band together to defeat dungeons and raids but also to just talk to each other or to help others out. Sometimes guilds even get together offline…

I can't believe I stayed up all night. *All night!* And I didn't even realise it. But now I'm standing behind the counter of the flower shop I really do feel it. I'm exhausted and there is just not a lot to do. I don't know if it's the time of the year or what, but we've barely had any customers yet and it's almost twelve. I'm almost falling asleep standing up, which is a skill not unknown to me.

I'm not sure if levelling that new class was worth not sleeping all night, but talking to Alex definitely was. He's smart and funny and knows so much about Destruction of Elysium and other videogames. He totally made me forget about what time it was and it wasn't until he mentioned it that I realised how much time had passed. Typical. Of course… I'm having to pay for that now.

A customer walks into the shop and when I look up I realise it's not a customer at all but my best friend, Jade. She dawdles around the shop for a moment before she comes over to the counter. "Morning." She looks me over, way too awake herself.

"Ugh." I have very few words this morning, especially to people who are too chipper and who I don't have to be super sweet to so I won't scare them out of the shop.

"You look like you haven't slept in days." Jade laughs.

"Just not last night." I lean onto the counter, hoping that a change in position will help.

"Why?"

"Videogames."

"Uh-oh." She pulls a face. She doesn't get my interest in them, but that's okay, we share other hobbies, like TV show fandoms.

"Met a guy online yesterday and we played all night." I want to talk to someone about this and no way I'm telling my parents or one of my 'mother approved' friends.

"Is this like... normal play or adult play?" She looks at me with her perfectly shaped eyebrows raised.

"Normal play..." I shake my head. "We just played the game. Nothing fancy."

"Fancy enough to keep you awake all night though..." She wiggles her eyebrows, her dark eyes shimmering in delight.

"He's just really interesting. He's like a year older than we are, so in his last but one year of secondary school and he's like really, really good at the game." I know it sounds silly, but I was impressed. And for some guy to be interested in me... That doesn't happen often. Usually I'm just the girl in the corner who nobody pays attention to, the one girl at a party not to get much interest from the guys. And I don't mind that much, it gives me more time for games and other fun stuff.

Jade laughs. "Well, sounds like your type then..." She turns around and looks at the shop. "What else do you know?"

"He plays a lot of videogames and he runs one of the best raiding guilds in Destruction of Elysium. And he invited me to play together with them last night." I can't help but squee a little. The thought that I may be good enough to run with them is still a little unreal to me.

"That's good, right? Like, really good?" She may not get my obsession with videogames, but she sort of gets that they mean a lot to me and she did catch some of my rambling about game mechanics, I think.

I nod. "Really, really good."

"How was it?"

"I can't even explain. Running that raid... *Wow*. So much going on, but then these people with me were like veterans at this raid, so I had to make sure I kept up with them and all. And I'm still like this newbie and everything..."

"Well, if he thought you could do it."

"He did. And he was right, even though it was scary... But we made it until the end." I take a deep breath, frowning. "He asked me to play again this evening."

"And that's a bad thing, why?"

"I promised the girls I'd go out with them. I also told my mum I would go with them." I sigh. "I don't mind, usually, but today... I don't know. I wish I didn't have to. But if I cancel now, my mum's going to be annoying again all week."

"True." Jade sighs. "But still, you'll be tired."

"You don't think my mum cares about that, do you? If she finds out I stayed up all night gaming again... I don't know what she'll do." I don't want to deal with that. Not now, not again.

Last time was bad enough, she took my internet away for three days, both the internet for my computer and the wifi for my phone. I don't know what 'responsible' way she'll come up with to punish me this time.

It's just stupid. I'm sixteen, I can have some responsibilities, you know? But, of course not. Not me. Not little me. Little me with a track record of making stupid mistakes... Stupid forgetful mistakes. Well, sorry for not having the same brain as she has, a brain that can remember things normally.

"Well, then you'll have to go." Jade doesn't exactly sound that sorry though.

"Yep."

"Need me to get you some caffeine?"

"Yes, please." My parents won't like it, but I don't care. Caffeine is on my 'no-no' list, but my parents are not here and I need the energy to keep going today. I'm only halfway through my work day, I'll have to get through the whole evening too.

"I'll be right back. Don't fall asleep." She grins, wiggling her fingers at me as she turns around.

Like I can.

Right as Jade walks out, two customers come in. Each of them wants a bouquet of flowers, but, of course, none of the ones in the shop appeal to them. So I have to put them together myself. I like doing this, the finding the right flowers, making the bouquet look the fullest and prettiest it can be. It's fun to do. But the exhaustion also pulls on me, which makes this all a little harder.

"There you go. Have a lovely weekend." I hand the bouquet to the second customer and she leaves the shop with a big smile. That's the best part, making people happy.

My boss, Andrew, comes through from the back. "How are you holding up?" He carries in two more bouquets and puts them into buckets.

"Pretty good."

"Did I hear Jade earlier?" He comes over to the counter.

"Yeah. She'll bring you a coffee too, don't worry."

"Too?" Andrew looks at me pointedly.

"I'm working all day and then I'm out with friends tonight. I need the caffeine." I shrug. "It's that or sugar."

"Caffeine is fine." Andrew rolls his eyes, smiling. I may only get a little jittery from caffeine but I seriously start bouncing off the walls after too much sugar. He knows, he's seen it before.

Just then, Jade comes back into the shop, carrying three coffees. She hands me the iced coffee and then hands Andrew one of the other cups.

"Thanks, I owe you one." He stretches as he walks to the back of the shop. "You two, don't go breaking stuff. Thanks."

I look after him and roll my eyes. Right... because that's what we do. Break stuff. Well, not usually anyway.

I take a sip from the coffee, the cool drink clearing my mind a little. At least this is nice. Now, if I could only survive the rest of the day...

W A S D

I stumble into the house. It's late, but at least I made it through most of the night. I'm so exhausted that I slump down on the stairs to take off my shoes.

Dad opens the door to the living room. "You back?"

"What does it look like?" I sigh and I stare at him, too tired to even come up with a smarter remark.

"You look like you're home. You want something to eat or drink? We're watching a film, want to join?" Too awake for my brain.

"No thanks. I'm off to bed." I've been awake for more than thirty-six hours by now and that includes a day of school *and* a day of work.

"Okay. Goodnight." He smiles and goes back into the living room, closing the door behind him.

"Night," I mumble at the door and then start climbing the stairs. During times like this I wished I had a bedroom downstairs.

I've been mainlining coffee all day and just crashed on my way home. Which is what happens after so much caffeine. I close the door behind me, slumping onto the bed, but even as I almost curl up, I reach out and hit the power button on my computer. I may be exhausted, but I still want to go check out DoE.

As the computer boots I pull myself out of bed and slide into the chair. Then I start the game and log on, typing the password wrong twice before I get it correct. Because, of course, lack of brain power.

As soon as my character appears and the world forms around me, a purple message shows up and my heart skips a little.

    AlexTheDestroyer: I thought you wouldn't be online today?

I laugh. Yeah, I remember saying that. But Alex has been on my mind most of today and I just couldn't not check in.

    BelleFleur: Just checking my market place and messages.

Sort of...

> **AlexTheDestroyer:** Did you survive today without sleeping?
> **BelleFleur:** Ehh...
> **BelleFleur:** Something to do with a lot of caffeine.
> **AlexTheDestroyer:** Whoops.
> **BelleFleur:** Yes.
> **BelleFleur:** What did you do today?
> **AlexTheDestroyer:** Hunted down some members for their contribution for the guild meeting in three weeks.
> **BelleFleur:** Meeting?
> **AlexTheDestroyer:** Yeah, the guild and some of the members who raid with us a lot get together and we're having a barbecue and stuff.
> **AlexTheDestroyer:** It's fun. We get to see each other face to face instead of just talking through a program or seeing each other in the game.

Seeing Alex in person? My heart does that 'skipping a little' thing again. Would it be too forward to ask where it is? If it's close to here…

> **AlexTheDestroyer:** Would you like to come? I know you've only been part of the guild for like... a day, but it may be fun.

Really? Could I? Would my mum even let me?

But at the same time, depending on when it is or where it is or if it's already summer break… It shouldn't be too hard to make this work...

And I'll be able to see Alex. Which feels a lot more exciting than it should feel, right?

> **BelleFleur:** Where is it?
> **AlexTheDestroyer:** It's at a barbecue grill place near my home in Groningen. It's just the afternoon and into the early evening. We've got people coming from all over

the place, so we can't make it too late because they'll
have to go home again.

Groningen?

BelleFleur: That's just an hour away for me.

That close? Alex lives that close?

AlexTheDestroyer: Really?
BelleFleur: When is it?
AlexTheDestroyer: Saturday, three weeks from now.
AlexTheDestroyer: Though, I guess Saturdays would be
hard for you...

Yeah. Saturdays aren't the best for me to work with, but I
get why they'd do it on a Saturday, better connections with buses
and trains and stuff.

BelleFleur: I could see if I can leave early from my job,
and it's only an hour away, so...
AlexTheDestroyer: So, you'd like to come?

Does he sound excited about that? Or is he just being
friendly? I wish I knew, but asking might be a little weird,
especially if he's just a friendly person. *Argh.* I wish this was
easier. I wish there was like an option to check someone's 'friend
level' with like a click of a mouse like you can in dating games
sometimes. Like, this person is 'friendly', 'slightly interested',
'flirting', or whatever you want to come up with.

BelleFleur: Yeah. Though I don't know if I'll be allowed.
Parents and stuff...
AlexTheDestroyer: I get that.
AlexTheDestroyer: I guess I could just write you down as
a maybe. And if you do come, you can bring money
with you for the drinks and food and stuff then. Sound
good?

This is actually going to happen? Like. Actually? He's not just being nice, but he's actually asking me to come?

> **BelleFleur:** Yeah. Thanks.
> **AlexTheDestroyer:** Great!
> **AlexTheDestroyer:** Are you coming to join us in a dungeon or raid, or are you going to sleep?
> **BelleFleur:** I'd love to do a dungeon.
> **BelleFleur:** But I should go to sleep.

Because every time I type, I have to retype each word three times before anything makes sense. I may really want to join them, but I need sleep.

> **AlexTheDestroyer:** Sounds like a better plan.
> **AlexTheDestroyer:** Sweet dreams, Flower.

This *is* flirting, right? I'm not just making things up? I'm too surprised and don't know what to reply right now.

> **BelleFleur:** Have a good raid.

I quickly log out, my face burning.

Have a good raid? What kind of dull goodbye is that?

But my brain may have gone into a little bit of a haywire status, because even though I'm so exhausted I'm almost falling asleep in my chair, my brain is in overdrive and my heart isn't far behind.

Dammit. I'm supposed to be going to sleep, but now I'm not sure how easy that will be.

I may be seeing Alex in three weeks. I'm already excited and I don't even know if I'll be allowed to go…

6
Alex

DPS = Damage Per Second = Shorthand to refer to classes that are damage dealers. Their most important attribute is their ability to do as much damage to monsters as possible in the least amount of time, so they have to have a high Damage Per Second. I sometimes think more of them as 'those who can't tank or heal', but I'm biased, I prefer being a tank mainly and a healer secondary. I'm no good as a DPS class, I always die.

"Was it a stupid idea?" I lean back against the bed in Troy's room, my laptop next to me as I stare out of his window.

"Asking Fleur to come to the meet?" His answer is slow, he's apparently actually doing his homework, something I've been trying all afternoon and failing.

"Yes."

"You're asking me this, again. After I've given you an answer six times already?" He now turns to me, frowning.

"Yeah?" I've asked him that often? I thought it was only twice, maybe. Hmm.

He rolls his eyes. "Asking her was fine. She can choose if she wants to come herself. Just, don't get your hopes up too much." He turns back to his desk.

"Why?"

"You may have fallen head over heels, but that doesn't mean it's the same for her."

"I know. I know." It's not like I'm not aware of that. It's just... Meeting a girl like Fleur and having her be a healer who matches my play style and she just sounds so sweet and she's like… sexy smart. I guess it's the perfect recipe for me. And I guess I'm just ready for a new girlfriend, no matter how silly that sounds.

"Now. Do your homework or you're going to get written up. You can't have that happen in the final weeks. Not after being good all year."

"Fine, fine." I grab my laptop, searching for the assignments we have for the week. There's not much, it's the final weeks of the school year after all, only two weeks away from exams. But still, the weather is so nice, I don't want to do my homework.

I wish I was better at making the jump from knowing what I should be doing to actually doing something. After I open the assignment I look up for a moment, out the window. "Do you think the weather will be good for the meet?"

"Alex..." Troy turns back to me. "Go do your homework, or at least let me do mine. If I get written up, you know my mum isn't going to let me come to the meet, which means, no showing up for you either." He looks at me flatly. "So, whatever, but just let me do this, yeah? You promised you wouldn't distract me if I let you do your homework here."

"Yeah, yeah." I push myself up, standing up and taking a few steps around the room. He's right. I tried doing homework at home, but it didn't work, so I begged Troy to let me come and do it here. "It's just..." Hard to concentrate. Different from usual. I'm too easily distracted.

"I know." Troy's been my best friend for years. The only reason he puts up with me is that I'm the only one who can kick his butt at games he knows he would be best at otherwise. "But don't let this year fall into the gutter just for that. Yeah? You can talk to Fleur later today. But you do have to pass this year or we're going to have to find another tank for raiding." He turns back to his desk. "And you know how hard that's going to be, especially because I don't know if Fleur will want to stay in the guild if you're not there." I can hear the teasing in his voice, but apparently that's what I needed to hear. Because I sit down again, grab my laptop and scan the assignment for next week.

I can do this.

I hope...

W A S D

BelleFleur: I asked my mum, but I'm still not sure if I'm allowed.

I frown at the screen. It's only one week until the meet. One week of exams almost twice a day and then we've got the guild meet. And one week until Fleur will or will not show up.

I get it, but that doesn't mean I'm not frustrated. Fleur's a year younger than me and even my mum won't let me get to these meets on my own. But it's still annoying that I won't know if she'll be there until she actually shows up, or not. I guess I'm just nervous.

I wish I could make it easier on Fleur, but I know that talking to some random person, me, won't help her parents feel safer about her going.

At least I've got Troy. Somehow, having a boy with me makes my parents think it's safer. Though… I don't know if it has to do with me being a girl, or my *slight* issue with hyperactivity and a lack of impulse control. Maybe they're just scared I'll get lost or something. Which… I don't know. It's much more likely that I'll have to find Troy in the middle of nowhere when he gets himself lost yet again rather than the other way around. But with parents… you never really know why they think some things are safer than others. And I've kind of stopped asking them 'why' when it comes to their insistence that I don't go places on my own.

AlexTheDestroyer: Well, we'll just have to hope for a
while longer.

Right? That's not weird to say? I don't know anymore. How do you talk normally to a girl you've just met but can't forget about? Because I'm sure that I haven't had to deal with this awkwardness in a long time, at least not with butterflies like this. It's making me jittery.

BelleFleur: Yeah.
BelleFleur: You've also got exams next week, right? Your
parents letting you play DoE during the week?

Like they can stop me. I almost say it, but reality is, they can totally stop me. If I don't pass my exams… Well, Troy was right, my parents would very likely do something to prevent me from playing this summer and probably even make it harder for me to play next year. Which means the guild would have to find a new tank to do raids with, which isn't easy and could pull the whole guild apart.

My parents only let me play so easily because I've got good grades and I can prove to them I'm taking my classes seriously while also being somewhat responsible in my sleeping patterns. It's still a learning process...

> **AlexTheDestroyer:** They don't care as long as I keep getting good grades.

Better answer and still the truth.

> **BelleFleur:** I wish it was that easy for me...
> **BelleFleur:** But at least they're letting me on in the evenings. So we can still play.
> **AlexTheDestroyer:** Good.

The butterflies in my stomach do a little hyperactive dance. Playing together with Fleur in the evenings will be a nice reward for working my butt off during the day. Which I'm going to need, especially since my mind will be all over the place from exhaustion. Knowing that I'll be able to play together with Fleur will keep me motivated, I hope.

> **BelleFleur:** Well, hit that queue button so we can go play.
> **AlexTheDestroyer:** Sounds like a plan.

I click through a couple of menus and sign us up for a random dungeon to run, not too complicated, but enough to keep us entertained.

I really don't want to think about the exam I'll be having in about twelve hours. I just hope I have prepared enough for this, because it's going to be hard. These are the last exams before my final year. Next year will be what everything depends on, what University of Applied Sciences I can get into and everything.

A screen pops up and I click to accept the invitation for the dungeon. Okay, game mode back on.

Nothing but the mobs, the bosses and the other players from here on out.

One last night before the real stress starts.

⌨ W A S D

"Alex?" Aaron's voice pulls me from my thoughts as he suddenly speaks in the group voice chat.

"Yeah?" I stare at the screen in front of me. I'm looking over some exam notes for tomorrow's exam while hanging out in the voice chat, since I bore easily.

"You've got everything set up for the meet, right?"

"Yes. Got the venue, got people's payments, got all I need, I think. Why?"

"Dunno, bored." He sighs. "There's nobody here."

I look to the side, at my phone. "It's almost four in the afternoon. Everyone is studying, taking exams or working."

"Ah, maybe."

"No, not maybe. Pretty definitely." I laugh a little. "Go make some triangle flag banner thingies or whatever if you're bored." Braining goes really well after two exams and now studying for tomorrow's exams.

"Really?"

I shake my head. Why is Aaron so surprised by my idea? "If you want to. I'm not going to carry it over there for you though. You can do that yourself. But yeah, if you're bored, go make banners or something game related to put on the tables or whatever."

"You studying French by any chance?"

"Oui," I grumble.

"Ah." Sounds like that solves his mystery.

"Why?"

"You get grumpy when you have to do French." I can hear him moving around. "Okay, fine. You go study, I'll entertain myself until Troy comes on."

"He won't be on for a few more hours." I can't help but snicker, Aaron isn't that good at entertaining himself.

"Why?" This time it's Aaron who sounds suspicious.

"He's got an exam until five and then has to do stuff with his family."

"Fine. I'll wait for someone else then. You go study your French." I see him log out of the program and get back to my notes.

Why my parents want me to study French, I don't know. Apart from France being one of the countries my parents love to visit, I don't really have a connection with it. This was the one class my parents thought would be a good idea for me to take for some reason, and they kept insisting. I only took it since I had to choose an extra language class anyway...

I grab my book and start walking through my room, trying to memorise the words on the page. I've been at this for at least two hours but I still feel like it's not going to work and that makes me feel even worse about French because I just want to pass all my classes, even this one.

When my phone rings, I take the distraction. I put the book down and pick up the phone, seeing it's Cerise. "Hey."

"Oh, you sound relieved." Cerise laughs. "Still studying?" Cerise is one of our DPS from the guild. She's a mage, like Owen, but she isn't around as often since her Higher Vocational Education classes and her part-time job kind of make it harder for her to be on every evening.

"Yeah," I grumble, letting myself fall onto the bed. "What's up?"

"Just checking in on you. Making sure you're actually working."

"And you're interrupting my study time for that?" I side-eye the book I just dropped.

"Yeah, you can't study for hours on end anyway. You're in need of a break."

"Okay. So what was so important for you to break my study session?" I make myself comfortable. I like talking to Cerise on the phone, she sometimes seems to understand me better than the guys do. The guys can sometimes be a little... brute-ish.

"Well. I was thinking..."

"Hmm, hmm." It's never a good thing when she starts like that.

"You know how it's my birthday in like... two months, right?" Cerise's voice goes up.

"Yes..."

"And you know how I usually don't really celebrate it, right?"

"Yeah..." Normally we just exchange gifts at a guild meet or something like that. My birthday is also over the summer, so it's easier. That way we don't have to try to get together three times over summer break.

"Well. I was thinking... Since we've got to know quite a few new girls in DoE, maybe we can do like a girls' night, or a girls' weekend or something? What do you think?"

"Ehh. What did you specifically have in mind?" Because in my mind, there's just pink and nail polish and stuff like that when I hear 'girls' night'.

"Well, I have a good internet connection and I can probably get my parents to give me the house for a night. And you've seen how many people we can house round the dining room table..." She lets out a laugh. "I could, of course, add pink to it and we could do a face painting competition to find out who can make themselves look the most like a game character..."

"Very funny. But I like the idea." I shake my head, also laughing. "Of the party, not the face painting. Though, you can go ahead with that if you'd like to." I shrug, though I know she can't see it. "Were you thinking about a shared party?"

"Yeah. If you'd like. It's not as if I'd invite people you don't know, it's just gonna be the girls from the guilds. Unless you've already planned something?"

"I'd planned not to do much at all, really. It's not like it's going to be important for me and with the guild meet and stuff so close to it. This sounds way better."

"Good." I can hear the smile in Cerise's voice. "We'll talk specifics at the meet. I need to go now. There's people expecting stuff of me." She lets out an exaggerated sigh. "And, hey, did I remind you yet that Fleur *may* be at the meet this weekend? Just, you know, to stress you out. Bye!" And she quickly disconnects the line, but I can still hear her laugh before she does so.

She's so evil, so mean. Like I need the reminder. Like I don't remind myself of that every moment. I've talked to Fleur a few times this week, we're both so busy with exams that it's not easy. But even though it's annoying for me, at least I know I'm going to the meet. And no matter whether or not Fleur is coming, it'll be a fun day anyway.

But for Fleur... To not know if she'll be able to come or at what time... I can't imagine how frustrating it must be for her, but at the same time... Yeah. Parents...

I really wish this was easier. I wish I could talk to her or meet her. But for now, it's all just in game and it may have raised my hopes a little too much...

Maybe.

Probably.

Argh!

7
Fleur

Patch = Update for the game, like patching up something broken. Usually they come in two variations. The first one is weekly updates where they fix bugs and things like that and the second one is almost more of an upgrade than an update. These bigger patches often include more dungeons and other content between big game expansions. One of the things often added during these are raids and endgame dungeons.

I'm bouncing my leg as I wait for DoE to update. Of course, it's the day before the meet and the game needs to update even though I'm itching to log on... My final exam ended late and I got home just in time for dinner. But now I'm done. Today was my final day of term before summer break and there's nothing I want to do more than spend the whole evening with the guild.

I stand up, the update is going to take a while apparently, so I walk downstairs and grab a cool bottle of fizzy drink from the fridge. Then I step out into the garden where Mum and Dad are still sitting in the sun, the plates from their desserts still on the table between them.

"Mum?" I lean against the door.

"Yes?" She looks at me, her sunglasses reflecting me like a funny mirror.

"Do you know about tomorrow yet?" I try not to sigh, because that only makes her annoyed, and when she's annoyed I'm likely not getting anything at all.

"This again?" She turns back. "Like I said. I don't know yet. I'm not sure if it's a good idea at all, you know that."

"I studied. I went to all my classes. I worked hard. I deserve some fun."

"Yes. You deserve fun. But why does it have to be with people you've only met online and you've never actually talked to? You can have fun with Hannah, Sydney or even that girl, Jade, from your work. Why do you have to look online for that?"

"I didn't look for them online. They're just other people who also play the same game and we play together a lot. They're not scary or evil or whatever. We just wanna hang out in real life for once." We've been having this discussion every time going to the meet comes up. "It's not like it's somewhere scary, they've just booked the outside tables at a barbecue grill place and it's only an hour away by bus."

"You've got work tomorrow." Which is a lame excuse, as she always bothers me that I should go out with my friends, at least the ones she approves of, after work all the time.

"I wish you'd consider it." I turn back to the house, escaping. Because as long as she's not said 'no', there's still a chance for a 'yes', even though I know that the chance is slim at this point.

I make my way up the stairs and lock myself in my room. The game wants me to log in again, which means the update has finally finished.

Right on time...

I sit down and as soon as I appear in game, a message from Alex appears.

> **AlexTheDestroyer:** Any news yet?
> **BelleFleur:** No.
> **BelleFleur:** I just wish she'd make up her mind. This is driving me crazy...
> **AlexTheDestroyer:** Yeah...
> **AlexTheDestroyer:** Anyway, how did your final exam go?

I laugh. Sure, leave it to Alex to ask the hard questions first.

> **BelleFleur:** I think I did well enough. You?
> **AlexTheDestroyer:** Destroyed it.

I can't help the smile, a fuzzy feeling in my stomach, which happens every time he makes me laugh at one of his lame jokes.

> **BelleFleur:** Right...
> **AlexTheDestroyer:** Hey, you got any preference for drinks or snacks or whatever? Or anything you can't eat?
> **BelleFleur:** Nope. Luckily not.
> **AlexTheDestroyer:** Cool.
> **AlexTheDestroyer:** So, you want to group up and get some dungeons done or something?
> **BelleFleur:** Yes, please.
> **BelleFleur:** I want to get this crazy thing called school out of my head and dive into the not-so-normal world of dungeons and monsters and magic.

I make myself comfortable as I wait for Alex to invite me to his party, but when I click the accept button, I see it's just us.

> **BelleFleur:** No others?

Ah. Yeah. With me not knowing if I'm going, even though I really want to, we kind of stopped discussing the meet a few days ago.

Now it's just nerves, nerves about yes or no for going and nerves about what would happen if I'd be allowed to go...

WASD

"Hey!" Jade prances into the flower shop, a big smile on her face. "I see someone is dressed for the summer. Or is it a date?" She wiggles her eyebrows.

"Don't say that..." I close my eyes. "I don't want anyone to put that idea in my mum's head, even if she's not here. This morning she looked at me and actually asked me if I'm dressing up for someone special today. I, of course, denied it, but I don't want to give her any more reasons to tell me I can't go."

"Still a no then?" She leans onto the counter, looking at me.

"She had this *great* idea this morning..." I sigh, playing with a few flower petals on the counter. "She may allow me to go. But... she wants to come too."

"What?"

"Yeah. I don't want her there when I'm meeting Alex for the first time. 'Hey, I'm Fleur, I know we talk and joke all the time online, so much so that I'm doubting if we haven't been flirting or something. Oh, and this is my mum...'" I groan.

"Well, it's some progress..." Jade shrugs. "But she doesn't have to go to the actual meet with you, right? She could just drop you off or something and stay nearby?"

"Yeah, I said the same. But she answered with more of a 'we'll see' than a 'yes' or 'no'. So I have no idea, still."

"So are you looking forward to finally meeting Alex? Meeting Mister Funny-and-Cute?" Jade grins, leaning closer. "You gonna jump him and kiss him when you meet?"

My cheeks heat up immediately at that thought, my mouth opening, but no sounds coming out. "Don't... I don't... I don't know." I put my hands on my cheeks, but it's no use, they're scorching under my hands, even in the heat of the shop.

But Jade just looks at me, a glint in her eyes. "Busted! You've thought of it. You want to jump his bones."

"I don't. I don't even know him. I just know he's funny and sweet. I don't know anything else about him." Not that I wouldn't like to. Not that I wouldn't like touching him and seeing where things will go.

Though, with today's weather, probably not very far. It's already hot and the day has just started. I can't imagine how hot it will be this afternoon when the meet actually takes place.

I let out a deep breath. "Is this going to be good enough? I don't want to look overdressed, but I also don't want to look like I just threw something on." I look down at my dress. "Alex said the meet would be outside, so there should be a little breeze, right?"

"You're going to wear that?" Jade steps around the counter, looking at me.

"Without the apron, of course." I laugh as I hold it aside to show the whole dress. It's just a simple summer dress with big flower patterns on it. It's probably the 'most summery while still decently covering' dress that I have.

"Looks pretty." Jade nods appreciatively. "Do you have like... a hat to go with it or something?"

"A hat?"

"Yes. Against the summer sun, but also, this dress requires a hat. A big summery hat."

"I don't have one." Because, when would I ever think of that?

"No worries. I'll get you one before the end of the day. Just make sure you personalise it with flowers or something. Make it more *you*." Jade checks her phone. "Okay, got to go. Break's over." She smiles and I can see a little mischief in it. "We'll get you an amazing outfit, and maybe even a little bit of makeup before the end of the day. That way your mum *has* to let you go."

"Sounds more like she'd have all the more reason not to..." I shake my head, excited and scared at the same time. "Okay. Fine. You do what you think is best. It's not like I've got much experience with dating, or even going on dates..." Not that I have no experience with it, but guys usually just aren't that interested in me, especially not when they can have one of my friends. And when I do have one of those dates, I always know what to wear because I know the type of things those guys like, the same person my parents would like me to be.

"You'll get there." Jade waves at me as she leaves the shop. "This is going to be awesome!"

W A S D

I look at my phone again. Andrew let me out of work more than an hour early, it wasn't busy anyway and I think he got a little annoyed with my jumping all over the place with nerves.

Which means I can get to the party earlier, I could grab the bus and leave. But, instead, I sent a text to my mum and she said she'd come pick me up. I don't want to push my luck, so I didn't ask what she meant exactly.

Then my mum's car turns onto the street, slowing down and stopping as she reaches me. I open the door and quickly slip inside, taking care that the big summer hat Jade was somehow able to find for me doesn't get bunched up or broken on my way in.

"Hey." I rearrange my things so I can sit more comfortably.

"Hey. How much did you say that meet-thingy costs?" She drums her fingers on the wheel of the car, looking thoughtful.

"Thirty euros. But that includes food and drinks and everything." *Wait.* Does this mean that she'll allow me to go?

"Okay." She rummages through her bag and hands me some money. "Should cover the costs for the meeting and then some for maybe something fun or nice or whatever."

"You're allowing me to go?" Really?

"Yes." She holds her hand up before I can say anything. "But, I'm going to be dropping you off. I will go and have a drink at the place itself to see everything going on and if everything seems okay, I will go visit a friend and then I will pick you up at ten. Are we clear?"

Hells yes! "Yeah. Thank you so much!" Wow. This really is going to happen. I want to squee, but I know that Mum hates that and I can't piss her off right now. I want to tell someone but I can't even send a message to Alex to tell him I'm coming. So annoying. But I can send a message to Jade. 'I'm going to the meet! Mum's dropping me off!' I just *have* to share this excitement with someone.

Mum starts driving and laughs a little in that way which tells me she's aware of my excitement and thinks it's cute.

Then my phone buzzes and I see that Jade has sent me a lot of emojis and moving stickers, from happy faces to fireworks to a whole row of hearts.

I feel my cheeks heat up a little. Yes. *Hearts.* I'll be seeing Alex. *Oh, help!* I check myself out as well as I can in the mirror, pulling at my dress a little, making sure there are no stains on it. But even if there were, I'm not going to be able to get changed anyway.

"That hat, did you make it yourself?" Mum glances at me for a moment as she drives through the city.

"Jade got me the hat, but I put the flowers on it myself." So, I guess it's a little bit of both.

"Very pretty. It looks lovely with all those fresh flowers on." She smiles. "You're really looking forward to this, aren't you?"

"Yeah!" Like my asking and begging for the last couple of weeks wasn't obvious enough.

"Anyone in particular who's coming. I thought you mentioned an Alex?"

"Hmm, hmm." I play with the hem of my dress a little. "Yeah, he'll be there too. He's the one organising the meet."

"Oh, that's nice. Have you told him yet that you're coming?"

"I don't have his number. We always meet in the game, so we didn't actually swap numbers." Especially since I sort of don't want to ruin the surprise of who I am. Or maybe just because I'm scared... What if he isn't as hot as I imagine him to be? Or what if his jokes are much less funny in real life? Or maybe he's just annoying or something?

I kind of didn't want to ruin the dream before I really met him. Or ruin whatever his idea of me is by being all plain and boring...

Dammit. Now I'm scared. What if I'm this huge disappointment to him? This plain little girl who has crappy social skills when out in a group...

How can I be scared and excited at the same time?

This is going to be one long drive...

8
Alex

Caster = A type of class that doesn't do physical attacks but instead relies on magical spells. A healer is a caster, though they rely on healing, not damage attacks. Mages and bards are two types of caster DPS classes, they do magical attacks from a distance. Out of all the DPS classes, I suck least at playing a mage probably because, like a healer, you don't want to stand anywhere near the monster you're killing.

It's hot. It's way hotter than I expected it to be today and I'm glad I took a strappy top with me instead of just my t-shirt. I lean over the table, my head on my arms. It's too sticky to sit like this, but also too hot to keep sitting up, even in the shadows.

"Troy…" I don't even lift my head. "Get me something to drink, will you?"

"Why should I?" He puts his sweaty and hot hand on the bare skin of my back and I groan.

"Too hot."

"Well, yes. It's summer." I can almost hear the evil grin he's making at me. "Summer means hot."

"Summer is evil." I sit up, glaring at Troy. "Go get me something to drink. I'm your guild leader."

"Ah-hah." He raises his eyebrows as he pulls a face. "And I've known you since you were small enough to eat sand pies and were considering adding spiders to your diet."

"Ugh." I sigh. I don't want to get up, it's too hot to move. I'm hoping that it will be cooler when we go home in the evening.

"Hey, did you hear from Fleur this morning?"

I shake my head. "She had to work and didn't know if she could get out early. And it sounded like she didn't know if her mum would let her come anyway..."

Which sucked. I really want to meet her, we've been spending so much time online that I *really* want to see her. But I get it. Meeting people you only know from online is just not something that many parents would allow you to do... Especially as a teen girl, which I know everything about. The only reason my parents allow me to come to gatherings like this is because Troy is with me. I don't know why, but somehow they trust him to protect me or something...

"Bummer. I know you *really* want to see her."

"Troy..." I glare at him. "Don't go there. I just have a lot of respect for her as a fellow female gamer and she's a great healer."

"Hmmm, hmmm. Keep telling yourself that. Keep telling yourself it's about *respect* and not something more primal." He grins and I kick at his leg. Which is way too much moving in this heat.

"Shut up." I groan and drop my head onto my arms again. It's too hot to argue with him today.

Troy's finally quiet for a while, but then I feel him move next to me, sitting up straighter. "Eh, Alex?"

"What?" I'm not lifting my head up for some stupid question.

"I think she's here." Something in his voice tells me that he's not joking, unlike the ten times he's tried this same move this afternoon.

My heart starts beating like crazy and I look up. Okay, so maybe I'm a bit more excited than I'd like to admit…

At the door there's a girl in a brightly coloured summer dress, her hand on her big sun hat as she lifts the front to look over the group.

I can only stare at her. She's like a vision. She wasn't joking when she said she loves flowers. Her dress is covered in them and I can even see some flowers on her hat, which I think may even be real. I don't know, it would fit Fleur to do that. She really is so much like her character, maybe not in actual looks, but definitely in the aura she gives off.

I watch the girl take a deep breath, nodding to herself, and walking over to Aaron, who's standing on his own at the table with drinks.

They chat for a moment and then Aaron looks our way, pointing at us.

I'm not sure if I'm breathing anymore right now.

Fleur smiles and then comes over to us, but as she comes closer I see she has her eyes on Troy and my heart sinks. Fleur eyes me for a moment but then flashes a brilliant smile at Troy. "Hi, you're Alex, right? I'm Fleur."

Troy lets out a little laugh. It's not the first time people expect him to be Alex, especially when it's just the two of us together. I have to admit, he does look like he could be a tank called *AlexTheDestroyer*, and, sure, I guess he looks good. But to hear the girl I've been talking to, the girl who has been on my mind for weeks now mix us up... it hurts, it stomach-pain-inducing hurts.

Troy clears his throat. "Actually, I'm Troy. This is Alex." He wraps his hot and sticky arm around my shoulder and I shrug him off as quickly as I can. Too hot and not good.

"Oh." Fleur's face falls some and then she puts on an awkward smile. "Hi."

"Hey." My voice is rough. "Nice to meet you." The happy feeling inside when I first saw her is gone now. She didn't expect a girl, she expected a guy like Troy. A guy who's built like a wall like AlexTheDestroyer, not a plain frail girl like me.

"Sit down. Sit down." Troy motions at Fleur, his voice is forced upbeat, then he stands up. "I'll go get you two something to drink. What do you want?"

"Water." I can't help but grumble a little. There's a beautiful and smart girl sitting right across from me and all she wants is a guy like Troy. *Fuck. My. Life.*

"Me too, thanks." Fleur's voice is careful before she meets my eyes. I can see her confusion, and her disappointment.

"I'll be right back." Troy walks off and when he's out of hearing-range, I speak up.

"I'm not who you expected." No question, fact. I wish it didn't hurt as much as it does.

Fleur shakes her head and takes her hat off, playing with the rim in her hands, her hair falls forward a little, hiding her face. "No." Her voice is soft, quiet among all the rowdy voices around us.

"I'm sorry. You thought I was going to be a guy. Like Troy, or Aaron." I feel my throat close up, making it hard to breathe. "Sorry. I didn't mean to deceive you."

I stand up. If I stay here any longer I'm going to cry. I don't want to cry in front of Fleur. It was all just in my head. Everything that happened was only in my head and I can't just force my feelings onto her because I had the wrong idea.

I'm a girl, I fall in love with girls, but other girls usually don't fall in love with me. I'm used to it, but it still hurts.

I make my way to the back, to one of the snack tables, looking at everything but not seeing it, my whole vision going blurry.

"Oh, Alex." Cerise comes over, wrapping an arm around my waist as she pulls me against her side.

I quickly cover my mouth with my hand as I take a shuddering breath, big fat tears slide down my cheeks. "I don't want to cry. I'm not supposed to cry."

"I don't care about supposed to or not. You like her and it seemed like she just turned you down. Pretty sure crying is a normal response." She leans in a little, her closeness comforting, her voice soothing. "I know it's no use to you right now. But, you're amazing and you have amazing strength in you. You know I'd date you if I was into girls, right?" Her voice is soft and makes me laugh a little, even though the tears don't seem to be drying up just yet.

"I know. I'd totally be into you if you weren't a DPSer." I laugh, but it's raw, not a happy sound.

Cerise is great, but no matter what, I don't feel for her what I feel for Fleur. It just didn't happen, just like it didn't happen with Aaron or Owen or any of the others I met in the Destruction of Elysium. It's just been Fleur. Fleur's the first girl

I've met online who I've fallen for immediately. But she expected a guy, not me.

"Hey." Cerise plays pretend-offended. "I can't help being a crappy tank or healer."

"I can't help being born a girl." I smile at her tone, at the look in her eyes. Cerise always knows how to make me smile.

"Exactly." Cerise steps around me, leaning in front of me, looking at my face with soft eyes. "And you're an amazing girl. Don't ever forget that." Cerise reaches out, wiping at my cheeks. "And you'll find someone who will realise that and fall in love with you. Don't give up." She smiles, then her eyes flit to a point behind me before she quickly grabs something from the table. "And I'm out."

I'm about to ask her why, when there is a voice behind me.

"Alex?" Fleur's voice is anxious and I quickly wipe at my face before I turn to her, trying to wipe the last tears away.

"Yeah?" Looking at her just hurts again. She's beautiful, she's exactly as I expected her to be, and just seeing her now hurts.

"I'm sorry. I didn't mean to hurt you. I didn't expect…" She raises her hands a little moving them nervously, before dropping them, her eyes averted.

"You didn't expect a girl?"

Fleur shakes her head. "Which is stupid, because why wouldn't I? We never exchanged other information apart from our names and you know, age and stuff. And really, Alex is just as good a girl's name as a boy's name." She lets out an awkward laugh. "I just… I had this idea about who you were and it didn't fit the reality. That's not your fault. That's my fault. And I'm sorry for that." She takes a breath, facing me. "You didn't deceive me, I deceived myself. I'm so sorry for hurting you." She frowns and bites her lip, running the edge of her hat through her hands. A nervous tic that's becoming more obvious.

She really does look like she's sorry and I get it. The stupid thing is just that this happens to me way more often than I'd like… and this is not the first time a girl I like likes my personality, or my humour, or anything else, but can't get over my being a girl. "Thanks. I'm sorry for over-reacting."

She shakes her head, her hair bouncing around her face. "You weren't at fault. I acted like an idiot, so of course I hurt you. That's on me, not you." She takes a deep breath, like I saw her do before, standing up straight, holding out her hand, a real smile around her lips this time. "Let's try this again. Hi, I'm Fleur. I play a healer and I sometimes do stupid things that hurt people, even when I don't mean to."

I take her hand. "Hey, I'm Alex. I play a tank and I…" I don't even know what to say right now. The only thing I can come up with feels silly. "And I sometimes play videogames all night with a girl I just met online. Sometimes so much that I get her in trouble." I smile and Fleur laughs. I hold my breath for a moment, she's so beautiful when she laughs. Dammit, this is not going to be easy.

"As long as that girl is just me." Fleur smiles softer now, maybe even teasing a little.

"Yes. Just you." I nod. The butterflies in my stomach seem to have resorted to playing high-speed-jet instead of fluttering. Maybe not all is lost? Maybe we can be friends?

Fleur's cheeks colour a little at that, nodding slightly. Then she almost jumps a little. "Oh!" Fleur's eyes sparkle instantly. "Did you hear about the new night quests? Like, they'll only spawn during night-time in the game. What did you think about that announcement? I thought it was genius, but I saw some people complain about it..." She looks at me like what I'm saying will really matter.

"I..." I'm taken a little off-guard by the sudden change in topic, gathering my thoughts. "I thought it was interesting. Though, I totally hope they come with special night gear or something. I hope this isn't one of those experiments they run and then totally forget about. Although..." I step closer. "I did hear that the next raid may be connected to the whole night-time thing too. Which could be interesting."

Fleur nods, letting out a little gasp. "Definitely." She smiles, then looks around. "I'm kind of hungry." She pulls a face. "Just got out of work and wasn't able to eat much today. Too nervous."

I laugh. "Well. Let's get you something to eat and drink then. Follow me." I walk to one of the tables where there is more food-food instead of just snacks. "What do you want?"

Fleur's eyes keep sparkling as she looks at everything on the table. "Oh. My. God. Ribs!" She rushes for them and as I follow her, I quickly grab some paper napkins, stuffing them into my pocket. We'll probably need those later. She turns to me, her eyes big. "You want some too? What flavour do you like?"

"Do they have something spicy?" I step next to her. I haven't actually checked the menu yet, too nervous. And suddenly it almost feels like we're back to how we were before, how we act in the game.

"Eh." She looks at the different plates. "Yes. Something with jalapenos."

"Yes, please." I grab a plate, but she pushes her hat into my hands and starts stacking multiple racks onto her plate, then she turns to me.

"Where do you want to sit?" She smiles broadly, looking much too cute.

"Eh." I look around, finding the only table sort of in the shadows to be the table where I sat at before. "Let's sit there. I see shadows there."

"Oh. Definitely!" She starts walking and I grab two bottles of water from a table with drinks nearby before I follow her.

So, this means we're sharing the plate. Right? I'm not misreading this situation? I'm not being stupid?

But I push the thoughts from my mind. This is food. This is sharing ribs.

Well, that and finding out that Fleur apparently loves spicy food as much as I do. Which is definitely a good thing. *If* we'd date, that is. Or, you know, just hang out as friends…

Dammit.

9
Fleur

ADHD = Attention Deficit Hyperactivity Disorder = I can try all I want, but sometimes my brain doesn't do what I want or need it to do. It will focus too much or too little on things, making mundane tasks difficult to complete and even conversations hard to follow, but also allows me to shift my focus around in videogames so I always know what is going on where. I guess it could be one of the reasons why I'm a pretty decent healer.

I feel a little strange. I try to wrap my head around the idea that the Alex I've been talking to, the one I thought was a boy, is actually a girl. I know I didn't behave nicely to her, and that troubled me, especially when I saw how upset it made her. And it wasn't even Alex' fault. I was the one who had different ideas about who she was than what she told me. I filled in the blanks about her in the wrong way.

But at the same time... Seeing her that upset. I felt so bad. Because I knew that the person who'd made me laugh so hard for the last few weeks was now in pain. And it was by my own hand.

So I gathered all the courage I had and apologised. Because if there's one thing I'm good at these days, it's apologising. I'm too impulsive and a little socially awkward at times, so I have to apologise on a regular basis.

Only, when she looked at me again, when I saw the pain in her eyes, not only did I feel bad, I felt a little flutter in my stomach, a little bit of the same feeling I got when I talked to Alex online. But that was just relief, right? Relief that she didn't actually hate me. It has to be.

We start digging into the plate of ribs. I'm hungry, really hungry. But it seems Alex is just as happy to keep munching away, to keep eating and digging through the huge stack.

I thought I may have grabbed a few too many ribs, but I couldn't help myself. When I read jalapeno ribs, I just had to have them, and when Alex also wanted them... Well, I guess I got a little too excited and just kept grabbing more. Not unusual.

I take a deep breath, trying to wait a moment for the food to settle, and then I take a sip from one of the bottles of water that Alex grabbed us. I lean back a little, looking at the girl sitting opposite me.

Alex' eyes flit up to mine for a few moments, but then she looks back at her hands, at the way she's pulling two ribs apart. Then Alex' phone starts beeping and she nearly lets out a curse, quickly looking my way before she cleans her hands and taps at the screen. She picks up her phone and sends someone a message.

A few tables over, I see the guy she was sitting with before, Troy, grab his phone, and then look around. Alex also looks around for him, but he's already coming over to us, holding a bag.

"Bag?" Troy puts it next to her on the bench, then he sits down, looking at me for a moment and smiling.

"Thanks." Alex flashes him a smile, grabs a strip from a pocket in her bag, takes a pill out of it, and then puts the strip away.

"You good?" Troy stands up again, apparently done here.

"Yeah. Thanks." Alex nods at him. "Thanks for always taking care of me."

"No problem. Better this than the alternative." He winks. "Okay, I'm going back. You two have fun." He smiles and walks off again with the bag.

Alex eyes the little pill in front of her, sighing and then takes it with some water. She pulls a face and then grins at me, a little mischief in her eyes. "Gross."

"Are you okay?" I'm not used to people being this unfazed by having to take medication.

She nods, taking a deep breath. She opens her mouth for a moment, then closes it. She seems to try to say something, but she also looks a little lost on how to.

"You don't have to tell me." I don't want to make her feel uncomfortable.

"It's not that. Just..." She shrugs, sighing. "I guess I can tell you. You'll figure it out soon enough anyway, and the others already know. It's not a secret."

That makes me worry a little, my stomach constricting.

"I have ADHD. I take meds so I don't do stupid stuff, or so I can actually focus on what is going on, like, having conversations." Alex doesn't look at me anymore, instead she's looking at the table. "Things like this exhaust me, so many impressions, so many people all talking at the same time. So I take my meds to make things a little easier.”

I reach out, touching her arm as a laugh bubbles up in me. I thought it was something bad, something serious, but this…

“What?” She looks a little confused, and a little annoyed.

“Me too.” I can’t help the relief that floods me. “I also have ADHD. Well, without the hyperactivity, technically.” The words all run together a little, and I swallow hard, taking a deep breath. “I get it.”

Alex grins, she turns her arm, sliding her hand into mine, making sparks rush all the way up my arm. “Really?”

“Yeah.” I look at our hands, at the way she holds me, how careful she is. “I took my last dose on the way here. Didn’t want to have to deal with it surrounded by strangers. But I totally get it.”

Alex nods, then she lets go of my hand, instead grabbing her phone. I don’t know why, but I wish she hadn’t let go just yet. “Look.” She shows me a screen on her phone. It’s got a lot of different timers on it, all set for different hours. “My secret to taking meds on time.” She winks and I laugh.

Of course, the one funny thing about taking medication which helps you focus and remember things, is that you kind of need to set reminders to remember to take it…

“I have two computer screens so I can watch TV series while I play videogames, otherwise I get distracted.” I shrug a little, my own way of refocusing my focus.

“Smart. I just have the voice chat in the background, so there are usually other people around while I’m doing things. But the second screen is a good idea too.” She thinks for a moment, her eyes sparkling. “To think the girl who is naturally good at being my healer, would also have the same attention span issues

I have... Interesting." She looks at the now empty plate between us. "Want more?"

I shake my head. "Too full. But maybe we can get dessert later."

"Good call." She pushes the plate aside and then the girl she was talking to before comes over too.

"Hey. I don't think I've introduced myself yet." The girl holds out her hand and I take it. "I'm Cerise, I'm a mage in DoE. And you must be our new healer?"

I nod. "Fleur. Brand new healer and a little overwhelmed by the number of people here." I smile at her and she nods as she sits down.

"So you decided to sit with our ball of energy? Makes *total* sense." She bumps her shoulder into Alex, who pushes back.

"You're just trying to flatter me." Alex grins, then she leans over, her eyes shining. "Okay, so I read that—"

W A S D

It's interesting to watch Alex interact with people, and also to meet all the other members of the guild. After the odd start, the rest of the evening goes much smoother.

I really like talking to everyone and it seriously makes me consider getting a headset so I can talk to them in DoE too. Especially now that summer break has started and I'll have a lot more free time to actually play with them. And having finally met them, it's no longer as scary.

Alex stays close by all evening and she seems to really include me when she talks to other people, making me feel welcome. I like talking to her, watching her react, looking at her as she enthusiastically moves around as she talks. I thought she was talkative in DoE, but she is really talkative in real life too, probably even more so.

"Fleur?" Alex looks at me, her eyes curious.

"Yeah?" I'm sure I've missed something.

"Are you good?" She smiles, coming a little closer. She's pretty, and so bubbly.

"I'm good. Just a long day." I check my phone. "My mum is picking me up in five or so minutes."

"Ah." Alex' face falls. "Let's get your things then, I'll walk you to the front."

I nod, standing up, addressing the whole group. "I'm leaving. See you all in DoE." I grab my bag and my hat, holding it instead of putting it on. The sun is too low to really matter anymore anyway and it keeps my hands busy.

"See you!" A lot of people wave at me, calling their goodbyes. I'll probably have forgotten half their faces and online names before I'm even back home, but that's okay.

Alex is waiting a little distance away, and I catch up with her before we go through the restaurant to the front. We stop near the parking spaces.

"Thank you for coming. I loved meeting you." Alex' eyes don't shine as much anymore, but I guess we're both a little tired now.

"I loved being here. Again, sorry for all the mess at the start." I play with the rim of the hat in my hands.

"It's okay." Alex lets out a little laugh, putting a hand over mine, stopping my movements. "At one point, we'll laugh that this ever happened. Don't worry. I'm just glad you enjoyed yourself."

"Yeah, I did." We fall quiet for a bit, Alex' hand is still on mine and I turn mine around, taking hers carefully as my heart beats like crazy.

Alex looks up, her fingers tensing around mine, her gaze is surprised, confused and maybe even a little scared, but I can also see happiness there too.

I feel like that too. I don't know what or why. I've never felt like this around a girl before, or, really, around anyone. I thought I liked Alex, back when I thought Alex was a guy, but now... knowing that she's a girl... It complicates things a little.

"I..." We both look up and speak at the same time, which makes us burst out laughing and the tension is broken.

"You first." Alex smiles.

"I'd like to meet up again." I look behind us. "Maybe not as a group, though."

"Me too." Alex' smile grows. "And it's not like we live that far away from each other. I live just on the other side of the city from here."

I reach up, pointing either way.

"East."

"Oh. That's actually closer to my place..." I meet her eyes, and then look down again.

"Really?"

"Yeah." My heart does a little flipflop at the hopeful sound in Alex' voice. "Which makes meeting up even easier." I can't help smiling at the idea of just spending time together with Alex. She's smart and funny and so easy to be around.

"Definitely." She takes her phone. "We should exchange numbers and stuff. DoE is great and all that, but I'd like to be able to just talk to you..." Her voice trails off at the end, uncertain. "If you're okay with that…"

"Sounds good." I grab my phone and add her number to it, then we also exchange friend invites in the voice chat program which the guild uses. I may not have a good microphone, but I've had an account for a while, although I only use it for text-based chatting.

"We'll have to see when we can meet then." Alex looks my way and I nod.

"Yeah." My stomach does weird things under her gaze. "We should."

"Actually. If you're into films... There's an action flick coming out this week or next. We could go together." Alex immediately starts tapping at her phone, looking for something. I can't help but laugh at it, so familiar to watch. "Yeah. It comes out at the end of the week. Starting on Thursday. We could go..." She looks up, raising an eyebrow. "What?"

"Nothing. I'd love to. I'll have to ask my mum."

"Of course." She lets out a breath. "I'd really like it." There is a vulnerability about her now.

"Me too." I reach out, touching her hand, and she slides it into mine, holding on. I like this, this feels good.

Then I see Mum's car drive up and we walk to meet her in a spot just down the road where she can park more easily. A few steps before we reach her, Alex lets go of my hand, instead stuffing it into her jeans.

Mum opens the door for me, looking at Alex, smiling. "Hi."

"Hi." Alex nods, I can see she's a little uncomfortable.

I climb into the passenger seat, organising my dress, hat and bag in a way that leaves me some space to sit.

"Did you make new friends? And did you get to see the Alex guy you really wanted to meet?" Mum immediately starts with the questions. "Did you thank him for inviting you yet?"

Alex steps a little closer. "I'm Alex, actually." She puts on a polite smile. "And thank you for letting her come today. We had a great time."

"Ah." Mum looks between Alex and me, a little confused. "Well, I'm glad. It's never easy for Fleur to meet new people."

"No, it's not. Which is why we do these meets." Alex is putting on her best charm, now that I know her a little, it's easy to spot. "This way new members can meet other people. It makes playing together more fun. And you get to meet face to face, instead of just an online persona."

"That's definitely true." Mum nods, thinking. "Well, we have a drive home to make. We should get going."

"Have a safe trip." Alex smiles, stepping back, her eyes on me. "And I'll talk to you soon."

"Yes. Talk soon." I can't help my own smile. "And I'll message you about that *thing*."

"I'll check with my parents too." Alex nods.

Then Mum drives off and I wave at Alex until we round the corner.

"She seems like a very responsible and thoughtful girl." Mum looks my way for a moment. "And kind too."

"She is." I look at my phone, at Alex' contact details which I've just added, my head a little light. "She really is."

I came up here excited to meet the funniest guy I'd ever met and now I'm leaving having spent the evening with the sweetest and prettiest girl I've ever seen.

Talk about life changes…

10
Alex

Melee = A type of class who does primarily or exclusively physical close-range damage. Think a boxer hitting someone in the face or a knight cleaving someone with his sword. That kind of stuff. While with casters, you're basically always under threat of getting hit by them. With these guys, you need to be in range of their weapons (or their fists) to get hit.

I watch Fleur drive off with her mother, and, for a moment, I don't want to return to the party. Watching her leave, seeing her get into that car and be driven away, it makes my chest tighten, even though I know I'll see her again soon.

How did this happen? I take a deep breath, looking around for a moment. How have I fallen for that girl even more, especially when she looked at me and smiled, when we laughed together about both having ADHD. I don't know what, but I feel like this may be something special.

"Alex." Cerise is standing a little way off.

"Hey." I put my phone away, turning to Cerise, waiting for her to reach me.

"And?" She smiles and I know she worries about me.

"I think we're going on a date next week." I can barely believe it myself.

"A date?" Cerise's eyebrows rise.

"Okay, we're going to see a film together. But it *could be* a date." I lick my lips. "She's... really special." I feel that tightening again, and at the same time a fluttering in my stomach. "I really like her."

"I can see that. *Everyone* can see that." Cerise laughs softly. "She seemed interested too, though she may not have realised it herself."

I nod. "Maybe. We exchanged numbers, so we'll see, I guess." Just then, my phone buzzes and I grab it again. When I unlock the screen, I see it's a picture from Fleur. It's from her shoulder, where she pulled the strap of her dress to the side and you can obviously see she's got sunburnt today. I let out a laugh.

Then I get another message from Fleur. 'So red. That's going to burn!'

I reply quickly. 'Looks like it hurts. Take care of it!'

'Will do. You also make sure you take care of yours.' Yeah, I guess I may have got sunburnt too, especially since we were side by side the whole time.

"You're in *so* deep." Cerise's voice is soft. "Don't get hurt."

I nod. "I'll try." Then I look back at the rest of the group. "Let's see if we can stir up some trouble together." I grin. It's not a guild meet without Cerise and me doing something stupid.

"Good idea." Cerise walks in front of me. "Wouldn't want to disappoint the masses."

It's already late by the time I finally get home, but I still turn on my computer. Some part of me hopes Fleur will be online. Even though I wouldn't be surprised if she's already asleep by now. She hasn't sent me another message since the one in the car, but I was really busy at the meet, so that's not totally on her.

As soon as I log on, I get a purple message.

> **BelleFleur:** You're here!
> **AlexTheDestroyer:** Yeah. Checking in a little.

Hoping to see you. Though I don't type the last bit.

> **BelleFleur:** It was so cool today!
> **BelleFleur:** I never expected there to be so many different types of people.
> **AlexTheDestroyer:** Gamers really are all different. Yeah.

I lean back in the chair, exhaustion setting in, but my heart is beating fast from talking to Fleur.

> **BelleFleur:** Hey, ehm...
> **BelleFleur:** Did you mean what you said about going to the cinema?
> **AlexTheDestroyer:** Yes. If you want to.

Is she going to cancel on me? Is she going to say she was just caught up in the moment?

> **BelleFleur:** Cool. Just... you know. Wanted to make sure.
> **BelleFleur:** I wasn't sure if you really meant it.
> **AlexTheDestroyer:** Yeah. I really meant it. If you still want to, that is.
> **BelleFleur:** Yes. I'd love to.

Oh, this is weird. I've never felt so nervous before. How can this be so scary? I've been on dates before, it's not like this is the first time I've asked a girl out.

But a little voice in my head tells me that I know why this is different. This is different because I may know Fleur from playing a videogame online, and we've already chatted so much, and I know so many things about her, but today was the first time I actually met her. This was the first time that I could talk to her face-to-face and maybe, just maybe, I've already fallen for her.

But I'm also strongly aware she didn't realise that I was a girl, and seeing me kind of freaked her out, even if just a little. And I don't think she's ever been in this position with another girl. Not ever. Which makes everything a weird combination between trying to have a friendship and also trying to let her know that I'd like more from her...

I do want more from her, especially after I saw her today. The butterflies still haven't settled and I can't stop bouncing my leg with the nervous energy.

BelleFleur: Alex? I'm going off. I need sleep.

I let out a little laugh. Yeah, sleep.

AlexTheDestroyer: Good. Me too. Night night!
BelleFleur: Sweet dreams!
AlexTheDestroyer: You too!

I see her log off and I sit up too, closing the game and then shutting down my computer.

Just as I'm about to climb into bed, my phone lights up.

I grab for it, finding a message from Fleur, well, more like a picture. She's sent me a picture she took through her window, looking out over her back garden. It's beautiful and dark, but there are some lights visible. Then, a moment later, a message comes in. 'Kind of calm and quiet here, so different from the meet.'

I sit up, looking out of my own window, but it's just the street in front of the house, which is not interesting at all. Instead I turn to my computer and take a picture of my desk and the lights that swirl and blink on all my hardware, even when the computer is off. Then I send the picture, quickly following it up with a message. 'I don't know which lights are more interesting.'

Fleur sends me a winking smiley. 'Well, I guess we're going to have to compare that someday.'

My heart beats fast, having Fleur in my room? Would that really happen? 'Sounds like a good idea. Sweet dreams!' Because if I keep thinking about this, I probably won't sleep at all tonight, and I'm really exhausted, especially now my medication has worn off.

'Sweet dreams!' Her message lights up the screen one last time before I put the phone away.

I curl up on my side, closing my eyes. Meeting Fleur today. Spending time with her. And she actually wants to see me again… I guess that may be more than I could have hoped for.

My heart keeps beating like crazy, Fleur's smile popping into my head and her laugh running through my mind. She's captivated me, more than she did before. Knowing her mind, her thoughts, that's one thing. Knowing her whole personality, spending time with her… That's a whole different thing.

And she's caught me, captivated me, has me.

W A S D

"Alex?" Mum's staring at me as she sits down at the table.

"Yeah?" I look up, trying to keep my voice normal. I've been zoning off as I'm eating breakfast, my mind both stretched too thin from all the impressions yesterday and at the same time filled with a certain girl.

"How was yesterday?"

"Good." I feel a blush creep up my cheeks.

"Hmm? What happened?" She raises an eyebrow as she smiles a little.

"A girl from the game also came. She's a new member, our new healer."

"I think I heard you and Troy talk about her before. But I take it she's even more interesting in person than she was online?" Mum knows I'm into girls, she may not get it, but she knows that I've fallen in love with girls before. She's even met a couple of them, with mixed results.

"Yeah. She's very interesting to talk to." *Understatement of the year.*

"Talk... Right." Mum winks.

"Sure. Fine." I roll my eyes as I let out a dramatic sigh. "She looks good and she's very sweet."

"Good." Mum stands up again. "Don't forget to drop by Troy's today. His mum wanted to borrow a book, I put it on the table in the hallway."

"Will do." I quickly finish my breakfast. "Anything else?"

"Do I get to meet her?" Mum turns around in the doorway.

"Maybe. Someday." I put my plate on the counter and then push at Mum a little so she'll step out of the doorway and I can pass her. "But not right now. I don't want you to scare her off."

"I don't scare people off."

"Yes, you do. You're a psych. You can't help asking questions and that scares people." I sigh, standing on the stairs. "I love you. But I'd like to ease this girl into our little world of insanity." I wink and then bounce up the stairs.

Sure. I'll drop by Troy later. But first, I get to play DoE, since school is over and I can do whatever I want.

Win! Win! Win!

When I got online, Fleur wasn't there, which was a bummer. Though, I guess she may have been sleeping in. I don't know.

I consider sending her a message, but if she's still asleep, I may wake her up or disturb her while she's doing other stuff. So, instead, I run a couple of Titans and even queue for a raid.

But as I'm waiting for the raid invite to pop up, which, even as a tank, can take a while as you need multiple tanks and healers for this, I hear a sound in the background.

It takes me a moment to recognise where it's coming from, and even then, a moment longer to respond to it. It's the voice chat program and someone is trying to start a voice call with me. I don't generally get calls, as the guild just has a group voice chat server, so we don't have to call to each other, we just drop by as we log on. Which I hadn't even done yet, enjoying a little quiet after last night.

I tab out of the game and in the middle of my screen I find a message, a calling screen, telling me that Fleur is trying to call me. My heart jumps as I click on the green 'connect' button.

"Alex!" Fleur's excited voice nearly deafens me. "Guess what I did?"

"Call me?" I laugh, then I click back into the game, not wanting to miss the pop-up screen for the raid.

"With my new headset!" Her excitement is cute, and very contagious. Then it dawns on me what she's saying.

"You bought a headset? Just to chat?"

"Yeah!" Which sounds more like 'duh' in tone. "I went out this morning to get one. This way I can still talk to everyone, even when I'm at home."

Everyone. For a moment that stings, she bought the headset so she could talk to the guild, not just to me. "Right. Well, I could probably walk you through setting up the guild server connection, if you want to."

She's quiet for a bit. "Thanks. But I like talking to you first. Ease into this and all that." Her voice is softer now, not as sure.

"Well, I'm happy to do that too. Though, I am waiting on a raid, so I may have to focus on that in a bit." I check the screen again but nothing is showing yet.

"I can wait on that." I hear her move a little. "Hey, I really liked meeting you. That was so much fun and I thought everyone there was awesome."

"Thanks. I loved meeting you too." Though, I'm pretty sure we've had this conversation before, like, yesterday when she left. "Did you think about the film yet? Did you ask your mum?"

"I haven't… yet." She lets out a little laugh. "I thought I'd let her get used to the idea that I went to a guild meet first, before springing on her that I want to go out and see a film with someone from there. Though, she thought you seemed responsible."

"Wow. High praise." I laugh too. "Well, I haven't asked my parents yet either. But we should, soon, or all the tickets will be sold out for the first days."

"Yeah. Hey, would it be okay if we like... went out to eat together before, or afterwards?" She's sounding nervous, insecure.

"You want to spend more time with me after being cooped up in a dark room, in slightly uncomfortable seats, for hours?"

"If you put it like that... Yeah?" She lets out a laugh again. "It's just... I don't get to meet many girls who also play videogames, at least not as much as me."

96

Again, that friends thing... That 'you're cool because you're a girl who plays games too' not 'you're cool because you're you and I would like to get to know you more intimately'. I don't know what to think of it. Am I misreading what she's saying? Am I misreading what she means? Am I just seeing things that aren't really there?

Argh. Why is this so confusing? If she'd been Cerise, or any of the other girls I've met online, I wouldn't have worried about this. But I am with her.

Fleur's making my brain go all mushy.

11
Fleur

Crafting = The making, or crafting, of items. The levelling of this skill is often separate from the levelling of your main class. Crafters can make things with the items people find around the game or with items that gatherers (from the gathering skill) specifically look for. The crafting skill I'm focusing on right now is tailoring, because it can make gear for my healer but also bigger bags I can use and sell. I love crafting, though I prefer gathering most of the time, it's more calming and requires fewer steps.

"Hey." Alex' voice surprises me for a moment.

"Yeah?" I blink. I was so focused on getting my tailoring skill up and which items I'd need for what, that I almost forgot Alex is in the voice chat with me.

"I'm going over to Troy's for a bit. Need to drop something off for my mum. Will I see you later?"

"Yeah. I'll be on later. I don't really have much to do today anyway." I click around in the game, bidding on a few more items I need in the market place.

"Cool." I hear her moving around a little. "I'll see you later, then. If I don't go now, my mum's going to get annoyed." She laughs and I totally know what she means.

"Good luck." I can't help but laugh too.

"Thanks. See you later."

"Later."

And then I see Alex log out of DoE, just as I hear her leave the voice chat too.

This morning, as early as possible, I went to the store and picked up a headset. Last night, after I said I was going to bed, I actually spent a good amount of time on my phone looking up headsets and which ones would be the right ones for talking to everyone and stuff. My old one was too crappy to use any longer, but I did have enough money saved up from working at the flower shop to buy a decent quality new one.

After meeting Alex yesterday, I just really wanted to talk to her more, and I realised how much easier doing raids and dungeons with guild members would be if I'd actually had a headset. Though, I guess the talking to Alex thing got me more excited… Not sure what to think of that.

My phone buzzes and I look at it, finding a message from Jade. 'Where are you?'

'At home?' I frown, I thought that would be pretty obvious, as I can't remember we're supposed to meet up today. Which doesn't necessarily mean anything, with my brain and all…

'Cool. I'll be right there! I want to hear all about yesterday!'

Uh-oh. I look at the message, and then think about the things I've told Jade about Alex. Things that were, well, not correct, mostly by my own fault. But to talk about that now? I dunno.

But I also know that telling Jade 'no' today won't stop her from asking questions until I either answer them or blow up at her. She's curious, which I normally like about her, but not always. Also, I do kind of need to talk to someone. Jade seems like the best person for that since I don't think I can talk to Mum about this, or any of my other friends.

I shut down DoE and turn off the voice chat program, then I quickly make sure my clothes are all either in the closet or the laundry basket and there isn't any food or rubbish or whatever thrown all around the room.

Because there is one thing I'm absolutely certain about, I do not want to have this conversation downstairs in front of my mum... *Nope. No Way.*

It takes just over ten minutes before Jade is knocking on my bedroom door, right as I'm shoving some boxes under my bed. "Come on in."

She opens the door, looking around before stepping in.

"Why did would you knock?" She never knocks, she just barges straight in.

"Just making sure you weren't hiding any sexy boys in here." She wiggles her eyebrows.

"I wouldn't have let you come over if I was." I stand up, grinning.

Jade shrugs. "True." She lets herself fall onto the bed. "So... How was yesterday?"

I sit down in my chair, running my hands over each other, trying to come up with a way to describe the guild meet the best. "Ehm."

"What?" She sits up, more serious now. "No good? Was he horrible?"

"Alex is not a he. Alex is a *she*." I pick up my phone, showing Jade a picture I took yesterday of Alex, Cerise and me. I'm standing in the middle between them. "Alex is the girl on the right."

"Whoa?" Jade takes the phone, looking at the picture closer. Then she shrugs, smiling, handing it back. "At least she's still cute."

Cute... I look at the picture again. I guess she is. But it's different when Jade points it out.

"What happened? Was there drama?" Jade grins a little, apparently already over the reveal.

I take a deep breath and then walk her through everything that happened from the moment I left the flower shop until Alex and I ended up eating spareribs together. I don't go into detail about the parts after that, especially not the part about the ADHD. It's not like that's of importance to her anyway and I don't think sharing information like that with Jade would be okay.

"Wow." Jade's eyes are big. "So, then what?"

"Then we hung out for the rest of the evening with Cerise, the other girl in the pic, and the other people from the guild."

"You mean, you talked videogames all evening?" Jade frowns.

"Yeah. Pretty much." I shrug. What else were we supposed to be talking about? We're gamers. This was a guild meeting. The one thing we have in common is our love for videogames, Destruction of Elysium to be more specific.

"And to think I thought you couldn't get any more geeky." Jade laughs, before turning more serious. "So, meeting sexy and funny *hunk* Alex was a bust, then? Do we need to like... have a night with junk food and rom coms to heal your broken heart?"

That takes me by surprise. Heal my broken heart? I hadn't even thought of that. Apart from those first few moments, broken hearts hadn't even occurred to me, apart from not wanting to break Alex' that is. I hadn't even thought about what Alex not being a boy meant to the... Okay, to the *crush* I used to have on her.

Used to?

"Fleur?"

I realise I've been quiet a little too long. "No, it's okay." What else am I supposed to say? Jade is right. I liked Alex, back when I thought she was a guy. I should have been heartbroken now, right? Heartbroken that the guy I liked doesn't exist. But, instead... Every time I think of Alex, Alex the *girl*, I get flutters in my stomach.

"You're blushing!" Jade leans forward, coming closer. "You're actually, honestly, blushing." She angles her head, looking at me even closer. "Wow."

I push at her, hiding my face behind my other hand. "I'm not." Though I can feel the heat in my cheeks. "I'm *not* blushing."

"You *are*." She takes both my hands, pulling them away, and I realise that while Alex taking my hands makes my stomach do weird flips, I do not have the same response to Jade. This stops me for a moment. Jade laughs, finally letting go of my hands. "Fleur, blushing, like this. I thought I'd never see it." She leans back, looking smug.

"What?" I can't make sense of what she's saying. I blush. I regularly blush over things, it's not that uncommon.

"You don't normally blush over *someone*. Sure, when you're in this 'crushing and not knowing someone well yet' phase, before they can disappoint you. But like *this*, after having spent time with them... You don't blush, usually anyway."

I shrug. Suddenly extra aware of the way I respond. "So?"

"So, this is interesting. This is good." Jade smiles again. "*Wow*. Fleur, my normally pretty neutral friend, being actually struck enough to blush, just thinking of a person."

"Enough." Maybe this is different for me, but that doesn't really mean anything. Right? "There's nothing going on. We're just friends." We are, right? I may not know her that well, but we're friends, right? "We're going to see a film next week. Just as friends."

Jade raises her eyebrow. "And who was the one who came up with this idea?"

"Alex. She wanted to see this film, she just asked me to come along with her. Nothing else." Sort of.

"Nothing else? She asks you out on a date, to go see a film, and you think there's nothing going on?"

"Date? Like... a *date*-date?" My thoughts grind to a halt.

"Is there any other kind?"

I shrug. "I don't know. I don't think... I didn't think..." Well, yes. I *didn't* think. I was excited about the whole idea because it was a film I'd wanted to see anyway, and going with Alex would be fun. But... a *date*-date. That never really occurred to me. A date-date with another girl.

"You didn't think she meant it like that?" Jade's voice is softer now. "Did you ask her about it?"

I shake my head. "I was just really excited to go."

"Do you want it to be a date-date?"

I shrug again. "I don't know. I really, just, don't know." Do I see Alex like that? Like I could go on dates with her? Like... a girlfriend? "I've never thought about that. I've never..."

"Never been interested in a girl before." Jade finishes my sentence and I shake my head.

"I haven't."

"Would you?" Then she reaches out, putting her hands over my fiddling fingers, stilling them. "Don't answer that. You don't have to. I'm just..." She shrugs with one shoulder. "Surprised, I guess. And happy for you."

Happy for me? About what? My confusion? What is there to be happy about that? "Do you think... Do you think I should cancel the film?"

"Why? You want to go, right?"

I nod.

"Then go. See if this is want you want, or if this is what you expected it to be like. You don't have to do anything, or decide on anything. Go have fun together. It's probably not a film I'd want to see together with you anyway, right?" She raises her eyebrow.

I shake my head. "No, not really. Explosions. Fights. Stuff like that." Which was one of the reasons why I was so happy that Alex wanted to see it. It meant I could actually go see it in the cinema without having to go on my own.

"Right. Not my kind of thing." Jade lets out a laugh. "So, have fun. Go have fun together and don't worry about things that are or aren't there." She leans back. "Talking about things that are or aren't there... Weren't we supposed to finish that TV series we started way back? With exams over and everything, it seems like the perfect moment to finish those last couple of episodes."

I stand up, glad to have something else to focus on. "Yes. You're right. Let me just move some stuff." I turn one of my computer screens so we can see it more easily from the bed, and then I put the series on.

It's some American crime detective kind of thing, but it's fun to watch and we both like it a lot, and it doesn't require too much thinking, which, after last night, is a good thing.

W A S D

The rest of the afternoon, and then a good portion into the evening, suddenly have passed before Jade leaves again, telling me not to worry too much and to tell her if anything changes, or if I just need to talk. After I've closed the door behind her, I take a deep breath. Well, if I want to go see that film at all, I'm going to have to talk to my mum about it first.

I make my way to the living room, where Mum is sitting on the couch, watching some drama on TV. "Mum?"

"Yes?" She looks my way.

"Can I go see a film with Alex on Thursday?" I play with the hem of my shirt behind my back, not wanting to show how nervous I am.

"Alex? Oh. That girl from yesterday?"

I nod. "It's not a school night and I can pay for it myself."

"I'm not really liking the idea of you making the trip from Groningen back here late at night." She frowns.

"We're not going over there. We're going to the cinema here. She's coming this way."

"Hm. It sounds like it should be fine. But I don't know about you going off with someone you barely know."

I try not to sigh, I get her point. "We've talked for weeks. I saw her in real life yesterday. We're not really strangers. And if I don't get to meet with her more often, we won't be able to get to know each other anyway."

"Fine. On one condition. I get to meet her again. I just want to properly introduce myself and talk to her for a moment."

"You can drop me off at the cinema, if that helps?" I'm not a little kid anymore, but she seems insistent on treating me like one.

"Sounds good." She smiles a little. "Then, I'm fine with you going. As long as it's not an X-rated film."

"Mum!" I feel my cheeks heat up like crazy. "It's not!" I rush out of the room. I don't even want to know what she was thinking, asking that...

That's so not... No. *No.*

Why would she even say something like that apart from wanting to make me blush?

Mums...

12
Alex

Buff/Debuff = A common term in MMORPGs to refer to status effects that are helpful (buff) or unhelpful (debuff), these are not specifically things that heal or do damage (which would be other types of spells) but more spells that boost or undermine your character. Buffs are generally things like increased defence, increased speed, increased healing possibility and things like that. Debuffs are generally the reverse, so they make you more susceptible to damage, or lower your attack rate or your damage itself, but sometimes it's something like being feared so your character will run away without your input or being turned to stone where you can't move at all. Buffs are awesome, debuffs suck, especially ones that the healer can't dispel.

This time, when the sound of the call comes through, I immediately recognise it for what it is. I jump out of the game, connect the call and jump back into the game.

"Hey!" Fleur sounds really excited. "Guess what?"

"What?" I laugh as I side-step a monster which is trying to attack me.

"My mum said yes to me going to the cinema with you." She almost squeals and I don't know if she realises it herself.

"Awesome. My mum said it was fine too, but she wants to pick me up afterwards. She doesn't want me to go back home on my own by bus or whatever." I grumble.

"Well, that makes them even. My mum wants to see you before we go to see the film."

I let out a short laugh. "I guess it's not that bad. At least they're not insisting on coming with us."

"No. But my mum did say that we weren't allowed to go see an X-rated film." Fleur sounds like she never would have even considered that. Cute.

"We could pretend that we are..." I try my best not to burst out laughing.

"No!" She sounds so horrified that I can't keep my laugh inside anymore. She's quiet for a moment and then lets out a slight growl. "You're teasing me."

"Yes. Yes, I am." I keep laughing because she sounded so horrified by the idea, like it would have been the worst offence in the world to her. "Sorry."

"Meany." I can hear the pout in her voice.

"Sorry. Better you know this now than later." I take a few deep breaths, stopping the laughing, but I can't help the smile when I imagine the way she's looking right now.

"I can't believe..." She lets out a deep sigh. "You're mean."

"No, I have a wicked sense of humour." I think so anyway.

"Same thing."

"Awwh. I'll make it up to you. There is something in your in-game inbox. If you haven't seen it yet." Which she probably hasn't because I didn't see her come online in DoE.

"What is it?" I get why she may be a little suspicious.

"You'll see. It's good." It is. It's one of the items we need for the quest line for the next raid.

"Fine. Give me a second." I see her come online, and I wait as she hunts down a mailbox to get her item. "What?! How did you...?"

"Found it." Sort of.

"These are like... totally hard to get."

"I had time. And I was waiting for a different item to drop anyway." For the preparation quest for the new raid, we need to collect some crystals of different drop rates in the final three endgame dungeons, and somehow I got lucky by getting two of the lowest drop rate crystals, so hardest to get, while trying to get one of the medium-difficulty drop rate.

"Have you finished the quest yet?"

"Nah. Still need the last one from the minotaurs dungeon." I shrug.

"Wanna do that one? I still need that one too, and since you got me the most difficult one, I only need one more after that." She sighs. "Which should be right in time for release on Tuesday."

"We can try." I eye the guild voice chat. "You want to join in the main chat, we can probably get a couple of us together to run it."

"Sure. Sounds good."

"Okay, lemme get the details." I start clicking around the chat program, trying to find how to add another person to it, since it's been a while since I did it last.

Well, now we can at least finish this quest together. It will be interesting to see how, or if, we can actually do the new raid as a guild immediately when it comes out. We're normally one of the first ones to finish it, but I know Fleur isn't that confident yet...

⬛ W A S D

Finishing up the quest was quite easy, and while we were waiting for the update, we also ran a couple more dungeons and raids so we could deck everyone in the guild out with the best gear possible. Apart from making sure we're in top form to run the new raid, the only other thing we can control is having the best gear going into the new raid...

And that is where we are right now, going into the new raid. Since it's summer break, we were able to get a full raid group together in the early morning. This means we don't have to wait until the evening to start playing it.

This raid focuses on a story of travelling into the underworld and we'll apparently be facing some chimeras and other half or fully mutated creatures. I think I saw Cerberus as our final boss.

"Wow! This room!" Troy is loud, but what else is new?

I look around, waiting for everyone else to arrive. The starting area is bright, though it won't stay like that.

Supposedly, we start in a field of some sort, and then we'll move down underground as the raid progresses. The area keeping us locked in the beginning room dissolves and we all start running to the first room with actual mobs.

People slow down a little as we get closer, letting us tanks pull the mobs before they start attacking. The first group of mobs may be big, but they look a lot like the ones we encountered in the dungeons we ran over the weekend. Of course, this being a raid... They're a lot stronger and apparently now have a special cleave attack that makes me extra susceptible to more damage.

"Fleur? Can you take the debuff off?" I keep checking my health bar, which seems fine, but I don't like the extra damage debuff blinking in the top of my screen.

"No. Doesn't work."

"Crap." I sidestep the next cleave attack, now aware of when it happens, and luckily, by then, the monsters are down.

We rush to the next room, which is a boss battle. *Good.*

There doesn't seem to be any special mechanics in the room itself, it's just a simple room and the boss is waiting in the middle. It's a huge creature, it reminds me a little of the minotaurs, but this one looks a lot more horrific.

We all pull up our buffs and then the healers also apply some group-wide buffs.

A yellow message appears on the screen.

Who is the main tank?

I reply without thinking.

AlexTheDestroyer: I am.

"Alex!" There is a glimmer of fear in Fleur's voice. "I've never done this before."

"Just heal and stay out of any flashing areas." I totally forgot about her being new to this, but I'm so used to being main tank. I start running, taunting the boss to attack me.

And, as the boss focuses on me, I see the others attack the boss. Everything seems to be going well until I see flashing areas and then hear the others in the chat curse loudly.

"What happened?" I check the screen and most of the raid is dead.

"Some area attack, but it was too quick to get out of," Aaron answers.

"Should I resurrect them?" Fleur pipes up.

"No." I check my own health and that of the few other people still alive. "We'll be wiped in the next attack anyway." And right as I say it, three other people also die, including Fleur and I wait out the last two attacks from the boss to finish me off.

Crap.

"What was that attack?" I wait for my character to resurrect and then run my way to the first boss again.

"Something big," Cerise answers. "I saw it, but it had such a short cast time."

"Okay. So, any areas where we can stand that are safe, apart from in front of the boss with me?" Which would be hard to time with the huge frontal cleave attack I caught right before it.

"A small area to the side, but by the second round we were gone there too." Fleur seems a little dispirited.

"We can work with that. Make your way to me when that attack is about to happen, maybe that helps." I stretch my fingers. "Ready?"

"Sure." I hear in the chat, but I already start running as soon as I see the buffs go up for everyone.

The second time is a little easier, but we still get wiped by the area attack, though this time more of us survived that first round.

I don't particularly like dying constantly, but getting to know new content, being so involved in finding the mechanics of a new raid or dungeon is really exciting. This is the kind of stuff that I really, really like.

It takes us seven tries in total before we've finished the first boss. Not our best, but definitely not our worst first encounter in a new raid. Although... this was just the first boss, we've got another three or so coming up.

Awesome!

And that isn't sarcasm.

W A S D

It takes us all day and multiple instances, because the raid timer ran out and that meant we had to start over from the beginning. But on our final run we finally got through all of the bosses. Mostly by luck, though. We only had two people still alive when the final boss went down, a tank from a different party and Cerise.

It's insane, which is why I love it so much. But at the end of a day like this... I'm exhausted and my fingers hurt like hell.

"Guys, I'm going offline for a bit. I think Mum's got dinner nearly ready." I log out of the game. "Later!" And then I also log out of the voice chat.

I stand up, but then crawl onto my bed. My brain hurts, too many things going on, too many flashy lights and too many things to keep track of. But it was a pretty cool raid. Even though I know it will take days before we fully understand all of the mechanics. So many of them are about moving around, staying out of areas, keeping track of 'area of effect' attacks or adds and stuff like that... It's not too complicated, it's just time consuming to figure out the order of everything and the timing between the different mechanics.

"Alex! Dinner!" Mum calls from downstairs and I groan as I sit up.

Right. Dinner. Food. That stuff which keeps us alive. I go downstairs and slump into my chair, Mum and Dad are already waiting there for me.

"Good raid?" Dad asks, eyeing me as he spoons some pasta onto his plate.

"Pretty cool." I nod. "Tiring though."

"Aren't they always?" Mum laughs and I shrug. That's true, they generally are. But I feel like this one is more complicated than the ones before. Or maybe that's just my brain thinking it is.

I finish dinner as quickly as I can before I give my dog Yukio his food and wait for him to finish it. "At least you don't care if I talk about raids and mechanics. As long as I talk to you." I look at him, watching him eat, watching his joy.

Then he comes back over to me, looking at me expectantly.

"Yeah, yeah. Just let me grab your lead." I stand up, putting on my shoes and grabbing his lead. I clip it on his collar and we walk out the back of our garden, through the alley that runs past all the back fences of the houses around us, before we're on the street.

It's still so light out, even though it's past seven in the evening. I like it when it's like this. This way I can walk wherever I want and, today, I need a walk. Sitting in a chair for so long is not comfortable and makes the need for moving in my body so much more uncomfortable.

My phone buzzes and I take it out of my pocket. It's a message from Fleur. 'You coming back to raid later?'

I frown. I could... But I feel like doing something a little bit different tonight. 'Walking the dog right now.' I take a picture of the streets in front of me, the mostly empty streets. Then I also take a picture of Yukio, sending both to Fleur.

'Ah! Cute dog!' She sends me a whole load of heart emoticons and I laugh.

True, he's cute, he's always been really cute. 'He needs a long walk.'

'Cool. See you later, then.'

'Later.' I put the phone back in my pocket, walking on for a while before I take it out again. When I turn around the corner, I'm about to walk into open fields. Really nice and big open fields.

I take another picture, the open fields, the space of it, the blue sky. This is the best part of walking Yukio on summer evenings, this moment of total calm.

13
Fleur

Wiped = When a whole party or raid is killed and nobody can or wants to resurrect them. This generally means that the group will have to start the room they were in all over again. This is common during boss battles, both in dungeons and in raids. When most of a group is killed one of the members will usually call out 'wipe' and members still alive at that time will wait to be killed off soon after so that the whole party can restart the room. I hate when this happens. I always feel like such a bad healer for not being able to keep everyone alive, but sometimes it happens, no matter how hard you try.

Seeing the picture Alex sent me, I totally get why she's not coming back to DoE soon. I'm tired too, my fingers are hurting, but I also still have all the excitement going through me from doing those raid runs all day.

I thought it would be much scarier than it really was. Which, yeah, a couple of weeks ago I thought the same about running end-game raids at all. But in reality, as soon as we were wiped by a boss a couple of times, we generally knew when different mechanics would hit and that made the next run a little easier. Though, still, that was so... *Eep*.

I'm no longer in the voice chat, and the silence is actually nice for the moment. It doesn't take long for me to become impatient and needing to do something else.

I boot DoE again, this time focusing instead on getting my gathering skill up, at some point I do hope to get the skill to max level. Or, at least, up high enough that I can use it to exchange items with crafters so they'll be able to craft me better gear and other items. And it's just really easy and relaxing to do when you're otherwise exhausted.

I look around the game and load up a guide which explains the fastest way to level my harvesting skill up. Then I put a TV series on to watch as I start the grind.

Relaxing, simple and I can do this all evening, even with half a brain.

W A S D

I'm nervous as I stand in front of my closet. Jade is sitting on the bed, giving comments on each item I grab.

"Dress, skirt or jeans and a shirt?" I turn to her. "What should I do?"

"Which do you like best?"

"All of them?" That's why I have all of them.

"What are you trying to convey to Alex?"

"Convey?" What the…?

"What do you want her to think when she sees you?"

My cheeks heat up immediately. "I don't know. I just want to go to dinner with her and see the film."

"Sexy? Sweet? Comfy?"

"Ehh. I don't know..." I've never really tried 'sexy', I don't think I'm very good at it, I usually just go for 'sweet'.

Jade sighs, standing up. "You wore a dress last time. So, let's skip that one." She looks around in my closet. "That means you've got the jeans or a skirt left."

"Yeah." I sit down on the bed, taking Jade's place. "Still a lot of choices."

"It will probably be a little cool in the cinema, but it will be hot when you go there." Jade picks up a few things and then puts them down again. "So, something that's easy to combine with a jacket of some sort." She grabs a skirt. "This one." It's a light green coloured skirt with an asymmetric style. "And with this top, and then a thin jacket." She hands me a tight black T-shirt. How does she do this so quickly?

I look at them both. "Are you sure?" It looks a little... plain to me.

"Yes. That t-shirt looks really nice on you. And you love the skirt." She shrugs. "And while the shirt is a little plain, it's also both sexy and simple enough that it doesn't matter where you're going out to eat, you will fit right in. It's a good shirt for when you have no idea where you're going out for dinner."

I guess she's right. "Shoes?"

"Boots or sandals. Depends on what you want. Boots give you a bit of an edge, looks cool, yet sandals are cuter." She sits down on the bed too.

"I don't know..." I sigh. "It's frustrating. I know I want to see her, that I want to meet her again. But at the same time... I get butterflies in my stomach when I'm near her, I get so nervous." I let myself drop back. "How do you deal with this?"

"With what? Falling for someone?" Jade lets out a laugh. "You've been on dates before. I've never seen you so nervous about them."

"I don't know if this is a date…" I sigh. "We didn't talk about that."

"Would it make a difference if it was a date?"

Would it? "Maybe I'd wear makeup?"

"So, wear it?" She looks my way. "You don't need to put on like layers and layers, or put on smudge-proof lipstick. But you can still put on a little."

"I guess."

"Is it because she's a girl?"

I close my eyes. Nodding.

"You're not sure if you're interested in girls in a love or relationship way?"

"I wish I knew." I guess I never really considered it, but I also never thought about it if I wasn't.

"What about Alex? Do you know if she is?"

"No. I don't know whether she is or isn't. We didn't talk about any of that either. I don't even know if she'd be…" A heaviness settles in my stomach. "I don't even know if I'm just over thinking things. If this is just me. Or if she's even interested in girls at all… It's just… It's confusing. I wish it was simpler."

"Simpler, like falling in love with a *boy* you met online?"

I push at Jade, which makes her burst out in laughter. "Not fair." She doesn't have to remind me.

"I think it's fair. I also think you're over thinking it. Go have fun. Go eat something nice. Go watch that film. And if something happens, it happens. If it doesn't… it doesn't."

"You're being too reasonable now." I laugh, then I grab the clothes and go to the bathroom, quickly changing. As I step back into the bedroom, I twirl, showing myself off to Jade. "Now you get to do my makeup."

She laughs. "Sure. Go sit down." She grabs my makeup bag, which she easily knows to locate. No wonder, she's the one who gave it to me, and most of the stuff in it too.

I don't really tend to wear much of it, usually.

W A S D

It's been a long time since Mum and I cycled somewhere together, but the weather is amazing and it will stay great, and this way I won't be dependent on bus schedules when I go home. We're riding in silence for a while, until Mum makes a sound.

"Hm?" I look her way, confused.

"I was thinking... You don't often make new friends."

I frown. Yes, I do. "What do you mean?" Because going against Mum in these situations only makes her double down on whatever she's saying.

"Well, you made friends at school, and then you have Jade, but I don't really see you around other people a lot." She looks my way for a moment and then looks back at the road.

"I guess I just don't see them that often, or, at least, not outside of like school or other things." Mum doesn't really approve some of the friends I have, so I tend to just hang out with them online or when I'm out somewhere, I don't tend to introduce them to Mum. Jade is one of the few people my mum doesn't seem to be able to intimidate easily, so she comes to my place regularly and I go to hers or we just hang out somewhere else. But I don't generally meet up with a lot of my friends outside of social occasions I'm going to go to anyway.

"Hmm." Mum seems to think this over for a moment. "And Alex?"

"What about Alex?" This is why I don't talk to her much, she always wants to know everything, even the stuff I don't even know, or want to know really.

"What does she do? What is she like?"

"She goes to school. She's a year older than me. Her parents both work. She has a really cute dog. And she plays videogames." Pretty sure that's all she really needs to know.

"What do her parents do?" Of course... This is why she wants to know. She wants to know if Alex is the 'right' kind of friend, like Hannah and Sydney are.

"I don't know. They live in one of the newer neighbourhoods in Groningen, pretty nice houses. I have no idea what they do." I really don't, why would Alex and I talk about stuff like that anyway?

"You don't have to get annoyed." Apparently, this conversation is now over. Which is fine with me, because we're just two streets away from the shop where Alex and I chose to meet up at.

We agreed that her seeing my mum would be best if it was somewhere that would be easy to recognise and easy to flee from for us later. Shops make great flee-excuses.

"Mum?" I already feel my heart beating loudly, thinking of Alex and of the questions Mum might ask her.

"Yes?"

"Please be nice to her. You've already seen her once and she doesn't need to feel like she's being interrogated."

"I don't do that." Mum sighs. "You just sometimes have friends who don't want to answer questions."

"Yeah, because not everyone wants to share their whole family history with you when they're just hanging out with me."

"I only want you to be safe. You know that, right? It's just so easy for things to get complicated and I only want what's best for you."

Now I feel like crap for saying something. "I know. I know. But I'm not five anymore. I'm sixteen, I can stand up for myself. I can leave a situation or a place if it's no good and I can save myself. I'm no longer a little girl who you need to pick up from playdates. You're not passing me over to an adult who you need to trust. I'm going somewhere with a friend who I already trust. Their parents' jobs or living arrangements are none of my, or your, concern."

We stop and park our bikes in one of the big bike racks that are located throughout the city centre. Mum is quiet for a while and that makes me feel like I may have overstepped some boundaries, then she looks up at me, sighing.

"I guess you're right."

"What?" Okay… Didn't see that coming.

"You're right. I'm treating you like you're still a kid, and you're not anymore. On the one hand, I let you go out partying on the weekend, but on the other hand, I may be a little too involved with your friends." She sighs. "Just… Do you understand that you meeting up with people you've only met online is scary for me? That it worries me? Because people can pretend to be someone totally different."

"Yes. I get that." She has no idea how well I get that, after the whole meeting-Alex fiasco. "And I do appreciate you being worried, but just… Can you not interrogate her? Please?"

"I'll try." She rolls her eyes at me and I roll my eyes right back, letting out the most dramatic sigh I can put on.

We walk the last bit to the shop and I already see Alex waiting in front of it, checking something on her phone, probably playing something or messaging people from the guild.

I've come to realise the guild is really important to her, that she does everything for them. It's something that I really like about her, her passion for the game but also her passion for the guild, her friends.

"Alex!" I quickly walk ahead of my mum for a bit and wave at her as she looks up.

Alex immediately breaks out into a grin. "Hey." We look awkwardly at each other for a moment, but then she opens her arms a little and I give her a hug.

It's a sweaty and hot hug, the middle of summer is not really the best time for hugs, but my heart is in my throat as I let her go and I can see a little pink on her cheeks that isn't from standing in the sun too long. Then she looks behind me. "Hello, Fleur's Mum. I'm Alex, we met the other night." She holds out her hand and Mum takes it.

"Hi. How are you doing? Did you get here easily enough?" Mum stands there like it's the most normal thing in the world, like she's not talking to someone who makes my heart beat faster...

"Yeah. It's just two buses. First one from two streets away from my house to Groningen train station and then a bus from there that actually stops right across the square." She points to the stop on the other side. "Quite simple, actually."

"That's good." Mum nods. "And at home, is that with your parents, or..." She looks expectantly and I groan inwardly.

But Alex doesn't even miss a beat. "I live with both my parents. My mum is a psychiatrist and my dad is a professor at the university."

"Oh." Mum blinks. "That's nice. Are you going to do that too? Studying at university?"

Oh, no... I thought that I'd asked her not to do this. I thought she understood.

14
Alex

Aggro = Agression/Agressive = also *hate* or *threat* = Used to describe how much focus a monster has on a player. In dungeons, tanks are supposed to have all the monsters focused on them, not on any of the other players. Generally, this is done as a percentage or level. But this can always change, if, for example, a healer is healing someone too much, out-healing the health bar of a player, it may pull the aggro away from the tank and to the healer, which, of course, is a bad thing. As a tank I have a range of skills to deal with this, but it's always better if other people don't do something that would pull the aggro away from me in the first place.

I can see Fleur isn't really happy with all the questions her mum is asking me, though, I have to admit, they're not as bad as the ones my mum asks... Fleur's mum is just trying to figure out who I am and this is apparently the only way she knows how.

My mum? She'll ask the weirdest stuff about people's thoughts and feelings and things like that... She seems to never really leave her job behind when she meets new people. That, or it's the only way she knows how to deal with people. Which of course is always a possibility too... It tends to freak people out a little when she does it.

"Mum." Fleur really has had enough now. "We need to go. I still want to visit a couple of shops and then we're going to eat somewhere before seeing the film. We kind of need to go now if we don't want to be rushed."

"Oh, yes. Of course." Fleur's mum smiles. "It was nice seeing you again, and talking to you for a while. Have a great afternoon and have fun at the cinema." She turns to Fleur. "Be safe, don't forget to turn on the light on your bike when you go home tonight."

"Yes, Mum." Fleur rolls her eyes a little. "I'm going to be fine."

"Good. Bye, Alex. See you tonight, Fleur."

"Bye." Fleur and I laugh as we both say the word at exactly the same time.

Fleur's mum starts walking off and I turn to Fleur, a little nervous now. Sure, meeting her mum was scary, but that's different from spending the day alone with Fleur...

"Where did you want to go?" I look her over.

"Oh, I need to pick up a couple of T-shirts that I saw online, but, after that, I'm free to go wherever." She smiles a little. "I'm so happy that you're here." Is that a little bit of a blush?

"I'm glad I came." I turn away, ready to start walking, then I turn back. "What shops do you want to go to?"

"I need to go to H&M." She points behind me and I let out a laugh. Of course, that's why we met up here in the first place.

She starts walking and I follow her. Now the nerves of meeting her mum are gone, I can focus a little better. Like, on the outfit she's wearing. A skirt, a T-shirt and boots, army boots. It's edgy and definitely not in a bad way, I like it. It's a little more 'rough' than the dress she was wearing last time I saw her. If she can change her style so easily, I'm curious what other outfits she's going to come up with each time I meet her.

"Do you need anything from here?" Fleur turns to me, walking backwards through the rows of clothes for a moment.

"No. I'm good." I'm just here for the fun, not for the shopping.

"Okay." She turns back around, right in time so she doesn't crash into a girl browsing the T-shirts on one side of the aisle.

I keep following her as she makes her way around the shop, picking up things, looking at them, considering them. I may not be interested in the clothes, but it's definitely fun to watch Fleur's face as she picks things up and puts them back down.

I think I could watch this for hours, which I probably will be doing today…

⬚W⬚ ⬚A⬚ ⬚S⬚ ⬚D⬚

The place where we're having dinner is a small pizzeria. The light is a little low, but it's cosy. And, since we're a little early, there aren't too many other people yet, so we can easily hear each other as we wait for our pizza to arrive.

We ordered a single pizza for the both of us, one with a lot of cheese and even more meat. We saw it on the menu and both went 'yes' at the same time. We decided that since we both want the same one anyway and we'll probably want some popcorn at the cinema, it would be better to share one.

Is it supposed to be this easy? Is finding someone you really like supposed to be easy? It's not like I've not dated girls before, but it was always more... complicated.

They didn't get my dedication to playing videogames. Or, they somehow couldn't seem to understand that I usually wear jeans and a shirt but I also like wearing dresses, I just don't do it often. I didn't fit their idea of 'butch', while at the same time, I liked things that they considered too 'boy-ish' to be girly. It was confusing and tiring.

Which is why it never worked out, I guess. But sitting here with Fleur, talking to her, this is so easy. This is so *very* easy.

And that scares me a little. It scares me how easy and comfortable it is. Because if it's this easy, doesn't that mean we may be better off as friends? Isn't friendship supposed to be the easier one of the two?

"Alex?" Fleur waves her hand in front of my face.

"Yes?" I blink, looking at her. I was totally zoning out, wasn't I?

"I was trying to ask you about DoE."

"What part?" Talking about DoE is easier, a much safer topic too.

"Raiding." She levels a look at me.

"Ah. What part of raiding?"

"The getting-killed-a-hundred-times part?" She frowns. "Isn't that like... really confusing, and also expensive on gear repair costs?" She frowns a little more.

I shrug. "It's the only way to really understand the mechanics, and the timing of them. Sure, you can watch videos about someone else explaining the mechanics, but when you're the first ones playing through a dungeon or raid, you're the one who's going to be writing those guides. And yes, the costs can add up, but with the item drops and the other stuff, you generally get more income from it than what you spend on repair costs."

She nods, thoughtful. "Still... As a healer, your whole party wiping over and over again, it's a little demoralising."

"True. It can get a little frustrating sometimes. Which is why I don't like to keep doing it day and night..." I smile. "I like figuring out new raids, but I also need to do other things those days too."

"Like what?"

"Levelling a gathering or crafting skill, or like, actually get away from my computer and stuff."

"You do things *away* from the computer?" Her eyes sparkle as she teases me.

"Oi!" I can't help but laugh. "Yes, I do. I have multiple hobbies that do not involve being connected to the internet, or even having a computer."

"Like what?" She leans forward.

"I like reading. I have a lot of different hobbies that I've collected and all tried for like... a couple of weeks. Ehhh..." I have to think for a moment, mentally running through all the different boxes with things in my room. "I guess reading is the one I still do the most."

"What do you read?"

Do I dare to tell? Not everyone responds well when I talk about this... "Romance novels. I've been reading a lot of paranormal romance novels lately."

"Really?" Fleur laughs. "That sounds... I don't know. I didn't expect that." She tilts her head a little. "I guess I expected you to read a lot of like... Hard science fiction or epic fantasy or something."

"Hard science fiction, no. Epic fantasy, yes. Just not recently. It's been a while since I read one." I kind of can't even remember the last time I read an epic fantasy novel. "I like reading romance novels, they make me happy."

"I guess I can see that." She nods. "I also read romance novels. Though, just contemporary stuff. I'm not into the monsters or shapeshifters or whatever. Give me a cute high school girl falling in love with a sexy sports-player or rich hunk any day."

Girls falling in love with guys... Of course. It's not as though the books I read are any different from that, but just hearing her say it like that, like it's normal... I don't know. It makes me really aware of our situation right now. I also almost always read about girls falling in love with guys, though I've been finding more books of girls falling in love with other girls, or guys falling in love with other guys. But, they're all a little... explicit. A bit more explicit than I prefer to read. Does Fleur read the explicit books? Although, the way she reacted to her mother joking about X-rated films, maybe not.

A guy comes to our table, smiling broadly. "Your pizza?"

"Thank you." I sit back a little, taking my drink out of the way so he can put it on the table between us.

"Do you need anything else?" He looks at us both, a big smile on his face, and Fleur gives him a sweet smile as she shakes her head.

"We're good." She looks at me, still smiling. "Right?"

"Right." I nod. "Thanks."

"Have a nice meal. And if you need any of us, just wave. We'll be happy to help you with anything." He bows a little, eyeing us as if he's very interested in helping us with 'anything', and then he walks off again.

This feels weird. I'm not used to guys looking at me like that, or at someone I'm with. A little bit of annoyance sparks in my chest.

Or maybe it's just been too long since I was out in the city without Troy by my side. I can't really remember if the same happened when I was on dates before. Or maybe it's just a different dynamic this time. Maybe we're now old enough to get this type of attention from guys? I don't know. Do the guys do this with all the girls who come in here together? Is it because we're both girls?

Is this even a *real* date?

"Alex?" Fleur's voice is teasing.

She's trying to get my attention again and I'm freaking out about this being or maybe not being a date. This whatever-it-is I'm on, with Fleur, who I apparently keep zoning out on as my mind keeps running in all different directions… *Whoops.*

"Sorry. I keep…" I move my hands, not sure how to explain or apologise right now.

Her eyes soften. "It's okay. I was just trying to tell you that you're on your way to push your phone off the table with your elbow." She reaches over the table, grabbing the phone, and putting it in the middle of the table, far away from my elbows.

"Thanks." I look at the pizza in front of us. "It looks good."

"It totally does." Fleur grins. "Who's gonna cut into it first?"

"You? This is your home town, and I did ask you to come to the cinema with me."

"Well, I was the one who came up with the dinner part, so you should cut it. You're a guest in *my* home town." She leans back, making it obvious she's not going to do it.

"Fine." I laugh and cut the pizza in half and then I cut a slice for myself. "Do you want me to cut a piece for you too?" I look her way.

"Yes, thank you." Fleur's voice is lower, her cheeks a little redder than before and she swallows hard.

Oh. My heart beats louder, and I quietly cut off a slice for her too. I slide it onto her plate and sit back again, a little awkward and very aware of the mood. It changed quite quickly.

We eat in silence for a while, both not saying anything and I don't know if it's because of something I said or did or if we're just a little too lost in our own thoughts...

"Fleur?" I watch her, watch the way she's focusing on the pizza.

She looks up, softly smiling. "Yeah?"

Do you like me? *Oh, hell, no. Can't ask that.* "Thanks for inviting me here. I really appreciate it." *And how's that any less awkward?*

She nods. "Of course. I didn't want to just go to the cinema. There's no point getting all excited about sitting in the dark for two hours." She smiles a little, then takes another bite of her pizza.

"Yeah." I take a breath. "Of course." That makes sense. It makes sense to spend a little more time here when it's an hour to get here and then back afterwards.

"And I like spending time with you. I don't know many girls who like playing videogames as much as I do. And you're probably even more dedicated than I am." She laughs and the awkward mood has lifted a little.

"Potentially." I grin. "But I've been playing this game since release. So, what? I've got more than a year on you?"

Fleur nods. "Yeah, sounds about right." She takes another slice. "But I'll catch up with you. I promise."

"I'll look forward to that. Tank and healer super duo. We'll take on any raid, just the two of us."

Fleur bursts out laughing, quickly covering her mouth and nose, then wiping at them with her napkin. "Don't make me laugh like that. My water nearly came out through my nose."

"Can't help being too funny that I'm a danger to my surroundings." It feels good, making her laugh like that.

Fleur rolls her eyes and shakes her head... Still laughing. "Right... Let's pretend it's that and not your overblown ego."

"Ego... Funny… I can live with either." I wink and Fleur wipes her mouth again as she shakes her head at me.

I love making her laugh so much that she can barely stop. She gets even more cute as she tries to compose herself.

15
Fleur

Gathering = The collecting of materials that can later be used by crafters. This usually includes herbs, pelts, metals, stone and other things. Of the non-fighter classes it's often a more time-consuming but also cheaper skill to train for a character. You can sell the items in the market place, but you can often make more money from them when you first gather and then craft something before you sell it. I like levelling my gathering skills as it's calming and easy.

Dinner was... fun and scary and totally confusing, all at once. I don't know if it was because we were nervous or something because we just kept saying things that were a little odd... I don't know.

Having Alex sitting across from me, laughing, talking, having her all to myself. I was very aware of her, I was very aware of the way she moved, of the way she looked at me, of the way she talked. And it made me do some foolish things, just because I didn't know how to act like myself... *Argh.*

But now we're on our way to the cinema, on our way to actually seeing the film that was the goal of this whole getting together thing.

It's still hot and bright outside, which is such a difference from the darkness of the pizzeria that we have to stand still, covering our eyes, for a moment before we can actually walk away from the place. It's not a long walk to the cinema, it's only five or ten minutes, but it feels like time stretches and compresses, both at the same time, when I'm with Alex.

"Oh!" Alex suddenly disappears from my side and as I turn around to see what's going on, she's already disappearing into a tiny shop.

I quickly walk back, following her inside. It's got all sorts of funny little things. Like small funny presents and things you can put on tables and around your house, all pretty cheaply... I don't even know exactly what made Alex suddenly jump into this shop. And as I look around, I have no idea where she's gone off to. So I start browsing, looking at the shelves with craft supplies and notebooks and pens and other things at the front of the shop. If she leaves again, she'll have to pass by me.

"Come on." Alex grins as she grabs my wrist and pulls me back outside, back into the heat, a white bag in her other hand.

"Sure." I let her pull me along and she doesn't stop walking until we're out of the sun and can stand in a slightly quieter area of the street, out of the busy stream of people.

"Okay. Open it." She hands me the bag.

"What's in it?" Did she just buy me something?

"You'll see." She looks so excited that I open the bag, and inside I find a fake red rose and a flower-shaped electrical fan.

"Eh…" I look at Alex.

"Take them out." She keeps grinning, so I do as she asks.

"The fan is so you won't overheat. And the flower is for in your hair." Her voice softens as she keeps smiling. Then she holds out her hand. "Can I put it in?"

I swallow, then I nod and give her the rose.

"Good, just stay still for a moment." She takes the little card off the rose and then starts bending the stem.

At first I flinch, so used to working with real flowers that I can't imagine that going right. But this is a fake rose with a bendable stem. Then she walks around me and braids the stem into my hair a little, making it stay in place.

"There." She steps back in front of me, looking at her work. "Looks pretty." She smiles.

I reach up, touching the rose, the way it's in my hair, then I grab my phone and use the front camera to look at what Alex did. It's pretty simple, a rose stuck into my hair, just over my ear, but the stem keeps it in place securely. But it also looks really nice, it looks kind of cute. "Thank you." I can't help the blush spreading over my cheeks, or the hot feeling I get when I remember that Alex just touched me to put it into my hair, or the big feeling in my chest over Alex buying me something just because she thought it would look cute on me.

"And now you can use the fan to cool down, with those red cheeks of yours." She winks.

"Cheeky." I laugh. I'm not sure if that was the exact reason she bought both of them, but it's funny anyway.

"I do try." She starts walking again, and I turn on the fan before I follow her.

I may not need it for the blushing, but the fan is really nice in the sticky summer heat, and it gives me some coolness while we make our way to the cinema.

Alex just bought me things, just because she saw them and thought they were cute. This is something you'd normally do for a friend you've known for a long time, but more likely, something you'd do for a... a *lover*.

And now I really need that fan and hope Alex doesn't look too closely at my face in the coming minutes, because I'm burning up at that thought, the implications...

My cheeks feel so aflame that I'm sure everyone walking past me knows exactly what's going through my mind.

Like you'd do for a lover.

⟦W⟧⟦A⟧⟦S⟧⟦D⟧

We reached the cinema early enough that we had time to buy some popcorn, even though we just had dinner. It's not a real cinema trip without popcorn, Alex and I agreed on that.

We made our way to the actual screen where we were going to be watching the film. The doors were already open, so we sat down in our seats and just looked around.

"This one is different from the one in Groningen." Alex sits up, looking at the back.

"Bigger, smaller?" I've only been to the one in Groningen a handful of times, but I've never been in one of the main screens, since I don't usually go there to watch a film that has only just been released.

"About the same size, actually." She looks around again. "But the arrangement of the chairs is different, as are the lights and the whole layout of the room. Interesting." She now properly sits down. "Interesting to see how two cinemas from the same company can be so different."

I hadn't really thought about that, but I guess it makes sense. "Do you go to the cinema often?"

Alex shrugs. "I sometimes go see some with Cerise, when she's in town anyway. These days, she's attending a University of Applied Sciences in a different city, so I don't see her as often anymore. Troy... Meh. Sometimes I can get him to come with me, but he's not really that interested in seeing films in cinemas. He prefers to watch them at home." She rolls her eyes. "The guy just doesn't get the excitement of seeing an action film on like... the huge screen. Right?"

"Duh." I laugh. "Yeah, I sometimes see one with some of my friends, or with Jade, my best friend, but if it's an action film, I'm generally on my own."

"Awh." Alex reaches out, taking my hand. "If you ever get lonely when you're seeing one of them, just tell me. I'll come support you in your *difficult* times." She laughs, but my heart is beating so loudly that I can barely focus on her words and I'm sure my hand is sweaty in hers.

I don't want to let her hand go, so I keep holding it, squeezing a little and Alex squeezes back. "I'd really like that." I manage to find my voice.

"I'm always available." Her voice also sounds a little different, in a way that makes me want to reach out and touch her a little more, but I don't, I'm too scared.

"Good." I sit back, still holding her hand, hoping she won't pull it back. "Have you seen the other films with the main actor?" I try to find something to talk about, to break this awkward mood.

"Him? Not so much. But the actress I've seen in a lot of action films. If she's in it, I usually try to see it in the cinema." Alex laughs a little. "There is just something to the way that she can kick butt and demand all the attention on her."

I think for a moment. I agree with Alex, the actress is really good at kicking butts, though I've never really thought about it that way. And I guess I've seen her in a lot of films, but that's what I get for binge-watching so many films while playing videogames. "Yeah. She really does. I think she's sometimes even better than the guy."

Alex nods. "She has to be. She's the one who has to do all the real fighting. He usually just gets to use his superpowers and expensive gadgets."

"True." And then I realise something else, Alex is focused on the actress, talks about the woman, about watching everything *she's* in, not him. I get differing tastes, but if I talk to one of my 'Mum approved' friends, they'd turn the subject to another actor who they'd prefer if they didn't like the one in the film we're discussing. They'd talk about another *man*. But Alex doesn't, she just switches to the *woman* in the film. Is that... Does that mean...

"Oh!" Alex turns to me a little, still holding my hand. "Did you see the other film she was cast in? It's like... a sort-of action film, but it also has a bit of a romance plot in it... I'm just hoping they don't totally ruin her for it."

"What do you mean?" Jumping subjects, we're good at that, but even if both our brains do it, we still sometimes get confused when it happens.

"Quite often, they turn these really strong actresses into these weepy princesses if they give them a romance plot in a film. Like, suddenly they can't stand up for themselves even though they're normally the ones kicking the most butt." Alex seems so annoyed by it. "It's just so unfair. We love watching them, and we love the type of characters they play, and then as soon as they're supposed to play a character who's in love, they have to give up their strength. I don't like it." She sighs, sitting back again, frowning.

"Is it really that bad?" I don't really think about this usually. I like romantic films, or even 'chick flicks', but I get her point on some of the characters that the actresses have to play. Some women just seem more naturally a fit for a kick-ass character, not the cutesy princess some of the romantic films require them to be.

"When I like an actress because she's great at kicking butt, I don't really like to see that power taken away from her just so she can play the lead in a romance flick." She frowns a little more. "It just feels unfair, both to the actress and to her fans."

"I guess so. I don't think many people really worry about that when they see actors. But I guess when it's an actress, it's different." I don't tend to watch many of the romance films where actresses I enjoy watching in action flicks play a lead role.

"There are so many generic 'cool action hero' or 'damaged action hero' actors out there, like, sometimes I even forget who is in what." Alex' voice raises a little. "But for actresses, there just aren't that many. There aren't many who get to play these kick-ass women and to then change who they are for a film just because they now have a love-interest just because the people in charge believe that's what the viewers want... I don't know. Like..." She lets out a disapproving sound. "They try to appeal to female viewers with a romance sub-plot, but then ruin the character who they love so much because the people in charge don't believe that romance lead and kick-ass heroine somehow go together for female characters." She sighs, squeezing my hand a little. "Sorry. Just... Something I can get worked up over and then I start rambling."

"Do you..." I swallow, but it's still not enough of a rest to stop me from blurting out the question. "Do you like girls more than you like guys?"

I quickly close my mouth, my heart going into overdrive. I pull my hand from Alex' to cover my mouth, preventing me from saying more stupid things.

Alex stares at me, surprise in her eyes, and I wish I could take my question back. I wish I could take my stupid question back right now.

Because, right there, that look, that fear, that confusion, I don't want to see it. I don't want to hurt her. And I did.

Again.

16
Alex

Currency = Most games have different types of currency. There is the global system that is basically 'money'. Depending on the game this can be a system with bronze, silver and gold or other metal coins, basically Euros and cents, other games use only one type of coin, like how the Japanese Yen works. But on top of that, most games also have special currencies that gamers collect from quests, dungeons, raids and other things and those can be exchanged for special gear and items at specific NPCs. Collecting enough currency is usually one of the reasons why people run the endgame dungeons so often, just so they can get a full endgame gear set.

What? How am I even supposed to answer that? Especially to Fleur... Especially when I have no idea what she thinks about me right now, how she *feels* about me... Would me answering ruin even the small bit of friendship we've started to build?

She looks so surprised by her own question, but I can also see the curiosity in her eyes. She does want to know. I don't know why, I don't dare to hope to know why... *Argh*.

I move in my seat, the hall is filling up with more people, and I don't want to make a scene. "I don't know."

It's the best I can give her right now. Of course, I know the answer, but I don't know how she'll react to it and I don't want her to hate me. I don't want her to act differently towards me. I don't want that.

She looks at me, her face falling a little, disappointed, and then she sits back in her seat, staring ahead. The silence stretches between us and I don't know how to fill it.

This just got a whole lot more awkward, more awkward even than when she saw me for the first time. It feels like I may have ruined any chance I had at shrugging this off. At acting like the question means nothing to me.

The silence between us keeps stretching and the hall darkens, the screen lighting up, starting to play commercials. I start fiddling with the hem of my shirt, trying to sit still, trying not to make weird movements, but I just don't know what to do, how to fix this.

I glance in Fleur's direction and she keeps looking ahead, her eyebrows drawn up and her eyes appear to be looking in the direction of the screen, but I can see how she's not actually seeing any it. Her eyes are blank. She's trying to act normally, just like I am.

I gave the wrong answer, didn't I? I lean in and Fleur looks at me, a little surprised. "I'll be right back, need to use the toilets."

She nods, her eyes on my face, searching it for something. "Okay."

"I'll be right back." I stand up and make my way through the rest of the row and then out of the screen. When I'm in the hallway, I take a deep breath, trying to calm my heart a little, and grab my phone. I send a message off to Cerise. 'She asked me if I liked girls more than boys. I totally choked up. Help!'

Then I go to the toilets, locking myself in a cubicle. I can't believe I totally choked up. I can't believe I freaked out like that. I should have just answered with the truth. It's not like me to freak out about my sexuality… It's so unlike me.

My phone buzzes and I see Cerise has sent a message back. 'What did you say? How did she react?'

'I told her I don't know. She went quiet after that, like she had to think about that.' The way she went quiet, the way she started thinking, lost in her own brain, that's what's making me worry most.

'You don't know?!' Cerise adds surprised emoticons to her message and I can't help but smile a little.

Of course, *I* know. I've always liked girls the most. There was no surprise or question about that for me.

'Was she thinking in a doubtful way, or in a confused way?' The message makes me look up again.

'I have no idea. I can't read her right now. I don't know if I even want to know. What if it's bad?' I don't want to lose Fleur. I realise more and more that I really don't want to lose her. Not as a friend, but also not as potentially something more than a friend.

'Don't you think she would have responded differently if it was bad?' How can Cerise be so sensible about this?

'I have no idea.' I keep repeating myself. But I'm just as confused right now. There is a fine line to walk between not telling and actively hiding who I am, and I don't know if I can really walk that line around Fleur. I don't want to walk that line.

'Why are you messaging me instead of talking to her?'

'I locked myself in the toilets. We're at the cinema.' It's childish, but at least here I can message Cerise without anyone knowing.

'She's still in the hall?'

'Yes. I left her there during the commercials.'

'Go back in. Don't be a wuss. She didn't freak out at your answer. So just go back in.'

'What if she hates me but doesn't want to say it? What if she now thinks I'm just here with her to hit on her?' I can't do this.

'Aren't you?'

'Not in a predatory way. I just like her. I want to be with her.'

'Then, go be with her. Go have fun together and stop freaking out. I'm going to ignore any more messages you send.' *Pushy. Pushy.* Cerise is right, but I don't feel like I have the courage to go back just yet.

Then a new message pops up, not from Cerise but from Fleur. 'Are you okay?'

My heart skips a beat, just from receiving the message. Am I okay? 'Yeah. I'll be right back.' Suddenly I feel both so much more scared, but also so much more... in love. Fleur sent me a message because she was worried. She cares, even if it isn't in the same way that I do.

I stand up, leaving the stall, and washing my hands, just to have something to do as I make sure I'm not going to burst out crying. I don't want to be this emotional over just a small question. But I'm still kind of scared, and it's hard not to get all worked up over it.

"Alex?" The door to the toilets opens and Fleur steps in. She looks around and then sees me. "Hey." Her voice is soft, her eyes filled with concern.

"Hey." I go over to her, trying to stay calm. "I said I was going to be right back."

"I know. You just seemed a little off after my question." She looks around and then steps back out. She looks to the side and walks a little off to a corner where few people will be able to overhear us.

I follow her, my heart sinking. This can't go over well. How am I supposed to keep calm? How can this situation get any worse?

She turns to me, her eyes now softer, darker, looking at me for a moment before looking down at her hands. "I'm sorry for what I asked. I know it's not my place to ask things like that. It's not right. It has nothing to do with me. Please, just forget I said anything." Her voice is rushed, wavering a little.

"It's okay. It was a valid question to ask at the time." I was going a little gaga over actresses in a way that most girls who primarily like guys probably wouldn't do.

She nods, then shakes her head. "No. It was still stupid of me to ask. I didn't want to ruin the mood. And I totally did. I'm sorry."

My heart breaks, just a little, from seeing her this upset. "I..." Tears start forming in my eyes, I don't want to cry. I don't want to freak out. But I can't let her think that I took offence to her question. I didn't. I just freaked out a little because it came from *her*. And now I've made the whole mood weird. "I..."

She looks up, her eyes watery too, and her lip wobbles when she meets my eyes. We're a bunch of cry-babies. Is this just who we are anyway, or is this one of those bad emotional regulations that sometimes comes with ADHD? Or is this something else? She reaches out and I take her hands, squeezing.

I lick my lips. "I do like girls. Almost exclusively." I look at our hands, and instead of pulling away, as I'd feared, she squeezes them tighter, holding on.

"Thank you." Her voice is thick, and I look up at her, but her eyes are also on our hands. "I..." She swallows. "I..." Then she lets out a soft laugh, looking up and flashing me a half-smile. Then she pulls a face. "I haven't before. This is a first for me." Her hands loosen and I step closer, wrapping my arms around her and pulling her close. She wraps her arms around me too, holding tight as her breathing is uneven.

It's only then that I realise what she just said. She likes a girl, for the first time. My heart starts beating loudly, so loudly that I'm scared she'll be able to hear it too. She hasn't had a girlfriend before, or liked girls. Although, it would be egotistic of me to assume she's talking about me right now...

"I think I might like you." Her voice is soft and her arms around me loosen, allowing me to pull back if I'd want to.

But I don't want to. I don't want to, ever. I tighten my arms around her a little. "I *know* I like you."

Getting confessed to in the middle of the cinema, that's unexpected. That's new.

Then she lets go of me, slowly stepping back and looks up at me. Her make-up is streaking down her face a little. "I have no idea how to do this, though. I've never..." She shakes her head. "I've never felt like this before. It's scary."

I nod. I know. I get how scary really liking someone is. How utterly frightening falling for someone can be. "Let's get you cleaned up and then we can go see the film. Yeah?"

"Are you sure?" She looks a little confused.

"We came here for the film. I want to spend time with you. That's all. Unless you want to go somewhere else?" I can do either. I'm not that fussed. I'm just a little too glad that she doesn't hate me and that she even thinks that she likes me.

She shakes her head again. "I want to see it."

"Well, then. Let's go back. After we've taken care of your make-up." I reach out to her and she takes my hand. Holding on.

My heart is still beating like crazy. But I think this is a good thing. I think this could work out alright.

I think...

W A S D

The film was pretty good, though I didn't really watch all of it. I was a little distracted by Fleur's hand in mine. I was a little distracted by this new feeling going on.

I never really considered that my feelings could be returned by Fleur, and that this would get even more scary than when we were just trying to be friends.

"Alex?" Fleur turns around. "When is your mum picking you up?"

I check my phone, I got a message from Mum about half an hour ago. "Twenty minutes, half an hour. Something like that." I wish I could make this date even longer, but I know I can't. There will be an end to tonight.

Fleur confessed. She confessed to me, at least, that sounded like a confession. Right?

I look around, trying to find a place where we can sit or something.

"Let's go get my bike, and then come back here." Fleur looks around a little too, before looking back at me.

"Good idea." That way we still get to spend some time together, and I won't have to think about leaving her behind just yet.

We start walking in silence. The streets are not as busy as they were when we walked here on our way to the cinema, but the night is still nice and warm.

"What does this all mean?" Fleur's voice is low, slow.

"What does what mean?"

"This? Between us?" She stops and looks at me, her eyes a little scared.

"I don't know. What do you want it to mean?" I take a deep breath, pushing my own feelings to the side a little. This is totally new to Fleur, and I can't force her. "You said that you might like me. That sounds like you may not be sure. I already know that I like you. This means that it's up to you to decide what it all means to you."

She nods, her eyes guarded. "I don't think I can… like... *do* anything right now. I don't know how." Her voice wavers again and I take her hands.

I want to take that pain away, her fear, her confusion, but I know that it takes time, not me doing anything right now. "I'm happy just being with you, talking to you. Holding your hand, or even giving you a hug, that's all extra for me. I just really like being with you. I don't expect anything you're not comfortable with."

Why does the little flicker of relief in her eyes make me angry? Has anyone actually forced her to do things she wasn't ready for? Anger grows in me, but I push it down. That's not for now, I can only show her that it doesn't have to be that way.

"Let's go get your bike. I don't want to get you into trouble over getting home late." I try to smile, not wanting to think about having to leave her alone in about fifteen more minutes...

17
Fleur

NPC = Non Player Character = Characters in a game world that are not controlled by another player but are instead controlled by the game itself. Some are just there to fill the world a little, while others are there to give you quests, or sell you items and things like that. I love the funny things that some of the NPCs will say, but you'll have to stand near them to hear it.

Oh. My. God. I can't believe I said that... I can't believe I actually said that I might actually like her... And she said...

I can't keep my mind in a single direction. Alex is still walking next to me, holding my hand, as we're going to pick up my bike. My heart is beating loudly and I feel it's hard to swallow.

No matter how much I thought about this possibility before, no matter what Jade asked me... I'm not ready for this. I'm not ready to consider this is actually happening. Me, falling in love with a girl.

But Alex is looking so cool and grownup next to me. She looks so much older, so much calmer. I feel like a little kid now.

How can this change again? How can we get back to being equal? I don't know. I hate feeling like I'm the little kid… It always reminds me that I'm different, that I'm the one always lagging behind on things. I hate that.

"Fleur?" Alex pulls on my arm a little. "You still there?" Her voice is soft, and as I turn to her, so are her eyes.

"Sorry. I…" I'm just a little caught up in my own head. Though I don't think I actually have to tell her that… She already knows that. She understands things like this. She *gets* me, no matter what.

Alex smiles a little. "I actually wanted to ask you something. Cerise and I are having our birthday party in a couple of weeks. We're still trying to decide on the exact dates, but it will probably be a weekend thing. It will be girls only and there will be girls from the guild and other girls we know from playing videogames."

"That sounds… interesting?" A girl-gamer only party. I'm not exactly sure what to expect from it, but it sounds cool.

Alex shrugs a little. "We'll probably all be taking our computers or laptops with us, and we'll be spending most of the time playing DoE or other games. Cerise's parents have a big house and we can have a LAN-party there easily. Do you want to come?" There is so much hope in her eyes.

I nod. "Sounds like fun. I don't know many girls who play a lot of videogames."

"That's why we sometimes do this." Alex grins. "I'll let Cerise know you said yes."

"I'll still have to ask my mum, so I'm not sure yet."

"Fair enough. Though, I think she'll be fine with it, after today." She lets out a laugh.

I can't help but laugh too. "True. She seemed impressed with you."

"I'm good at impressing people." She winks and my cheeks heat up. That was flirting, right?

We reach my bike, and I unlock it, grabbing hold of it. Having my bike... I realise that soon I'll be going home, on my own. Away from Alex.

"Alex?" I'm not even sure what I want to say, but my voice is a little rough.

"Yeah?" She turns to me, putting her hand on the handlebar, near mine. She's quiet for a moment, and then moves her little finger over to my hand, sliding it along my fingers. "I was serious when I said that I don't expect anything special from you. I don't want you to be scared. I..." She takes a breath. "I really enjoy just spending time with you, no matter what happens."

My heart sinks a little. I don't want her to sound like that. I don't want her to sound like I may be scared of her. I'm not and I would never be. "I'm not scared. I'm just... confused." I slide my hand over, covering hers, squeezing a little. "I like spending time with you too. I want to spend more time with you." Why are those stupid tears there again? Why? Why do I cry so easily?

Alex reaches out, wiping at my tears with her thumb, then holding me for a moment. "We will. But everything in its own time." She smiles, then her phone buzzes. She takes her phone and frowns. "Mum's here."

I nod. "You're meeting her at the cinema, yes?"

"Yeah." She looks at me with sad eyes.

"Let's walk there." I tug on her hand which I'm still holding on the handlebar.

I don't want to leave. I don't want *Alex* to leave. But this day will come to an end. And that scares me.

Because what happens when I'm back on my own?

What happens when all the fluttery feelings that I get near her calm down?

W A S D

When we approach the cinema, a tall woman is standing in front of it. By the colour of her hair, and the way she's looking our way, I suspect that she's Alex' mum.

We stop in front of her, and the woman smiles at us both. She reaches out to me. "Hi, I'm Alex' mum. You must be Fleur."

I nod, taking her hand. "Nice to meet you."

She turns to Alex, and then looks at me again. "Did you have fun seeing the film?"

"Yeah. Was fun. How was work?" Alex is still standing next to me.

Her mum shrugs. "Not too bad. But I'll be happy to be in my bed soon." She does look tired. "On that note. We should probably go." She smiles at me. "I'm sorry I've got to cut this short, I only just got out of a long shift. You're always welcome to come over to our place. I'm pretty sure Alex wants that, anyway." She eyes her daughter.

I can feel my cheeks heat up again and as I look to the side, I see the same on Alex.

"Ah, so I *was* right." There is a tone of glee in Alex' mum's voice.

"Mum!" Alex raises her voice now and her cheeks go even redder. "You're *not* allowed to do that."

"I'm just glad to see you happy. That's all." Alex' mum grins. "I promised I wouldn't ask awkward questions. I didn't. You were the one who gave an answer to a question I didn't ask, no matter how involuntary it was."

Alex sighs loudly as she rolls her eyes and I burst out laughing. So her mum is as annoying as mine. I understand how Alex was able to deal with mine so easily.

"See? She doesn't seem to mind." Alex' mum still laughs.

"Ugh." Alex shakes her head, then she looks at me, smiling. "I'm taking her home before she starts asking actual awkward questions."

I nod, also smiling. The mood now much lighter. "I'll talk to you soon."

"Talk to you soon." She steps closer and we hug a little awkwardly as I'm still also holding my bike.

When she lets go, I already miss having her near.

Alex' mum looks at me. "Have a lovely evening. And get home safely. Are you sure you don't want us to drop you off at home? I can easily put your bike in the back of the car."

I shake my head. "Thanks. But I'll just cycle home. The weather is nice anyway."

"Okay. See you some other time." She smiles, then waits for Alex.

"Talk to you later." Alex runs her fingers over my hand, and I grab them for a moment.

"Talk to you later." My voice is low and I feel a tightening in my chest. But we both know that this is the end of the date, the date-date.

Alex steps back, then as she turns around, she waves at me. I wave back as I watch them walk off.

When they walk around the corner, I slump over my handlebars, letting out a deep sigh.

Today was exhausting. So much happened, much more than I ever thought could happen. And now I feel a little lost.

I grab my phone and send a message to Jade. 'OMFG!' I don't even know how else to put into words what's going on in my head.

'What?' She's pretty quick at responding.

'OMFG OMFG OMFG!'

I can imagine the face she's making at my messages. 'Where are you?'

'About to go home.' I sigh. I'm still too wound up to actually go home. Especially since I know that I'll just be there alone and Alex won't be home for another hour...

'Wanna come over? You need to tell me everything about the date!' Jade's place is much closer and on my way home anyway.

'Sure. Lemme let my mum know.' Or she's going to freak out and I don't want that. Especially not when the blame would be on Alex, if she doesn't know that I'm with Jade. And if I want to see Alex more often, that's gonna be annoying.

W A S D

I lock my bike and walk up to the back door of the house, but Jade's already pulling it open. A huge smile of excitement on her face.

"Tell me everything!" She pulls on my arm, but instead of going into the house, she pulls me to the bench at the back of the garden. She makes me sit down and then sits on it herself. "Come on. Tell me." She looks so excited.

I shrug, embarrassed. "I don't know what to tell you, really."

"You only sent me O-M-G. I need more than that!" She raises her eyebrow at me.

"I sent O-M-F-G, not just O-M-G." I can't help smiling now.

"Even better. Start at the beginning." She crosses her arms in front of her, trying to look sternly.

"She met my mum." I cringe a little at the memory. "You know what my mum's like... But Alex survived her well. Which... I actually met her mum too, just now. I get *how* she survived Mum now." I let out a breathy laugh. "Alex' mum is almost worse than mine. She was the best, or worst, really. I don't think I'll ever see Alex blush like that again. I didn't even realise she could." I feel my own cheeks heat up at the memory, of how cute it made Alex look. Alex, who usually looks so cool and even sexy, or at least much more grown-up than I feel, reduced to blushes and sounds of awkwardness. I know that I'll probably not see that again any time soon.

Jade is giving me that look again. That look that tells me she thinks I'm some special specimen or like I'm doing some weird new trick...

"Stop looking like that." I now try to frown at her.

"I can't help it." She smiles. "This is new. This is new for you, but it's also new for me to see you like this. You're excited."

"I'm always excited." I get easily excited, that's who I am.

"Not in the same way. You're excited about a *person*. You're talking differently, acting differently. I like seeing it. But it's also a little odd right now."

"If you're just studying me, I'm not going to continue my story." I lean back, crossing my arms in front of me, pretending to pout, which always gets to her.

"No, please. Tell me more. I haven't dated in a long time. I *need* to live vicariously through you right now. This is the closest I've been to a date in months." She also pouts, giving me the big puppy dog eyes.

"Fine." I roll my eyes, laughing. "So, after she survived my mum, we went shopping quickly, before we went for dinner." That had been interesting, if not a little scary sometimes. Being so close to her, I felt like I'd burst out of my skin at any moment and I couldn't help it. I just couldn't help feeling all those bubbles inside, those bubbles that made my brain go all weird and made me say stupid stuff a couple of times. "Have I told you yet that she's sexy? Like... When I saw her... Hmmm..." I wrap my arms around myself, grinning. "Gives me butterflies." I bite on my lip. "I can't believe I just said that out loud."

Jade bursts out laughing. "I've gotta meet her. I know you showed me a pic, but I really need to meet this girl who reduces you to a puddle of goo."

"Maybe." I look at her. "I don't know if that would be safe, for my sanity." I grin.

"Riiiight." Jade shakes her head. "So, what part of all of this was the O-M-*F*-G part of it?"

"I asked her if she likes girls more than boys." I cover my face with my hand. "Still can't believe that I did that."

"You, *what?*" I hear the surprise in her voice because I can't look at her right now. "What did she say?"

"At first, nothing... And then she fled to the bathroom..." It freaked me out too. I was scared I'd said too much. I couldn't believe my own stupidity.

"What?"

"I followed her. And she said that she does like girls better." I take a deep breath. "And-then-I-confessed-to-her." The words spill from my mouth in one long line.

"You—" Jade pulls my hands away from my face, looking at me closely. "You confessed?"

I nod.

"You said that you like her?"

"I said that I thought I *might* like her..." I look at my hands.

"What did she do? What did she say?"

"She said that she already knew that she likes me." I still can't really believe the words or that it happened.

Jade lets out a squeal and laughs so loudly that I curl up on the bench, trying to hide. "O-M-G. I can't believe it!" She turns to me, grinning. "She really likes you. Like, *likes*-likes you, like that." That's a lot of likes...

I nod, my emotions split, excited and scared at the same time.

"Congrats." Jade still grins and wraps her arms around me.

"What was that noise?" Jade's brother looks at us from his bedroom window, glowering, trying to act all tough. Though he never really got that good at it when it comes to us. He's always been too much of a softie as a big brother.

"Fleur's got herself a girlfriend!" Jade calls up at him.

"Right. Now, can you just keep the noise down?" He rolls his eyes as he closes the window again.

Jade and I look at each other and then burst out laughing. Leave it to her brother to just shake his head at us as he goes off doing something else again. Typical.

It also takes some of the anxiety away. His reaction, laughing, it all makes me happy, and less anxious. It makes me feel like I did around Alex a little, relaxed, but also a little nervous.

Because, I'm sure not everyone will respond to this knowledge in the same way...

And that's what really scares me... Not knowing how other people will react when they find out.

18
Alex

HoT/DoT = Heal over Time / Damage over Time = Most attacks or heals only happen when you cast the spell or hit something with your weapon. But some things also have the ability to do healing or damage over time. Like when you cut someone and they start bleeding, or when someone breaks your heart and the pain keeps coming… Those things, they're DoTs.

The drive home is filled with Mum trying to get more information out of me. Though I don't have much to offer… Not much more than what she already guessed at anyway.

I send Troy a message, letting him know that I'll be back online in not too long. This morning I told him I'd do another dungeon run with him when I got back home. We're levelling a new class each, trying to get maximum level on all the classes in the game. We normally play too much on our main and secondary classes, so the others kind of fall by the wayside. But now we have all the time to get back to this, with it being summer break and all.

'How did the date go?' Troy's response is kind of expected.

'Was fun. Film was cool and we had pizza.' I'm not giving him extras so easily.

'Boooring. What happened? Did something interesting happen? Did you kiss her yet?'

I nearly choke on my own spit and break out into a coughing fit. Did he *have* to ask it like that? From the corner of my eyes I can see Mum look my way for a moment. "I'm fine." I shake my head. Physically maybe, mentally is a whole different thing.

'Well?' The guy is insistent.

'No. I didn't kiss her. Get your mind out of the gutter.'

'I thought that that was the whole goal of today... Boring!' He sends a couple of frowning emoticons with it.

'It was a date. I didn't go for a make-out session.'

'Pfff. Why wouldn't you?' He's got a way with being annoying.

'Because she's never dated a girl before.' The moment I type the words, I realise how important they are. Fleur has never dated a girl before. I have, a couple of girls even, but she hasn't. And apart from the physical differences between boys and girls—hey, I've seen and play fought with Troy mostly naked often enough to know there is quite a difference between the two. At least, when it comes to certain areas... My cheeks already heat up when I think exactly of where those areas are and especially how I'd like to touch Fleur and hold her...

'Ah.' It's just a single word, a short reply, and I hadn't even realised I'd sent the message yet. But I know that he's got his own worry when it comes to this.

'What?' Not that I need to really ask.

'Nothing. Just that you're not making it easy on yourself, or on us.'

'Why?'

'She's never dated a girl before. Her healing style fits your tanking perfectly. What if she freaks out? What if she runs away? Then what? How long will it take for you to find a new healer for the guild?' He might sound like an idiot, but he's right.

I may want to date Fleur, but she's also part of our guild, a guild who also love to have her with them, and if I mess this up… it's not just me who will lose her. What will happen then? Will I scare her off?

I put the phone away. I don't want to think about those questions, I don't like them. I already know this. I already thought about what could happen if things went wrong. And I have no answers. I have no answers to any of those questions. Because Troy's right, if I scare Fleur off, it's not just me who'd be affected.

I bump my head against the window and look outside, at the fields passing us by. I know I won't be ruining just one friendship if this goes bad.

No matter how much I'd want this, Fleur's inexperience with girls means that it could go wrong very easily. And it's not like I don't have experience with that. It's not like I don't know what can happen when a girl decides she's not as into girls as she thought she was at first. It's not like I don't know that pain.

And is that worth it? Is that worth giving up something that could be a great friendship?

Ugh.

W A S D

I sit down in front of the computer, putting my headset on, but not going into the main group chat server. Instead, I check whether Fleur is online yet, and when she's still offline, I set up a private chat with Troy.

All the fun things that were swirling through my head have slowed down now, come to a halt. I need to reconsider what's going on, if this is all worth it.

I've already sent Fleur a couple of messages, nothing of consequence, just a few funny pics and emoticons. But she hasn't replied yet, which doesn't make me feel any better either.

"Hey, lovebug." Troy's voice is too upbeat and makes me flinch for a moment.

"Hmm." I boot Destruction of Elysium. "Can we go do the dungeon?"

Troy's quiet for a moment, but then he lets out a sigh. "I'm sorry for what I said before. I really am. I shouldn't have said that."

"No. You were right." AlexTheDestroyer spawns in the guild house, and Troy's character, PathTroying, is right next to me. "It's not like we don't know how this will end in the long run anyway." I click to put us in one party, my throat closing up.

"We don't know that." Troy declines the party invite.

"Hey! I thought we were going to play." My voice is going a little weird now.

"I thought so too. But you can't play like this. You can't play when your head is all messed up." He sounds so serious. "I really didn't mean anything bad by what I said before. I was just worried. And we don't know how everything will work out. You can't get down like this over something stupid I said. I'm sorry."

I shake my head, not wanting to reply.

"I was just scared for you for a moment. I said something stupid because I don't want you to get hurt again. I'm sorry."

I make a sound. "She said that she *thought* she may like me." Why am I repeating those words? Especially when they're so fragile that I know they could break at any moment?

"That's good, right?"

I shake my head again, tears threatening to roll down my cheeks. "I really like her. Like, really really. And she *may* like me."

"Were you the first one to confess?"

"No. She did. She was the one who said it first."

"That's a good sign then, right?"

I lick my lips. They've gone dry, and it doesn't help the sinking feeling in my stomach. "Doesn't have to be." My voice breaks at the end, pain running through me.

"Oh." He doesn't say anything else, because he knows exactly what I'm talking about.

I log out of Destruction of Elysium, and instead climb into bed, still wearing my headset, still being able to talk to Troy. He's the only one who really knows what happened before. What happened when I started dating another girl who had never been into girls before...

I met her at school, we shared some classes. We quickly became friends. We were young, I must have been thirteen or something, she was probably the same age. I'd never been very confused about who I liked. I'd realised early on that I liked girls over boys.

That had never been much of a confusion for me. Even my parents had been totally accepting when I'd told them about it a year earlier. They'd just shrugged, like I'd told them something that didn't really need explaining.

Though, my mum did sit me down not long after. To explain that liking girls, being a lesbian, came with dangers. Dangers from society as a whole not accepting me, or who I loved. And that there would be guys out there who would not be deterred by my sexuality, but that they would see it as a challenge. Guys who would try to force themselves onto me to make me 'change my ways'. She didn't really word it like that, I was twelve, so she used slightly different words. But it came down to the same thing.

She insisted that there was nothing wrong with me liking girls, but that not everyone thought about it the same way. That there would be people who wouldn't agree with me being able to choose who I loved. At least if the person I loved wasn't a boy, simply because of my gender.

Not long after that, I started dating my first girlfriend. She was two years older, and she was so cool. I thought anyway, at the time. She was nice and sweet, and she taught me about kissing, and opening someone else's bra in under three seconds. A skill I have made many girls laugh with later on, or squeal. Usually squeal first before laughing.

We loved teasing and joking around together, but what we felt wasn't love, we were just good friends who tried dating for a bit. She's been dating the same girl for two years now, they're even living together while they're going to university. It's so sweet.

But the girl in question, the first girl I dated who hadn't been interested in girls before... She was different. We became friends so easily, and she was very curious about my liking girls. There was something to her, something I couldn't resist.

We'd meet up in secret, meet after class, or on the weekends, things like that. Troy knew, of course, but nobody else was allowed to know, not even my parents, though I expect they quickly figured it out anyway.

Those short weeks changed me in many ways, but, above all, they taught me the one thing my mum couldn't warn me about. Some girls like the idea of dating another girl, but they don't actually want anything else. They may be curious for a while, but then will push you away like you're the biggest piece of trash in the world.

That's what she was like. She liked the idea of having a girl fall in love with her, and kissing and holding hands were perfectly fine with her, but only where other people couldn't see us. Every time I asked her for even a little more, she'd refuse. She used the excuse of Troy finding out about our relationship to break up with me. Telling me that she only 'put up' with me because I'd seemed so pathetic, that she really wasn't into girls. That I'd been imagining things.

That was... That was the hardest thing in the world. Her going off on me like that, in public even, right in the hallway during our lunch break. It was a life-defining moment for me, mostly in that I vowed to never date girls who didn't know if they were actually into girls ever again. Because those words, getting my heart trampled on like that, just hurt so much.

I don't want to be some toy or 'fun experiment' for another girl ever again. I don't care if a girl only has experiences with boys, I've dated girls like that. But I do care if they have genuine interest in me as a person, not just my sexuality. Lesbian, bisexual, pansexual, demisexual, heck, I've dated an asexual girl before, though she was biromantic, so we had great fun. And it's not just girls who were born as girls either, I've dated a trans girl, I've dated someone who was agender, though they mostly presented as female. I've dated a lot of cute people who mostly presented as female, no matter who they were born as. I really don't care about all of that. I just care that they see me as a real human being, not just some experiment, not just another item on their 'twenty things to try out before you're twenty' list.

I'm sure Fleur isn't like that. She seems genuinely interested in me, but she also first fell in love with Alex-the-boy before she knew who I really was. So how much of her interest is still her projecting her previous feelings onto the actual me now? How much of this is real?

I take my phone. She still hasn't replied to any of my previous messages. 'I'm off to bed. Exhausted. Night night!' I add a couple of sleeping emoticons to it and then sit up.

"Alex?" Troy's voice surprises me.

"Yeah?" The word barely leaves me.

"It will be fine. I promise." He can be so caring, even when he's a blockhead sometimes.

"Thanks. I'm gonna sleep now." I get behind my computer so I can turn it off.

"If you need to talk, or whatever. You can always message me."

"Thanks. Will do." I don't want to talk anymore. I don't want to talk to anyone. I'm exhausted in so many ways that I really don't even want to think anymore.

"Night."

"Night." I turn off the program and then shut down my computer.

I climb into bed, pull the covers over myself, even though it's really too hot for that. And then I close my eyes, hoping sleep will take me away soon, will take me out of this world soon.

Today started so well, but now... I don't know anymore.

19
Fleur

Critical Hit = An attack, or heal, that does more damage than the normal range of the attack. Nearly all games have a crit rate, or a critical hit rate, on weapons and spells. The higher the rate, the more likely you are to do the extra damage. Critical hits are great when you do them yourself, but mobs and bosses also have them, so you can suddenly get hit by them and get into more trouble than you thought you would be. Small things can have way more effect than you expect…

When I finally look at my phone again, as I'm about to leave Jade's house, I realise that I've had multiple messages from Alex. The final one from over an hour ago, saying that she's off to bed. I feel a little bad for having totally forgotten to check my phone for messages, but I was just having so much fun with Jade that I got lost in it all, which often happens when I'm with Jade…

So I quickly send Alex a message anyway, even if she's already asleep, she'll see it in the morning. 'Sorry, was at a friend's place. Sleep tight!' I hope it doesn't wake her up, if she has actually already fallen asleep, because that would be bad.

I get on my bike and quickly make the ride home. At home, my parents have also already gone to bed and I quietly go to my room. There, I lean back on my bed, trying to decide between going online or just trying to go to sleep.

Though, I really don't feel like sleeping right now... Too nervous, still too excited.

I quickly change into more comfortable clothes and turn the computer on. I log onto DoE and I immediately see people talking in the guild chat. They're all chatting about some dungeon event that will be coming up, and as I'm reading, I get lost in the game. I grab some gear from my bank and queue up for a dungeon. Not even seconds later, I get an invite straight away and dive right in.

The game makes me forget everything that happened today, just letting me focus on finishing the dungeon, and then diving in again to go for another round.

It's not until I hear birds outside and there is a little light coming into my room that I realise I've played all night. That I've not even gone to bed yet. So, as soon as the dungeon is over, I turn the computer off and climb into bed.

I don't know what it is, but there is an uncomfortable feeling settling in my stomach. I have no idea why, but it keeps nagging at me. It keeps popping up.

But in the end, I'm so exhausted that I fall asleep without much trouble.

W A S D

I sit at the table, trying to eat breakfast, as Mum is staring at me, frowning but not saying anything. I've only slept for three hours, and that wasn't enough. Obviously. But I can't go back to bed, at least not yet. Mum keeps looking at me, and since I just took my meds, I know that sleep won't be happening for at least the next couple of hours. I also forgot to take my phone with me downstairs, so I'm just sitting here, my only entertainment the newspaper, but I've long ago realised that I've got no interest in it. Not at all.

So, as soon as I finish my breakfast, I'm back up the stairs, booting my computer and finally finding Alex online.

I put on my headset and call her through the chat program.

"Hey." She connects the call immediately. "How did you sleep?"

"Meh." I shrug, logging onto DoE.

"Yeah." She laughs. "I heard that you'd been online until like... early this morning."

"Nothing ever stays a secret, does it?" I grin. Of course, people in the guild would know what time I was online.

"Not for the guild admin, no. Actually." She lets out another laugh. "It was on your profile. The guild roster tells when you were online last. I woke up and saw that you'd only logged off an hour before."

"What? So unfair. I should have stayed on longer."

"I don't know. This way you've at least had some sleep. Right?"

"Some..." I try to suppress a yawn, but fail miserably.

"Well, more than nothing, that's for sure."

"Yeah, true. Hey, you want to run a dungeon? Or a raid through the group finder?" I'm not sure if or how I should talk about what happened yesterday. I loved seeing Alex. I loved talking and being with her. I loved it so much. But I don't know how to bring it up again. Now I can't actually see her, touch her, I don't have the nerve to actually talk about it.

"Sure, let me grab a few things. I'll be right back." I hear her put down her headset, stumbling around her room, and then a door opens and closes.

I walk around the game, check the market place for items to buy and sell and almost jump when I hear a door again, looking around until I realise that it's on the headset and it's actually Alex' door I can hear. The headset makes some sounds and then she's back.

"Sorry, took a bit. Got some snacks and drinks." She laughs and I can hear some bags and stuff on her side.

"What did you get?"

"Wine gums and liquorice."

"Nice." I know my mum won't have those in the house, sugar and all that... And I'm too tired to go out and buy them right now.

"Okay. What dungeon were you looking at? How far along in the event are you?" Alex sounds focused now, focused on the game, on what we're going to do.

"I'm four into the eight dungeons. People were sleeping, so it wasn't easy to run all of them last night." I shrug and accept the party invite that Alex sends.

Alex laughs loudly and I love the sound. "Yeah, that happens when you're a night owl. So, I'm only two in, I need a couple more."

"I don't mind running the others first, so we're both at the same place."

"Cool. Let's get in." I see a timer start on my screen, showing when we'll likely be starting the dungeon and I lean back a little, waiting.

It's not going to take long, not when you're a tank and a healer waiting just for a couple of DPS players.

That's the biggest advantage of playing together with Alex, at least we never have to wait long for dungeons.

⟦W⟧⟦A⟧⟦S⟧⟦D⟧

"Ehm." It's late on Sunday evening. It's been four days since Alex and I went to the cinema together and we've barely spoken about it, apart from both of us saying that we enjoyed it a lot. But even those conversations seem to die out pretty quickly.

Did I read the atmosphere wrong? Did I expect more from Alex than we really talked about that day? I'm not sure what happened, but somehow I feel like we've taken a couple of steps forward and at the same time steps back.

I'm not even really sure what and where... Like, I feel closer to Alex, and we've been joking a lot more, but I also feel that she's taken a step back from me and isn't letting me as close as before, if that makes any sense.

"Yeah?" Alex sounds a little sleepy, which makes sense, we've been playing all day.

"You said something about a birthday party? Do you have more details yet?" We talked about this when we were on our date, so it's not really a surprise subject, and maybe it's a good way to talk about us a bit more…

"Oh. Yeah." I hear her move. "Cerise said we can have the party in two weeks. It will be on Saturday and Sunday, so overnight. Bring your computer, or laptop, and an airbed or something else to sleep on. And a sleeping bag and stuff like that, of course. I'll send you the address tomorrow, I don't have it here right now."

"Two weeks is when exactly?" I'm going to need more details if I'm to convince my mum so she'll allow me to go and I may have to take the day off from the flower shop.

"First weekend of August."

"And your birthday is?" Hey, gotta know these things.

"Two days after that." Alex laughs. "Though, apart from this, I don't actually really celebrate it. Just a dinner with family and stuff. Nothing special. I don't do much."

"Awhh. Well, I guess I'll have to change that, then." I'll have to see if I'll have enough money to take Alex out for dinner, or something. She can't *not* celebrate it.

"What?" Why is she confused?

"I can't have you not celebrate your birthday. Not letting you do that. Birthdays are special."

"Right..." There is a carefulness in her voice, and I'm not sure how to read it.

"What's wrong?" Something is different. It's been different for days, but it's kind of obvious now.

"Nothing. Just... I don't know. I don't like to plan that far ahead." I can almost feel her pulling back from me.

Huh? What's going on? This is her birthday, it's in two weeks. It's easy enough to just accept my idea without giving a weird excuse. Why would she do this?

"Fleur?" I've been quiet for too long.

"Why?"

"Why, what?"

"Why do you not want to plan for your birthday?" And why does the thought of that hurt?

"Oh." The sound is quiet, and she doesn't say anything for a while. "I just..." She lets out a breath. "I don't have great experiences with planning ahead for birthdays and parties."

"Okay." How can I take that fear away for her? "I really would like to do something special with you though. You're turning eighteen. We have to celebrate that."

"I guess. Thanks, though." She's still doing it, keeping me away.

"Did I do something wrong?" I'm starting to get a little emotional, tears stinging my eyes. I don't like it, but I also don't like Alex pushing me away, being so cold.

"Why would you think that?" There's that confusion again.

"You've been distant since we came back from the cinema. Did I do something wrong?" I feel tears fill my eyes.

"No." A gasp. Suddenly, Alex' voice isn't so steady either. "No. You didn't do anything wrong."

"Then, what? Am I no longer interesting? Did I disappoint you?"

"Oh. God. Fleur. *No.*" Her breathing speeds up. "Nothing like that."

"Why?" Because she's not denying something has changed.

"I'm just... a little scared." Her voice wavers. "I'm scared that in two weeks' time I'll no longer be interesting to you. But that's on me. That's *my* problem. I'm sorry."

Whoa? I can't keep my tears inside anymore, she really does sound scared. And it does make some sense with the way she's been acting. "I won't." My voice pitches.

"You don't know that. I'm a girl. I'm not a boy. I have a different body. I'm different. It's not the same. Not the same at all." She sniffs and I hear another shaky breath.

"I know." If there is one thing that I've already thought about, it's how different that could be, bodies and everything. But that doesn't stop me from liking Alex. I just like her, Alex as Alex.

"I can't be just an experiment to see if you could like girls too. I really like you." She lets out a sob. "I'm sorry. I can't do this right now. Just... I'm sorry. I really... I wish..."

"Alex." I try to get through to her.

"I'll talk to you tomorrow. Please, forget this happened." And the voice chat disconnects. Then I see her go offline too. No longer in the program.

I pick up my phone, ready to send her a message, wanting to tell her that things will be alright, that I won't hurt her. But I know that anything I tell her right now won't get to her.

I pull my headset off and hide under the covers. Letting out my cries, letting out my pain.

I don't get it. I really don't get it. I don't want to hurt Alex, but somehow, I've already hurt her. Again.

And I only want to wrap my arms around her and hold her. Nothing more. I want to hold and protect her.

But something she said also nags at me, she doesn't want to be some experiment, she doesn't want to be the one I hurt just because I may or may not like girls.

Before meeting Alex, I never even thought about this possibility. I never even thought about my sexuality. I just did what everyone else did and was fine with that. But with Alex, this won't be the same. And there is one thing that she's right about. It will be different. But not in the way that she thinks.

I actually get butterflies when I think about her. I've never understood the whole idea of butterflies in my stomach.

But now I do.

And right now they're burning me up from the inside out, because I hate that I hurt Alex, even without meaning to.

I hate that I hurt her, and I'm going to have to make it better.

I *will* make it better.

20
Alex

AFK = Away From Keyboard = Usually said when you step away from your computer for a while, or when you're having to tab out of the game. AFK lets other people know that you're probably not going to respond to messages, or be able to attack, defend or heal during that time. Some games will also automatically put an AFK tag on you when you don't interact with the game for a certain amount of time, making it easier for other players when you haven't actually marked yourself as AFK.

I stare at the computer, the screen dark, the whole machine quiet, something that doesn't happen that often unless I'm off to bed. And even then, it's not uncommon for me to have my computer on when I'm asleep.

I just blew up at Fleur...

I had to get away from her, I had to get away before I said something I'd really regret. There are only so many ways that you can tell someone that you're sorry and I'm pretty sure that I'll run out of them soon with Fleur. Or the different things I'll have to apologise for. Again...

'Alex?' My phone lights up with a message from Troy. 'Are you okay?'

I guess that suddenly leaving DoE and the voice program and turning the computer off may worry some people. Especially when they are actually expecting me to stay around a while longer for dungeon runs and such.

I'm not okay, but that's got nothing to do with Troy. 'I'm fine. Just don't feel like playing right now.' I don't want to talk to him. I don't want to talk to anyone. The memories, these bad memories, they're just mine and they keep haunting me. Will it ever get easier? Will they ever stop?

I flop onto my bed and wrap myself around my covers, hugging tight. I wish someone could tell me if it will always be this hard, this painful. Knowing that you're the reason something has to end, that you have to protect the other person, even just from yourself.

My tears start all over again, tears, sobs, cries. I don't want to think about the past, I really don't. I've been trying to ignore this feeling inside for days. I've been hoping that if I don't talk about the date or our friendship/relationship thing that Fleur won't say anything either, that she won't ask anything. That I can ignore all of this and forget that anything ever happened.

But that was too much to hope for, wasn't it?

Now she knows. Now she knows why I just can't do this. I can't invest in someone who doesn't even know if they really like girls or not. It's just too much. I don't want to break all over again.

I don't want to lose Fleur. I don't want to lose her as a friend. And if this all does go the wrong way, I'll have lost her and I won't ever be able to get her back. We can't go back to being just friends after we've started to date, when we really start taking those next steps.

I can't lose her friendship. She means too much to me.

I know what I'm going to have to do. I already know. So why does it hurt so much?

A loud sob leaves me and I hide my face in the covers. I can't stop the crying, because the pain is just too much. Way too much.

It's breaking me up inside, breaking me into pieces, millions of painful pieces, shards poking at my heart, at my insides, hurting.

W A S D

I haven't slept all night. I've just been curled up in bed and staring into the darkness. And now that the light outside has started to grow and the birds have started to sing again, I know it's time get out of bed. I don't want to, but I can't stay here either, I just can't.

There is a heaviness inside me that won't go away, I know that it will probably stay there for a long time. At least until I talk to Fleur and probably for a long time after that.

And the birthday party...

I invited her, but it means I'll have to see her again. I'll have to face her... Why did I do that? Why did I invite her? This is going to be so painful.

I sit up, looking around, and then grab some clean clothes and get dressed. Yukio has to be walked, and he won't mind going for a walk a little early. Maybe it'll help me keep my mind in check until I can bring up the courage to do what needs to be done...

The house is still quiet as I make my way to the back, where Yukio sleeps, and open the back door to let him out. Then, I grab his lead, and put it on him, before leaving through the back garden gate. It's so quiet here, people are still mostly asleep, even though the sun has started to warm everything up. It makes the world seem almost unreal.

It's too quiet, and also so beautiful, like the day after some big bad event in a dystopian film, right before you find out how messed up the world has become.

I put one foot in front of the other, walking, just moving my body and taking in the familiar surroundings. Losing myself in my thoughts, even if I don't really want to face some of them.

When I look up, I'm suddenly in the middle of the fields and the quiet of it all and the open space jolts me into action.

I grab my phone and open a message to Fleur. Looking at the empty line waiting for me to type something, the cursor blinking... 'I think it's better if we just stay friends.' I send it to Fleur and immediately turn my phone off.

I don't want to see her response. I don't want to see what she'll say. This is the best for both of us. This is the best. I don't know what else I'm supposed to do. I don't know what else I can do to make sure we both don't get hurt too much... Too much more...

I start walking again, my eyes on the road in front of me, though I don't really see what's going on. Instead, in my head, a compilation of everything Fleur has ever said to me, the times she smiled at me, when she held my hand, it all keeps spinning around, it keeps going and going.

That first time when her face fell as she saw me... I should have known then that this would be a bad idea. I should have stepped away then. I shouldn't have even tried after that. I should have stayed away.

But why didn't I?

Why did I have to hurt myself like this?

Why did I have to put Fleur through the pain too?

Why did I have to be so stupid?

I should have kept to my own rules from the start. When I realised what had happened, I should have just stepped away and forgotten about my feelings for her. That would have been the right thing. That would have been the best for us.

Tears fill my vision and I wipe at them, but they keep coming back.

I'm stupid.

I'm stupid for even getting us into this situation in the first place.

I'm so stupid.

W A S D

When I get back home, Mum and Dad are already awake, sitting at the kitchen table, having breakfast. They both look up at me, their faces worried but I don't come in and they don't ask. Instead, I give Yukio his breakfast and am out the door again. I can't stay at home today, I can't be here. I can't be alone, but I also can't be with my family. I just can't.

I grab my bike and make my way to Troy's. I have no idea what time it is now, and my phone is turned off so I can't check it, but I need to get away from home and his is the closest place where I can go right now.

As I ride through the city, I barely avoid crashing into at least four cars and two other bikes. The danger racking up my adrenaline levels and pushing away the dark feeling, even if just temporarily.

Troy's house is quiet when I arrive. His parents have probably already left for work and, knowing Troy, he'll still be asleep. I park my bike next to the garage and quickly grab the spare set of keys from the hidden hook. At least I can let myself into his house.

I open the door, and the whole house is quiet, as I expected. I take my shoes off and quietly walk up the stairs to Troy's room. The door to his room is slightly open, a slow gust from the fan coming through it from time to time, and when I look inside, I find him sprawled out on his bed, fast asleep.

I go into his room, sitting down next to his bed, where I always sit when I'm here, playing games or whatever. The same pillow is here on the floor like always, because Troy's mum doesn't think that sitting on a hard floor for hours on end is good for my back, or something like that.

At least it's quiet here, quiet and comforting. Nobody is making a sound, apart from Troy's steady breathing as he sleeps. I lean my head back and, finally, I calm down a little. The quiet and soothing sounds are relaxing me and dissolving the final traces of adrenaline and anxiety…

A hand against the side of my head jolts me awake. I hadn't even realised I'd fallen asleep.

"Alex…" Troy sounds a little confused, and when I look to the side, he's got his eyes only barely open, bleary-eyed. But he doesn't say anything else, just tugs at my shirt and then pulls one of his pillows from behind the bed and puts it next to his.

I climb up and also make myself comfortable on the bed. Troy puts his hand on my arm for a moment, but it's too hot to hug him. It's way too hot.

But I don't think for long, as I'm quickly asleep again. I shouldn't have stayed up all night, but at least I can sleep now. I'm safe here, nothing bad can happen when I'm here.

At last I can get some rest.

I'm safe.

W A S D

I wake up from an insistent beeping, beeping from a computer, and as I open my eyes, I remember falling asleep at Troy's place. The beeping is from his computer, someone trying to get his attention.

"Troy." I shake him. "Your computer."

"Hm?" He turns around, looks at me, groggily. "What?"

"Your computer is beeping." I don't want to get up.

"Then go check. I want to sleep."

"No. It's your computer. You go check." I don't want to check, I want to sleep, like he's apparently about to be doing again.

"Fine." He sits up, climbs out of bed and turns his monitor on. I can see the chat program open on it, though I can't read anything on it. He looks at the messages for a moment and then looks my way, frowning.

"What?"

"What did you *do*?" He quickly types a short reply and turns the screen back off, then he comes back to bed. He looks worried. "What did you do?"

"What do you mean?" Honestly, context is key here. It's not like I can magically figure out what he means, and I think we've pretty clearly established that I'm bad at not doing stupid things on a regular base.

"That was Fleur." He keeps frowning.

My stomach drops. "What did she say?" Of course, my biggest mistake of the last twenty-four hours…

"She asked if I knew where you were. She said that you weren't responding to her messages. That she's worried." He sighs. "Again, what did you *do*?"

Last night and then this morning, it all flashes through my head. Flashes of pain. Hitting me inside and ripping me apart. I don't even know where to start. I also don't want to really think about it. "I told her we were better off just as friends." I turn around so I don't have to face Troy, see his disappointed look.

"And you decided that on your own?" I don't need to see his face to know the way he's looking at me now.

"Yes. Because I know how this will end. Even if she can't see it." I shrug, but just the movement, the thought, brings me to tears again.

"Say that again." Troy's voice is thick now too. "Say that you're better off as friends, but now without crying. You like her. Heck. You *love* her."

I shake my head. "It doesn't matter. This is better." Tears make my voice sound strange, even to my own ears.

"Alex…" He puts his hand on my arm again.

"No." I pull my arm away. "This is for the best. Please."

"Alex…"

I can't do this right now. I really can't. This really is the best. I *know* it is.

Even if it breaks my heart into a million pieces...

But, instead of letting me go, Troy wraps a thin blanket around me and pulls me close, holding me tight.

And I really break into a million pieces, crying again.

It's not like I want this. I just know it's for the best…

I'm doing this to protect us both.

21
Fleur

Leeroy Jenkins = A player from *World of Warcraft* who is (in)famous for ruining a strategic plan for a raid by running into a room full of mobs and getting his whole party wiped. Later it was discovered that it was a fake video, though the idea stuck. Now mostly used as a joke term when a player runs into battle without much of a plan or idea of what they're going to do. No matter the type of battle...

I can't believe what just happened. I can't believe the message I got from Alex. That was so not a fun way to start the day, not at all. I never expected that Alex would so forcefully push me away and tell me that she only wants to be friends, nothing more than that. And she didn't respond to any of the messages I sent her after I saw it. And then she wasn't even online...

It made me worry. It made me so scared that something bad had happened to Alex. So I sent some messages to the two people who I knew would be able to tell me what was going on, or, at least, where she was and if she was safe, Troy and Cerise.

Luckily, Troy replied, saying that Alex was at his place and that he would try to get her to talk to me after she woke up, though he couldn't promise me anything.

The relief that she was not in any danger made the other part of all of this take over in full force, the pain. The pain of Alex pushing me away, of her wanting nothing to do with me. I broke down for real.

I was so happy when I talked to Jade about Alex after our date, finally knowing what I wanted. *Who* I wanted. Finally being able to see that maybe I could feel like this and that I *do* feel like this towards girls, or, at least, one girl in particular. But now everything has broken down. Now everything is different.

I don't want Alex to hurt. I don't want her to feel bad, but I don't know how I can tell her that she doesn't have to worry. That I really don't see her as some experiment, that I don't want to 'try' to see if I may or may not like girls *in general.* That's not why I like her. That's not why I want to talk to her or see her or hold her again. I want Alex because she's Alex and I like Alex. That's why.

Of course, my mistake of originally thinking that Alex was a boy will haunt me forever. Or, at least, it will forever stand in the way of Alex really trusting me. I hate that it happened, and I feel so silly over it, but I don't want to lose her.

I'm still curled up in bed. After Troy's messages, I climbed into it and haven't come out since. I have my phone with me, hoping that Alex will send me a message, any message, but she's still quiet.

Will this be the end? I don't want it to be. I don't want this.

But what can I do, apart from respecting Alex' wishes? What else can I do?

I have no idea, and that scares me.

I haven't talked to Alex alone in over two days. Whenever she is online she is in the group voice chat, and any messages I send her directly trying to talk to her on her own are politely declined.

Crap. This hurts. Being able to hear her, talk to her, but to not be able to actually have a conversation with her... I can't do it. I can't do it at all. And it hurts so much.

I know that others in the guild are also aware that something is going on. It's kind of obvious she's avoiding me after the way Alex and I used to be. Though, any questions they ask, I just avoid answering, I deflect them. I don't know what else to do. How am I supposed to explain this?

Alex and I were never officially dating. *Heck.* Even if we had been, it was what... one date? That's not something I should feel this upset over. That's not something that should be affecting me this much.

We barely knew each other. So why does it hurt so much? *Why?*

I've talked to Cerise a few times. She's really nice and seems to at least get what's going on, even though she refuses to talk to me about Alex and how she's doing.

And Cerise even asked me to still come to the birthday party in a few weeks. That she really wants to see me again and that it will be a fun weekend. That no matter what happens between Alex and me, she knows we'll still have fun.

Cerise seems really sweet but a little naïve. I don't know how things can be fun when Alex and I will probably be trying to avoid each other all weekend. I've already asked Mum if I'm allowed to go, and even though she hasn't given me a hard 'yes' yet, I think she'll let me.

It's just that I'm not sure if I actually will be going, if I want to go. Especially if Alex is not talking to me, at least not more than a couple of words to coordinate whether we're running a dungeon or not. That's not talking, that's tolerating.

Pain. Every time I think of Alex, my chest hurts.

I was so happy when summer break started. Weeks of uninterrupted time to play videogames. But now I hate the free time and empty days. How am I supposed to fill them when everything I do now reminds me of Alex? When everything I do feels so dull now I'm not sharing them with Alex?

I can't do this.

"Everyone, I'm going offline." I close DoE. "I'll be back tonight." I need to get out of the house. I need to *not* be here. It's only early in the day, but I can't play DoE when it keeps hurting.

"Later!" multiple people reply. "See you tonight."

For a moment I listen if Alex also says something, but she stays quiet.

I leave the voice chat, my tears close to the surface again.

I want this to stop. I need this to stop already. How long is this going to take?

I grab my phone, sending a message to Jade. 'Want to hang out?'

The reply is quick. 'Sorry, working today. Can't leave. What's up?'

'I don't want to be at home.'

'Ah. I don't think the boss-lady will appreciate you hanging out here, though.' She adds a smiley sticking its tongue out to it.

It makes me smile a little. 'Yeah. I'll figure something else out. Sorry.'

'Alex still not talking to you?'

'No.' I sit down on my bed.

I keep going through the same useless things in my head, wishing I could find a way out of this situation. Cerise may not want to talk about Alex, but she did imply that Alex wasn't happy either. So why is this still going on? 'She ignores my messages and calls.'

I've even tried calling her on her phone, seeing if she'll pick up then, it was a desperate attempt because I hate making phone calls. But half the time the phone is turned off, and the other half it just keeps ringing and ringing, without ever being picked up.

'Is there some other way you can talk to her?'

'Not really. She really doesn't want to talk to me. And I know that I need to respect that. But...' I keep running in these circles. I can't just let this go when I have no idea what exactly went wrong. How I can try to convince her that this isn't as bad an idea as she seems to think it is.

'I have a crazy idea.' Jade adds a row of silly smilies to it.

Uh-oh.

'You can hit me next time you see me if you hate it.'

Right… But at this point, crazy sounds good, even if it's an idea that's not going to work out. I can use the smiles and distractions. 'What is it?'

'You said that she only lives an hour away... Right?'

'Right.' My stomach drops, I'm pretty sure I know what comes next.

'Can you go visit her?'

'I don't have her address.' It was something I had considered, even for a few seconds. But it's no use.

'Can't one of her friends give it to you? You can contact them, right?'

What? That sounds almost like a sane idea. Even though... Who can I ask? I don't think Troy or Cerise would give me the address. They're Alex' friends. I can't abuse their friendship with Alex like that. I really can't. 'That would be unfair.'

'Why?'

'Would you like it if I gave your address to some guy you were trying to avoid?'

It takes a moment for her to reply. 'If we were as in love as you two seem to be? I may not like it. But if it's to protect me from myself... I guess I could overlook you doing it.' *In love?* Then another message shows up. 'Would you hate me if I gave your address to Alex if you were in the reverse situation?'

I look at my hands. Would I? 'Maybe for a while.'

'I'd deal with that, if it came to it.' And I know it's not an empty promise when Jade says it. 'But as far as I know, from what you've told me, both Troy and Cerise seemed to like the idea of you two dating. And you did say that they're both worried about Alex too.'

I guess. I don't even know how I'd do it. Or whether Troy or Cerise would tell on me before I'd even be able to get to Alex' place. But I want to see her. I want to talk to her. I need to tell her that whatever she thinks is going on, whatever she's scared of, she doesn't need to be scared.

I don't care about the consequences. I need to do this. *Need to.*

I check the time, it's just past noon. It takes at least an hour to get there, and Alex did say that it would be easy to get to her place by bus.

My phone buzzes. 'Go ask them. The worst you can get is a no. But maybe they won't. Nothing lost. You can only gain from this.'

'Okay.' I sit back behind my computer, clicking on Troy's name in the chat program first. He seems to be the closest to Alex and she was hiding at his place last time.

> **BelleFleur:** You there?

My heart beats loudly, adrenaline rushing through me. I'm doing this, aren't I?

> **PathTroying:** Yeah. What's up?
> **BelleFleur:** I have a question, and you can say no if you
>   don't want to do it.
> **PathTroying:** Sure. But I'm not looking for a girlfriend.
> **PathTroying:** Sorry. Bad joke.
> **PathTroying:** What is it?

My hands shake as I type my question, ignoring Troy's idiocy.

> **BelleFleur:** Can I have Alex' address?
> **PathTroying:** Her email?
> **BelleFleur:** No. Her home address.
> **PathTroying:** Why?

Well, I never expected it to be easy.

> **BelleFleur:** I want to

I shake so badly that I totally send the message too early.

> **BelleFleur:** I want to go see her.
> **PathTroying:** At home?
> **BelleFleur:** Yes.
> **PathTroying:** Why don't you ask her yourself?
> **BelleFleur:** She's ignoring all my messages. I haven't
>   talked to her since Sunday.

He doesn't respond fast enough and I lose steam, doubt creeping in.

> **BelleFleur:** Never mind. It was a stupid idea.

I shouldn't be doing this. I shouldn't have asked him.

BelleFleur: Forget I asked.

I can't do this. This is a bad idea. A stupid idea.

PathTroying: I'll give it to you.
PathTroying: Just promise me you won't hurt her. She's
been hurt enough.

Like I don't know that. Like I don't know that she's been hurting. That's why she's been pushing me away to begin with.

BelleFleur: I promise.
BelleFleur: I just want to talk to her.
PathTroying: Fine. Give me a moment.
PathTroying: I'm only doing this because I can't see her
in pain like this either.
BelleFleur: Thank you.
BelleFleur: Thank you so much.

Oh, wow.

This is happening! This is really happening. I can make this better again.

I can make Alex look at me and talk to me directly. She can't ignore me when I'm there, at her house. She can't just shut me out again, she'll have to listen to me.

I grab my phone sending a message to Jade. 'I'm going!'

W A S D

I looked the address up on my phone and then checked what buses I had to take to get to Alex' place. She was right, it's pretty easy to do.

After getting the address, I had to convince Mum that I wasn't going to do something stupid, somehow. But she's been on my case for being unhappy for the last couple of days and it's been really annoying, but at least this gave me a good excuse.

I told Mum that Alex invited me to go see some film at her place to cheer me up and that I wouldn't be back too late. She's seen Alex, talked to her and liked her, so she knows that I'm not just meeting some random person.

I changed into something pretty, something that I know looks good on me. I've gotta make a good impression when I get there, right? Woo Alex into letting me see her?

I take the first bus into the city, which takes me to the shopping centre where I work at the flower shop. And since the bus to Groningen, where Alex lives, doesn't come for another thirty minutes, I go inside. I want to give Alex something fun, have at least something with me to give her, convince her that I really do mean well.

Andrew, my boss at the flower shop, is surprised when I step into the shop and ask for a dozen roses. Well, more like I walk in and demand a dozen roses, chosen by me. He lets me do what I want, though he does keep asking questions about why I'd need them. He knows a little about Alex, but not about what happened between us since the weekend.

After some quick answers, he wraps up the bouquet I've picked out, making it look pretty. "Good luck." He nods at me. "You can do it!"

"I'll try, at least."

"No. You can do whatever you put your mind to. And with roses like that, she'd be stupid not to recognise that." Andrew grins.

I'm not so sure about that, but I don't have the energy to fight him. I need to save it all for when I see Alex.

Then I step into the shop next door and find Jade behind the counter. Her eyes go wide when she sees me, but then she smiles softly. "You're doing it."

I nod. "Yeah. I'm doing it."

"Good." Her smile grows. "Show her that you're serious. Show her that you mean it when you say that you like her."

"I'm just hoping I don't scare her off more first." I'm anxious. I'm the one who I need to convince that this will work. I'm scared she won't even look at me. That I'll be standing there in front of a closed door and nobody will open it.

"She'd be stupid to not even consider talking to you when you're dressed like that and carrying those flowers. Stupid, I tell you."

I shrug, I'm not so sure.

"Okay. Do you have two minutes?" She holds up two fingers.

I check my phone. "I have ten. Why?"

"Enough time. Good." She grabs my arm. "Come with me." And, as she starts walking, I realise she's dragging me towards the makeup section. "Let's make you irresistible."

Uh-oh. I'm not sure that it will make my nerves any less, sitting still as Jade does my makeup. But she's right. I'm going to have to show Alex that I'm serious about her. And I'm going to need all my courage to do it.

And if this helps me, even a little, I'll take it.

I'm going to do something crazy. And I have no idea if it will work out well. Because apart from going to Alex' house, showing up at her door, I have no plan.

Yikes.

22
Alex

Stun = An attack to stop another character or mob, often comes in a single or group version. A stunned enemy usually can't attack or defend themselves, making them an easy target for others. It's the equivalent to standing there, staring, not able to move or do anything.

I know that some people in the guild are annoyed with me. With me not talking to Fleur unless I have to, or just going offline for a couple of hours at a time when I can't deal with hearing Fleur any longer.

But I really don't want to deal with all their complaints right now. I only have to get through the first couple of days until the pain goes away. I know that it will happen at some point, I just have to get through it until it happens.

Cerise lets out a deep sigh in the group chat. "Alex."

"Yeah?" I don't like it when her voice sounds like that. It usually means that she's going to be sensible and act like she's my big sister. Either, or, both.

"Can't you just... I don't know... talk to her?" I know that she's trying to be supportive.

Aaron also speaks up. "It's not like something bad has happened, right? And you said it yourself, finding a new healer sucks. It could take weeks. But you two acting like this isn't going to make it easier on either of you."

"I know." It's not like Fleur being our new healer wasn't one of the reasons why I knew it was better that Fleur and I didn't do the whole relationship thing. This whole situation is exactly what I wanted to avoid happening. "But I just can't."

"Why?" Aaron sounds confused and a little frustrated. He doesn't know everything from my past, from before I became AlexTheDestroyer, before I created my own armour around myself.

"I just can't." I lean back in my chair, looking at my ceiling, trying not to cry.

"Why not? Alex. This isn't like you. This isn't..." He sighs. "It's just not like the Alex I know."

"Maybe you just *think* you know me, but that's just the wrong Alex." I snap, sitting back up straight.

"I don't think so. The Alex I know wouldn't hurt herself like this, or someone else." Aaron's voice drops, serious.

"Shut up." I shake my head, reaching up, about to cover my ears, which is of course useless as I'm wearing a headset.

"Alex..." Cerise sounds so sad now.

"No. Shut up." I stand up, taking my headset off and logging myself out of the voice chat.

This is why I don't want to be online right now. But online is the only place where I can hang out. I don't have anywhere else to go. Everyone I know is connected to the game. Everyone

I know is connected to Destruction of Elysium and that means they're all connected to Fleur.

I flop down onto my bed, hitting my pillow as hard as I can, but it doesn't help anything.

My phone starts buzzing and I grab it. It's Cerise. I decline the call and then turn the sound off. I don't want to talk to anyone. I just want to be alone.

But I don't. Not really.

I want to be alone but I also *don't* want to be alone. I just... There is only one person I want to be with, and I pushed her away. And that's all my own fault.

There is a knock on my door. "Alex?" Mum sounds worried, like everyone else lately.

"Go away." My voice is thick and I don't want to cry in front of her.

"There is someone here for you. Your friend."

"I don't want to see anyone." Though the way she said it makes me think it's not Cerise or Troy, she would have just let them come up on their own and they wouldn't have knocked.

"I think you'll want to see her." Mum's more resolute now.

Her? No. I don't care. I don't want to see anyone. I don't need anyone. "Tell her to go away."

I hear footsteps on the stairs and my heart starts beating louder. Army boots.

"I don't think she's going to do that." Why does Mum sound amused?

More knocking on the door. "Alex?" My heart skips a beat and I gasp. *Fleur!* "Alex? Can I come in?"

I stare at the door, the only thing between us, stunned. I can't believe this. She's *here!* "Yes." My voice breaks, and I wipe at my face with my covers, hoping there aren't any tears.

The door opens and I see Mum first, her face amused, then Fleur steps into my room and I can only stare at her.

She's like a vision again. Dressed in army boots, a summer dress covered in flowers and wearing delicate pink lipstick. I can't believe this. She's really here, and holding flowers. Flowers!

She closes the door behind her and holds out the flowers in my direction, only staring at her feet. "I got these for you." Her voice is a little shaky and it hurts to hear her like this.

I carefully get up, taking the big bouquet of roses. They're beautiful, ranging from dark red to pale yellow and some pinks, but they don't hold a candle to the way Fleur makes me feel just standing there.

"Thank you." I put the roses on the edge of my desk, not sure what else to do. "Fleur, I..." I shake my head, stepping back, trying to make sense of the situation. "Why are you here?"

"I wanted to talk to you, but you were ignoring me." I can feel her eyes on me even when I'm not looking at her.

"I just..." I still can't do this.

"There was no other way for me to make you listen to me. You weren't giving me a chance."

"I suck at listening." I'm not sure why I say it, but I sit down on my bed, needing to sit for a moment.

"Well, I don't care. I listened to you. I listened when you told me why we couldn't do this. Now you need to listen to me." Her voice gets stronger, and when I look up, I'm taken by her beauty, by the look in her eyes, by the fire that seems to come off her.

She meets my eyes and then looks away, a blush spreading across her neck and cheeks.

"I love you." I hear the words and it takes me a few moments to realise that they've come from me, because Fleur is looking at me in surprise, her mouth open, her eyes big.

Oops. I hadn't planned on saying that.

Time passes and it gets awkward, the way we stare at each other. Both trying to decide what to say next.

I've scared her off. Of course I have. That's what happens when you confess to a girl who's not into other girls. That's what I do, hurting myself and her, scaring her off.

Fleur's breath hitches and she lets herself slide to the floor, her dress spreading out around her, like a princess in a fairy-tale.

"I don't know." She looks up, her eyes watery and her breathing irregular. "I don't know how to answer that. I've never felt like this before. But I know that not being around you, not talking to you. It hurts. It hurts so much." She reaches up, tears sliding down her cheeks, she stops for a moment, but then runs her palms over her eyes, smearing the carefully applied makeup.

This is why I shouldn't talk to her. Because there is one thing I hate even more than her potentially hurting me, and that's hurting her, knowing that I'm the one who hurt her.

I get up, kneeling in front of her. "Fleur..." I reach out, but don't touch her yet.

"I don't know how I feel. This is all so new to me." She lowers her hands and looks at me, her makeup all smeared, but her eyes so sad. "I can't give you more than that. And if it's not enough, then I don't know. But I don't want to lose you." She sags down.

I wrap my arms around her, pulling her close. "I don't want to lose you either. I don't. I'm..." How can I even explain why I had to do what I did? How can I even try to begin to explain? I hold her tight and it feels so good. It feels so good to have her here, in my arms.

She wraps her arms around me too, holding on tightly. I can feel every shuddering breath she takes. I can feel every tear that falls onto my bare shoulder. I can smell her sweet scent. And I slowly break apart even more.

What are we going to do now? How can we keep going? It's all out now, there is nothing to hide anymore.

I love her.

She doesn't know how she feels about me.

And how is this supposed to be better than before? How is this pain supposed to be better?

Fleur moves a little and I feel her hot breath on my shoulder for a moment before she kisses my skin.

My heart almost breaks out of my chest, shocked, surprised. *What?!*

She pulls back a little, and then puts another kiss on my shoulder. Her lips soft and warm and a little sticky as she pulls back.

She does it again and finally, as she pulls back, she lets out a soft laugh. The sound surprising and so sweet. So innocent.

I look at my shoulder, at where she's just kissed, and I see pink lips on my skin. I swallow hard as I look at them.

They look so innocent, but at the same time... Fleur has marked me. In some part of my brain the thoughts keep running around. Faster and faster. Making me feel dizzy.

She doesn't know how she feels, but she also wants me and she kissed me, left her lipstick behind on my skin.

My breathing is shallow, my whole body burning up. This is... *Wow.*

I reach up, putting my fingers against her jaw, sliding them down until they slip off her chin.

Fleur looks my way, licking her lips, and then pulls a face as she tastes her own lipstick.

We both burst out laughing, the tension broken.

"Gross." She pulls a face again. "Shouldn't do that again."

"Right." I reach behind me and grab my makeup remover from a shelf. "Let's get you cleaned up. I don't think you meant to look like a panda."

Fleur shakes her head, smiling a little.

"Okay." I stand up and reach out. "Let's not do this on the floor."

She grabs my hand and lets me pull her up, though she doesn't say anything. We're standing really close again. So close that I can feel her breath on my skin, setting it on fire.

I put that out of my mind, though, and instead pull her towards my bed. She sits down a little awkwardly. She looks a mess, her makeup all spread around and streaky. "You did look really pretty when you came in." I take a tissue from the box. "Close your eyes."

Fleur closes her eyes, turning her face up to me a little. "Thanks." Her voice is still a little tearful.

"No problem." I wipe the tissue over one of her eyes carefully, each movement taking more makeup away, cleaning up her skin. I take a new tissue and then start on the other eye. "This is some stubborn makeup." I let out a little laugh.

Fleur sighs, smiling. "I know. Jade said that it was water-proof."

"Water-proof? More like cleaning-proof. Because it's not tear-proof at all." I can't keep my eyes off her as I try to take her makeup off as best as possible. She's so beautiful and the way she relaxes as I help her makes my heart grow. I can't stop it. "Almost done." I throw another tissue away. "Just your lips now."

Fleur nods, opening her eyes and looking at me, and I get lost in them for a moment, my breath taken away by the way she makes me feel.

I take a clean tissue and hold it up. "This is going to be gross."

She shrugs, smiling a little. "Better than what I have now." She reaches out and wraps her arms around my hips, leaning back a little so I can clean off her lips.

I swallow hard. Trying to keep my hand from shaking, or my brain from frying, as I take the pink lipstick off and reveal more and more of her beautiful red lips. I put my fingers under her chin and angle her face so I get a better view of how much lipstick I've taken off already.

I swipe the tissue over her top and bottom lip one last time and it comes away clean now. "I think we're done." I throw away the tissue, and let out a squeak as Fleur pulls at me and we fall onto my bed.

She's so close. So, so close. She rolls us over and suddenly she's hovering over me, looking at me, her eyes on my lips.

I reach up, wrapping my arms around her, holding her, but giving her enough leeway to get away if she wants to. "Fleur..." I'm not sure about what's going to happen, even though I know what I wish would happen next.

"I..." She bites her lower lip a little, her eyes shooting from my lips to my eyes and then back to my lips. "I want to kiss you. Can I?"

23
Fleur

XP = Experience Points = When killing mobs, handing in quests and other actions in the game, you get experience points. Points from gaining more experience in certain situations. They're like the real world, only you can actually see them in the game, we only know we've gained them in the real world because we get better at things… Or not, in some cases.

Oh. *Crap.* What did I just ask? I still, scared that Alex will push me away now. Her eyes widen in surprise.

Why did I ask if I could kiss her? Why would I?

Alex was so sweet, so careful as she cleaned off the makeup, so full of concentration. And that, after I just barged in here, demanding her attention. After… all that.

She was still so careful, so caring, paying close attention to what she was doing. It was hard to ignore the way she looked or how it made me feel. It made my heart swell and beat faster.

It made me so aware of her.

Of her soft lips. Of her careful touch. Of the curves of her body, so close to mine. Of her scent, making me want to get even closer to her.

When I pulled her onto the bed, on impulse. As a joke, partially. Just because I felt like it, partially. But mostly because I just couldn't help myself and wanted to touch her more, feel her more. When I did that, I knew everything changed right at that moment.

Alex' body is soft against mine, unexpectedly soft. And, so close to the covers, everything smells even more like her.

So, when I looked down, saw her lips, the pressure of her touch still lingering on my lips, I blurted out what came to mind.

"I... I want to kiss you. Can I?"

She doesn't do anything for a long moment, her eyes wide with surprise, but then she nods. She licks her lips, and I mirror it, pulling a face again, because even though the lipstick is off my lips, the residue from the makeup remover is still on them. *Ick.*

Alex bursts out laughing, shaking her head. Then she points to the desk. "There's lip balm over there." Her voice is a little breathy.

I nod, sitting up, looking down at her. "Stay here?"

Her eyes grow as she inclines her head, colouring a little.

"Good." I climb off, take the few steps to the desk and spot the lip balm easily.

I uncap it, it's strawberry scented. I didn't expect that, from Alex I'd expected some neutral scent or something. Then, as I swipe it along my lips, I realise that this lip balm has been against Alex' lips before, and I'm now giving her an indirect kiss... *Eep!*

I quickly put it down. With the force behind my movements, it wobbles a few times, before it finally stands still.

Alex is leaning up on her elbows, looking at what I'm doing, raising an eyebrow. "What?" She grins.

"Nothing..." I go back over to her, pushing at her shoulder. "You were going to stay there." Feeling a little braver.

"I didn't move." She winks, then wraps her arms around my hips as I climb back on top of her.

I'm so much more nervous now. Before, it was just me doing something silly, impulsive, not really a lot of brain involved. But now I'm actually getting on top of her knowingly, and it's so different. It makes me much more nervous.

She's slim, which I already knew. But I can feel it now against my own body and for someone who says that she hates sports, she feels pretty sturdy.

Alex reaches up, running her thumb over my lips, smiling. "I think I like neutral or red lipsticks best on you."

I nod, my breath stuck in my throat. Her touch is so delicate, so different from the raging feelings inside me.

Then I push forward and crash our lips together. It's awkward and slightly sticky from the lip balm and I think her lip got caught between our teeth.

I pull back again, my heart beating so loudly that I think it's going to burst out of my chest. I kissed her.

I *kissed* Alex.

Our first kiss.

I stare at her, frozen in place. Now what? Now, what am I supposed to do next?

Alex puts her arms around my neck and pulls me down, next to her on the bed, barely inches between us. She smiles, her eyes shining.

Then she moves closer, her breath on my lips, before I feel her lips again, softer this time. More careful.

They're short kisses, little more than pecks, so short. But it still takes my breath away.

I put my arm over her, feeling her against me. Face to face. Body to body. With Alex.

I pull my head back, needing to take a good breath, but no matter what I do, I smell Alex. I bet I'll still smell like her when I get home. My cheeks flame up at that thought.

"Are you okay?" Her voice is soft, her eyes only half-open as she looks at me.

"Yeah." I can barely hear my own voice.

"Did you like it?"

I nod.

"Good. Because I like it too. And want a lot more of them." She comes up a little, leaning over me some.

I nod again.

She comes closer, her breasts pushing against mine, and they're so soft, moulding against mine. It feels... different, but not bad, good even, definitely different.

Then her lips are on mine again, soft, but this time they're not just short kisses. Our lips are together, and then I feel her tongue tease along my lips.

Oh.

I tighten my arm around her as I open my mouth, letting her in. She's careful, curious, slow. She doesn't rush anything.

I slide my tongue along hers, the sensation sending sparks through my body. And I forget to breathe for a moment.

She doesn't taste like anything but the strawberry lip balm I just put on, which is kind of funny, and makes me laugh, having to break the kiss.

I can't stop the laugh bubbling inside of me, spilling out, making me wrap my arms around myself. I'm not even sure why it's so funny, but it just feels funny, good. All the stress from the last week leaving me.

Alex sits up, looking at me, amused, licking her lips a few times. "What are you laughing at?" She raises an eyebrow.

"Strawberry lip balm." I can't stop the laughing.

"Right..." She smiles, shaking her head a little. "Glad that entertains you so much."

I sit up too, leaning in a little. "Just thought it was a curious choice for you."

She shrugs with one shoulder. "I like strawberries, and red." She winks and my cheeks feel like they're trying very hard to take on the shade of Alex' favourite colour.

"Right." I lick my lips, still able to feel the ghost of hers on them.

"You're good?" She tilts her head a little, reaching out and putting her hand along my jaw.

I nod. The places where we touch are on fire, every movement shooting electricity through my body.

She leans in again, putting her lips to mine, soft pillows as she keeps pushing, and we're kissing again. Sharing a breath, two, more.

It makes my head swim and I hold onto Alex so that I don't lose my spot, or whatever. My brain is going mushy and weird.

Loud footsteps bang up the stairs. "Alex!"

We pull apart, startled, staring at the door.

Cerise opens the door, ready to bolt in, but she stops when she sees us.

Oops.

She looks kinda angry right now...

"Hi..." Alex looks at the floor, though I can see that she's trying not to laugh.

"Oh." Cerise lets out a breath, blinking a few times and then relaxes some. "You didn't pick up your phone..."

"Hmm. Hmm." Alex nods, eyeing her phone, but not picking it up.

"You were ignoring me." Cerise steps further inside and closes the door behind her.

"I was, at first." Alex looks a little sheepish right now. And I guess that I wasn't the only one she was ignoring.

"And then you got distracted." Cerise now properly looks at me. "I can see that now."

I nod, blushing. "It... It wasn't planned."

"Yeah. I guessed that." Cerise lets out a laugh as she shakes her head, sitting down on Alex' computer chair. "That explains things." She shrugs. "I guess it's good that you two made up."

I look at Alex, who looks at me, grinning.

"Or, made out, apparently." Cerise laughs again. "Not exactly what I expected to find here."

"Sorry." I stand up, now Cerise is here, maybe it's time for me to leave. "I guess I made things a little complicated. Sorry about that." I don't want to bring more problems.

"Wait." Alex grabs my wrist. "Stay, please? At least until dinner?"

I look at Cerise, who shrugs. "Okay." I sit down again, a little awkward with what we just did on this bed. Especially now Cerise is here. I feel like my cheeks will stay red permanently if this goes on any longer.

But it also feels good, being here with Alex. Having her at my side, and things not being weird... at least... not in the same way as before.

"Let us walk you to the bus stop." Alex grabs the lead for her dog, Yukio, and spends the next minute trying to put it on him.

It's after dinner. Cerise also stayed over, and I met Alex' dad, her mum already left for work. We had pasta with tomato sauce and sausages. Which Cerise had to make really funny faces at as she sat opposite Alex, who laughed while also cringing. But I think Cerise will probably have a bruise on her shin later if I have to go by the face she pulled after a particularly bad sausage joke.

I asked my mum if I could stay over for dinner, but I decided not to push my luck and also ask if I could sleep over. There are only so many steps she will let me take before she'll pull me back or suspects something else going on.

Plus... It's not like I've got anything with me to sleep in or a toothbrush. I don't really want to sleep in one of Alex' shirts. Just, no. Not the first night I stay over at hers. That would be too awkward.

"Okay, ready to go." Alex grins triumphantly, holding up the end of the lead as Yukio is on the other end, his tongue hanging out, looking very excited and happy.

I let out a little laugh as I grab my bag. "Me too."

"Good." Alex opens the front door and we step out into the warm summer evening.

It's still really hot and I'm not looking forward to sitting on a bus for over an hour, again. But I've got to, there isn't really another way for me to go home and my mum is definitely not gonna come and pick me up.

We walk in silence for a few moments, but then Yukio finds something fun in the bushes and we have to wait for him to do whatever he wants to do to it.

"I'm glad you came." Alex' voice is quiet and then she looks at me. "Really." She sounds almost relieved or something.

"I'm glad too. It was really scary though."

"Yeah. By the way, who gave you my address? I don't think I gave it to you." She raises an eyebrow.

"Promise you won't kill him?" I pull a face, already having given her enough clues about who it is.

"Him?" She still asks it.

"Troy…"

Alex rolls her eyes as she lets out a deep sigh. "Of course. That was to be expected."

"Don't kill him. Or get mad at him. Please." I really don't want her to, even though I know it may have been totally out of line for Troy to tell me.

She shrugs. "I guess. I'll be nice to him, for you." She winks.

"Good enough." Because I know that it's not really okay, the way I went about to get her address. But I had to see her, and this was the only way I could think of where she couldn't just lock me out, where she had to listen to me. Or, really, apparently, not do much talking with our voices, anyway. Kissing. Hmm.

"It also explains why I didn't get any messages from Troy, while Cerise blew up my phone." Alex doesn't seem upset or surprised.

We start walking again, Yukio is apparently done with whatever he's been up to.

"Yeah. Probably." I quickly check my own phone, but I only have a handful of messages from Jade, asking how things are going. I sent her a quick 'okay' right before dinner but I'll message her back with more details when I'm on the bus.

We reach the bus stop way too soon. I don't even realise it at first, but I also don't really want to go now.

"So..." Alex looks at the stop, then at me. "I guess this means I'll have to let you go, for now." She looks sad, even though she tries to sound upbeat.

"Yeah." I take a breath, then Alex is suddenly standing really close, sliding her arm around my waist.

"I want to kiss you. Can I?" She grins, repeating my own words back to me, but I'm not letting her say anything else smart.

I put my lips to hers, kissing. It's not as rough as our first time, or as sweet as the times after.

But it's right.

My heart flutters and I can't stop my smiling.

Yes. This is right.

When I pull back, Alex' eyes are glazed over and she gasps, taking a deep breath, before she flashes me a grin.

"I guess that's a yes?" She winks and I lean in closer.

"That's definitely a yes."

24
Alex

PVP = Player Versus Player = Opportunities in the game where players play against each other instead of against the game (mostly). This can either be a whole-world kind of thing where you can fight people from other or your own faction in the world you play in or in special instances where you're grouped together and have to fight other groups and teams. This type of stuff can be very intense, but also really fun, especially when you're grouped up with friends.

I don't really want to let Fleur go. I'm so happy to see her, to hold her, to have her at my side. But I also know that she can't just stay over, her mum probably won't allow it.

"I'll see you for longer than just a few hours in two weeks." Fleur smiles, leaning in a little.

"Of course, the birthday party. Do you know if you're allowed to go yet?" I keep holding her hand. *Yes, please?*

Fleur nods. "Probably. I've just gotta find presents and stuff like that. Well, that, and deciding what to take with me from my computer or how to game when I'm there."

"Can you get your parents to drive you? We usually take computers or laptops, depending on what's easier." I generally take my whole computer, it's easy enough to pack up, but that's because I made sure to get a computer that would make it easy.

She pulls a face. "I have a double screen setup for my desktop."

"Ah, yeah. Not sure that's a good idea to bring, especially since screens aren't so easy to transport."

"I thought so." She squeezes my hand. "I'll figure it out. No worries."

I nod, stepping in closer. "I'd really like for you to come, though. Really really."

"Me too." Her eyes glitter. "I heard something about Mario Kart competitions, and DoE PvP championships?"

"You were talking to Cerise, weren't you?" She's the competitive one.

"Maybe." She smiles. "I guess I'll need to practice. I'm a little rusty at Mario Kart."

"You've got two weeks." I shrug.

Then I see the bus turn into our street. It's time.

Fleur looks behind her and her face falls, then she looks back at me. "I guess..."

"Yeah." I squeeze her hand one last time. "Time to go home."

"Yeah." She nods.

The bus stops and Fleur steps away. "See you in two weeks. I'll talk to you online when I get home."

"Talk to you in a bit." I try to smile the best I can. It's just for a little while. It's not even two hours before she'll be home and I can talk to her again. Why does it feel so much longer?

"Later." She steps onto the bus, turning around one last time.

"Later." I wave at her as she finds a place to sit.

Then the bus drives off and she's out of view. She's gone.

It takes me a couple of moments before I move again.

Yukio keeps pulling on his lead, already impatient.

"Yeah, yeah. We're going." I start walking, Yukio now leading me.

I just have to entertain myself until Fleur is home. Cerise already went home after dinner, so it's just me and Dad right now. I guess I'll figure something out.

Fleur was right about one thing, I should probably also practise my Mario Kart skills if I want to come out on top this year. Last year Cerise and one of our friends, Izzy, shared the top spot in the competition.

I've gotta do better this year, I feel like I've got something to prove. Maybe, possibly.

A giddy feeling fills my chest as I think about the party. I'll be spending the whole weekend with Fleur!

W A S D

One week.

One more week until the birthday party starts. I can barely believe it, but it's really that close.

In the next week, I'll be doing a lot of shopping with my parents and Cerise's parents together and then helping reorganise Cerise's parents' place so that we get the most use out of the living room and kitchen and stuff. But this weekend is for raiding, like we normally do. At least, this Friday is.

Even during summer break, Fleur has to work at the flower shop on Saturdays and she's been sighing about having to go out with her other friends tomorrow evening.

I'm not exactly sure why she keeps going if she doesn't like it, but it's something her mum wants her to do, something about having the 'right' type of friends. I don't know if I'm just needy for wanting to talk to Fleur so much or if I don't know how to feel about Fleur's other friends.

Fleur comes online in the voice chat. "Hey." She sounds so excited.

"Hey." I can't help grinning. "You up for raids?"

"Yeah." She seems upbeat, but I can hear something in her voice.

"What's wrong?"

"Nothing. Just... stuff with my mum. My boss told me it's fine for me to take next Saturday off, but now Mum is being difficult. Apparently I haven't spent enough time with the 'right type of friends' lately. She thinks that I've been seeing you too often, and Jade too, but I haven't spent time with the people she actually approves of." Her frustration is so obvious in her voice. "I told her that it doesn't really matter, but then she started talking about how she wasn't sure if she should let me go to the party next weekend. Since I'm *obviously* ignoring my *very important* friends. It's like she doesn't even realise the only reason we're all friends is because we know our parents want us to be."

"Why?"

"Because they decided it was the best idea when we were like... really small. Their parents are the 'right type of people' who my parents like to be connected to socially. So, they've been making us have playdates since before we can even remember. It's a thing in like my parents' circles, their parents were exactly the same with them."

"And being connected to those people matters that much to them?" I really don't get it.

"Yeah, for my parents it does. Connections are everything." She sighs. "Let's not talk about this. I want to kill things."

I smile, definitely ready to change the subject. "Kill things or are you fine with me killing things and you just healing?"

"Either. Stuff just needs to get destroyed." There is a fire in her voice. "And I've gotta get as much Alex exposure as I can get tonight, if I need to be peppy and well-adjusted all evening tomorrow."

"I can do that." I can definitely do that. And I can't help but smile at her words.

Things have been going pretty well since she was here. We've been talking and I guess I can see this maybe working out. At least we both like games, so that's an easy connection and all.

Even if it doesn't really...

Let's not go there. I want this to work out, because I've never felt like this before, not ever. It's not easy to find a girl I can share something which is so important to me with, and who is also interested in me as a person, interested romantically.

"What raid were you looking at doing?" Fleur pulls me from my thoughts.

"Ehm. I think Troy was talking about the underworld raid, with Cerberus? I know we've run it often lately, but that's not too bad, is it?" I still want some endgame currency for it so I can stock some up for my secondary class or to convert when a new currency unlocks.

"Nah, that's fine. Killing things, or well, healing you while you kill things, and it not taking all of my mental energy will be fine." There is finally a smile in her voice again, and I can imagine the way she's looking, her eyes all glittering.

"Good." I add Fleur to my party in the game and then invite Troy too. Then I do a call out in the guild chat.

> **AlexTheDestroyer:** Anyone wanna do underworld?
> **CherryBomb:** Me!
> **BloodyBAaron:** Yes!
> **AlexTheDestroyer:** Cool, will add you.

I invite them to the party too, and then sign us up on the raid group finder. I also add everyone to the voice chat I'm in with Fleur.

"Let's do this." I grin. This is the type of party work I love. Everyone together, no matter what else is going on, we can just work together and get through whatever the game throws at us.

A group of friends, supporting each other, that's sometimes the most important thing of all.

W A S D

The evening went by way too quickly, and Fleur had to get to bed on time because of work. I'm still in the chat, a little annoyed with myself for being disappointed that Fleur isn't here anymore.

I'll talk to her when she wakes up and when she gets back in the evening. But I just wish I could spend more time with her. I just really wish that I could.

"Yo, Alex." Cerise lets out a laugh.

"What?"

"Looking forward to next weekend?" She keeps laughing and I hear the smile in her voice.

"Yeah. But I need to survive this week first. So much stuff we have to do."

"Of course. But I'll be there with you, for most of it." She thinks for a moment. "Hey, what games are you taking with you? I'm not sure which ones I should be focusing on to practice, you know."

"I don't know. Maybe a race game or a fighting game. I don't think I have many games that you don't also have, or are way better than me at anyway." That's what you get when you've been friends for a long time and when you like the same things, you know how good the other person is at certain games and which ones you're better at.

"Hmmm. True. No new games lately?"

"I just play DoE. Lots of time in that. How else do you think I got so many of my classes levelled so high?" Hey, I have my pride. And having most of my classes at least halfway to max level is one of those things.

"Lucky you. Wait until you also get to Higher Vocational Education, not as much time to game anymore then." Cerise tries to sound sad, but I still hear her grin.

"Riiiight. I'm pretty sure I'm seeing you more often these days, not less often."

"Busted." She laughs. "But I don't play as heavily as I used to, not doing much progression. I need a lot of down and slow time, even in the game. Some of these classes... they fry my brain."

"You chose them yourself." And I'll probably be following her next year. Cerise is studying Computer Science with a specialisation in software engineering. It sounds so complicated sometimes, but it really looks cool too, and since I like it enough, I'll probably be doing it.

It's not like I've got much of a backup plan. I like computer games, computers and ehhh... yeah... not much else. I don't think Fleur counts.

"Yeah, I chose it myself. And I'm totally helping you out when you start here, because some of these teachers..." She sighs.

She's been complaining about the teachers since she started. The worst one was a teacher she had for computer labs. She had to hand in assignments that she'd be graded on, but the teacher couldn't even read the code, he had to use an answer sheet to check it. So if you hadn't solved a problem according to the answer sheet, you got a bad grade, even if the coding was fine and the result was exactly the same, but you'd just got there a different way.

I can't understand why they'd let someone like that teach at a University of Applied Sciences, and I'm hoping I'll never get that guy for any of my classes. But Cerise also said there just weren't enough teachers in the department, because teaching doesn't pay enough in comparison to the money software engineers can make when they work at a company. So, yeah, they don't tend to get the best people. Sadly enough.

It made me doubt going to that university, but they seem to rank decently well and I'm not sure if other places would be much better, not that I've heard anyway.

Higher Vocational Education. It feels so far away, but at the same time, it's so close. It's crazy. Just one more year of secondary school left and I'll be off to a University of Applied Sciences. It's not even a question with my parents, they expect me to keep learning and stay in education until I at least have my bachelors degree. That's always been the plan. So it's not like I've got much of a choice, I just get to choose what I'm going to study.

"You'll have to tell me how I can get ahead."

Cerise snorts. "Yeah, no. You'll be busy enough with studying for exams this year, and I suspect that you'll want to spend the rest of the time with Fleur."

"Oi." That's not entirely untrue...

"You want to deny that?" There is a challenge in her voice.

I take a breath, but then give in. "Maybe. But it's not going to be like that."

"Not yet, you mean." Cerise keeps laughing.

"Hush." I can't help grinning too.

So what if I'd like to spend as much time as possible with Fleur? It's not going to happen. Not now. Not yet anyway.

But... if I could? I'd not leave her side, at all.

So, yes, maybe I'm crazy in love.

A girl can dream.

25
Fleur

Spec/Respec = Specification = The specific skill points your character has in skills, abilities, stats and other class-specific attributes, also called your 'build'. You distribute your points and attention during levelling your character and if you do a total overhaul of these points, it's called a respec, a respecification. You'll change as you level your character, just like when you grow up, and sometimes that gives you a better understanding of who you really are, or what you really like.

There is such a difference between hanging out with Jade or Alex and when I hang out with Hannah and Sydney, the girls my mum approves of me hanging out with.

We all know this. We all know that the only reason we all hang out at all is because our parents think 'it's important for us'. Well, that, and I guess we've got used to it by now. I've got used to hanging out with them and going to places that I know I probably won't enjoy. But we all deal with it, we all just put up with it because this is what's expected of us.

None of us are brave enough to go against our parents' wishes, we just smile and do what they ask. Even if we don't really want to. It's a part of growing up in 'high society' as we like to joke. Sort-of-rich people trying to make connections with other sort-of-rich people, and we're just one of those types of connections they can make.

So, tonight, I'm at a party of a friend of a friend of a... I don't know how far this goes, but it's not a place I'd normally go to and I know that it isn't for Sydney either. It's too... I look around. It's too strait-laced, too straight. I burst out laughing, which makes Sydney raise her eyebrow at me.

She looks after Hannah for a moment, who is getting us drinks. "What are you laughing at?"

I shake my head, trying to get my laughter under control. "Nothing."

"Didn't sound like nothing." She steps closer. "What were you thinking about?" One downside to knowing these girls for so long is that they also know me pretty well, even if I'd sometimes like to ignore that.

"Just that this wouldn't be a party I'd normally go to." I shrug, still smiling.

Sydney nods. "Yeah, it's a little... posh." She pulls a face. "But that doesn't have to be a bad thing. At least it's not some grimy place in the city centre where you have to wait in line to get in."

I'm not sure I agree with her, but by then Hannah is already back with our drinks. "Cola for Sydney, Sprite for me and a water for Fleur." She eyes me. She knows I'm not allowed to have sugar but she always complains that she feels stupid ordering water for me.

Of the two, I usually get along with Sydney better than Hannah, but they're both not people I'd normally choose to hang out with, but I still have to show up with them, keep up appearances. This whole party is filled with people my parents would love me to make connections with, all people my age coming from families with the right amount of money and the right type of education, and of course family values...

"Thanks." I take the glass, taking a deep gulp of it. It gives me something to do, and I'm sure they've got those mist machines or something in this place, it feels very dry in here. I check my phone, it's still early and the temptation to message Alex about how bored I am is very high right now.

"Fleur?" Sydney looks at me. "Why do you keep looking at your phone?"

"No reason." I put my phone in my pocket. They don't need to see the background picture of Alex and me together.

"We know you better than that. Did you get a new boyfriend?" Hannah steps closer.

A new boyfriend? I laugh again. Of course, that would be the first thing that comes to mind for them. Like anything else isn't a possibility.

I shake my head, smiling a little. "No, not a boyfriend."

Hannah frowns. "So, not a boyfriend? Then what?"

"Does it matter?" I shrug. "Does it matter why I keep checking my phone?"

Sydney also steps closer, leaning to me. "Well, you keep smiling, grinning, checking your phone." She looks to the side. "And there's a really cute guy staring your way since you came in, and you haven't even noticed him. Yeah, right now, it matters."

I follow her eyes, there is a guy looking my way but he's just… He's not my type. Truthfully, he's too 'peppy', too 'posh' like Sydney would put it, not my type at all. "Why would I notice him?"

"Because he's hot?" Hannah frowns. "He's like, really hot?"

"I'm not agreeing with you on that. But we have different tastes." I shrug, leaning back, taking another sip from my glass. "But if you want him, why don't you go over to him?"

"Because he's only got eyes for you." Hannah now steps between me and the boy. I'm not sure if it's because she wants him to stop staring at me or because she knows that her butt looks good in that skirt. "Anyway, back to the phone issue. Is there anything on it we're not allowed to see?"

I feel my cheeks heat up, even though it's already quite warm in here. "I… I don't really… think so?"

"Ooh." Sydney's eyes now begin to shine. "Now I *really* want to know."

"Why?" I'm not sure I can get away from these girls right now. I'm not sure I can get them to lay off their questioning.

"Because we're curious." Sydney steps next to Hannah now. "You haven't gone out with us in, like, weeks, and now that we're all here, you keep checking your phone. We're hurt." Of course, when it's of use to us, we'll always use our friendship to our advantage, even to each other.

"Well, and you really haven't told us much about what you've been doing lately." Hannah shrugs.

"I've been playing videogames." What else am I supposed to tell them? "That, and I've been working at the flower shop."

"And which of those two would require you to check your phone every two minutes?" Sydney raises her eyebrows.

"Neither? And it's not every two minutes." I'm pretty sure of that… I think.

"Okay. So, what is it?" Hannah's really getting into this, isn't she?

How much can I tell her? How much can I tell these girls without it getting back to my parents in seconds? Would it even matter? Would Hannah and Sydney even care?

"Is it a secret?" Sydney's eyes now go more serious. "Is it something we're not allowed to know? Or your parents aren't allowed to know?"

I shrug. "It's just… I don't know."

Hannah looks around us and then tugs on my shirt. "You wanna go somewhere else? Just to, you know, talk? You know we're here for you."

I swallow hard. Can I tell them? Would I even know what to say? But I nod. I guess that telling Hannah and Sydney about Alex would be a good idea.

I have to start somewhere, and with them is easier than telling my parents first. Of course, Jade knows, but she's different. She knows a lot of things about me that others don't. It's the perk of being a close friend, and one I actually chose myself, instead of being forced onto me by my parents.

Hannah starts walking along the wall to one of the back doors, stepping out onto the patio at the back where it's a little quieter and the air isn't as heavy.

She sits at one of the picnic tables, putting her glass down in front of her, her hands on the table. She waits until we all sit down too and then she looks at me again. "What is it? What is it that you're hiding?"

"I'm not… I'm not hiding anything." My voice trails off. "I'm not really hiding it. It's just…"

"You're not *pregnant* are you?" Sydney leans in, her eyes worried. "That's not the secret you're not telling us, right?"

I wish I didn't laugh. I wish that it wasn't the thing most out of the realm of possibilities for secrets I'm hiding right now. I really wish I hadn't started laughing because Hannah and Sydney are now glaring at me. "No. I'm not pregnant."

"You're doing badly at school? Something else?" Hannah keeps eyeing me.

"No. School's fine. It's just…" I take a deep breath. "I… I've got a girlfriend."

"Well, we all do." Hannah frowns. "We're all girlfriends, aren't we?"

I burst out laughing again. I surprise myself, how can I laugh when she's really misunderstanding me? "No. Not like that."

"You mean…" Sydney raises her eyebrows. "You kissed a girl, and found out you liked it?"

"Well, I liked the girl, and then I kissed her. But, yeah." I look down, I don't know how I can face them right now. I don't know how I… My cheeks flare up and I can feel the heat go down my neck too.

"You're a lesbian now?" I'm not sure how to read Hannah's voice. "Are you like… like, into girls now?"

"Well…" I play with my fingers, trying to come up with an answer. "I… Her… I'm not a lesbian."

"I don't get it." Sydney sounds confused too. "You have a girlfriend, that has to mean that you're into girls, but you're not a lesbian?"

"I…" I shake my head. "I'm not *just* into girls."

"And those boyfriends? Were they not real?" Sydney leans in. "Was that just *you* trying to be normal?"

I shake my head again. "No. I did… I did really like them at the time. I just, right now, I've got a girlfriend." Calling Alex my girlfriend is still a little strange. Good, but strange. And a little scary.

"Then, what?"

"I guess I like boys and girls." I try to shrug it off but this has been something I've been thinking about for a while. That I've been wondering about since I met Alex in real life. Way back, when I thought she was a boy, I already liked her. I liked who Alex was. And then finding out Alex was a girl, it shocked me, but it didn't change what I thought, what I felt for her.

"Is that even a thing?" Sydney now shakes her head. "Like, you're into girls *or* you're into boys, right?"

"No." I look up, making sure that I look at Hannah and Sydney, that I've got their attention. "You can like boys, girls, or both, or neither, or… well, none of the above? All of the above? It's not one or the other for me."

Sydney shakes her head. "Yeah, but what does it mean for you? Like, do you like, like one of us?" She motions between her and Hannah.

"No." I let out a little laugh, a little relieved how the questions are turning. "It's not like that. You don't like every boy who walks around here, right?"

"No…" Sydney looks around. "There are a lot of guys here who I do not like, like. A *lot* of them." She pulls a face.

"And I know you've been friends with guys before." I look at her. "Guys who you were friends with without ever wanting to kiss them, right?"

"Yes." Sydney thinks for a moment. "I guess you can be friends with people you *could* fall for and not fall for them."

"I hadn't ever fallen for a girl until I met Alex, either." Glad they seem to sort of understand me.

"Ooh. So her name is Alex?" Now Hannah is interested again. She loves gossip, and there is no juicier gossip than who is dating whom, especially the question of who is having sex with whom.

I blush, looking down, nodding. "Yes. Her name is Alex and she is also a gamer. I met her in a videogame and… that's where it started."

"Are you sure that she is a she? You know, with a name like that, and playing videogames. Are you sure that she is a she?" Sydney raises her eyebrows.

"Yes, I'm sure." That's a mistake I made before. A male game character, a male-sounding name, and a love for videogames, that's why I thought Alex was a boy at first too. She's not.

"Do you have pictures of her?" Having got over the surprise, Hannah now seems curious.

"Yes." I slowly take my phone from my pocket, opening up one of the pictures that Alex and I took last week. My heart beats loudly as I look at it, not wanting to spoil this feeling, but also, I'm a little proud. I'm proud because it's not been easy, and I never expected it to be. I turn the phone to Sydney and Hannah. "This is her and me."

"Oh. Yes, definitely a girl." Sydney grins. "Definitely. Also, kinda lesbian."

"You don't…" I sigh, turning my phone away and putting it on the table. "It's not like that. Just because she likes girls, or just because I like girls and boys. It doesn't mean that we look one way or another way. You can't *see* someone's sexuality like that."

"Well… It's just that…" Hannah shrugs. "She really *does* look like a lesbian and, you know, you *don't*. Are you sure you really are into girls? Are you sure that she's not just tricking you? Or you're not just projecting your feelings onto her because she looks butch?"

How does she… Why does she even think that?

Is that how people see us? Is that really how people see Alex? Or me?

Maybe telling Hannah and Sydney wasn't the best plan after all…

26
Alex

PVE = Player Versus Environment = Unlike PVP where players have to fight against other players, PVE is where players fight the environment. This ranges from characters fighting mobs, having to interact with certain elements of their surroundings, or interacting with NPCs. In MMORPGs most of the game is generally player versus environment. This is where the game works in standard ways, unlike the more unpredictable play style in PVP, because in PVP you're playing against other people, not pieces of code. In some ways it's like the real world, always interacting with what's around you. And some cases like social structures can be a lot like PVE, you do what is expected, you follow the rules. That is, until you don't, then, suddenly you're 'breaking the rules' and 'being different'.

Instead of sitting around, getting annoyed or bored because Fleur isn't here, I'm actually going out of the house too. Today, or rather, tonight, I'm with Troy and Yukio.

The weather is amazing, there isn't a lot of wind and the sun is still nice and warm, and I just knew that I had to get away from the house for a couple of hours. So I've got a backpack full of food with me and we're just about to leave my neighbourhood, walking out into the fields.

Sure, it's corny, 'girl going on walk with boy who she is very close to'. Unlike the trope though, we're not like that. This 'going places', is something we've done for basically as long as we've known each other. We like to do this during the summer, especially when we're bored or our parents really need us to, you know, not be inside all the time.

Yukio nearly trips Troy, who quickly grabs hold of my shoulder. The little devil lets out a happy bark and Troy glares at him.

"Why does he have to do that *every time*."

"Well, I'm pretty sure it's because he thinks it's funny. I think that he thinks that you like it when he does it." I shrug his hand off. "And don't lean on me, it's way too hot for that."

"Well, you're just so easy to grab. I just always know you're there."

"Yeah, but… I won't *always* be able to be there for you, you know."

"What are you being all gloomy for? What's got into you?" Troy just walks next to me now, no longer leaning on me.

"Well it's true, isn't it?"

"Yeah, but do you have to say it like that?" I can feel his eyes on me.

"Then what do you want me to say?"

"I was just thinking... I don't know. Something not-gloomy."

I shrug. "With Cerise, you know, her being off to university and everything. It's only a year for us now too."

"Yeah, so? Next year is not *now*. That's like, a year away. This is about Fleur, isn't it?" Troy looks thoughtful, which I don't tend to see often, but it has been happening more often since I met Fleur.

"Why?"

"Well… She's a year behind us, so even if you're off, she's still at home."

"Yeah. I guess." Though, I don't know, I'm not sure if that's a bad thing.

"Do you have an idea where you're gonna go?"

"I'm thinking of following Cerise. You know, computers and stuff." It's my best bet.

"Yeah, but won't that mean that you'll be closer to Fleur. Like, closer you are now anyway?"

I shrug. "Not really." It's an hour by bus from here. And if I study in Zwolle, where the school I want to go to is, it's still an hour away, just by train.

But if I'm going to get into Higher Vocational Education I'll get a pass for cheap and free public transport so it will make visiting Fleur a lot cheaper, and I won't have to deal with my parents telling me what time I need to be back. Graduating secondary school and moving out of my parents' place has a lot of advantages.

"So, where are you getting all this 'we won't always be at each other's side' stuff from? If you're going there, the same school as Cerise is going, we'll still be right next to each other. The only place I can study to be a physics teacher that's even remotely around here is right there at that school."

I stop. "I guess I'm just being gloomy. I guess I'm just…"

Troy pushes at my shoulder. "Yeah. Yeah, you were *just*. You're *just* missing Fleur."

"It's that obvious, is it?"

"Yes. Now, can we… go do this?" Again, Troy almost trips over Yukio, but this time Troy starts running and Yukio follows him, happily barking.

Troy's right, it's time to stop being gloomy and start having fun.

Fleur is at a party and I'm going to have my own right here.

WASD

I lean back on the blanket, looking around us. We're on top of a dyke—yeah, sure, go make fun of that—and we can see everywhere around us.

From here we can see some of the small villages in the low lands and fields around us. And we can also see every ship coming our way. Though, with weather like this, it's mostly just people in small boats. Who all greet us because that's what you do when you're on a boat and you see people.

Yukio keeps exploring the grass and bushes, and sometimes comes back to beg for something to eat or to drink from his bowl.

Troy's speakers change to a new song and I hum along to it. It's a song by the Japanese girl group Perfume called 'Spending All My Time'. I almost automatically start doing the hand movements the girls do in the video of it. I can't help it, it's *sooo* catchy.

Troy bursts out laughing, but then he synchronises with me for a few moments. "How do you…" He has to stop because he keeps laughing so much.

I shrug. "That's what you get from watching the video too much and not being able to sit still."

"True." He sits up and takes a handful of the chips. "You can never sit still."

"I can. Sometimes." I put my arms next to me, on the blanket and try to stay as still as possible.

"Right." Troy spews pieces of chips everywhere as he talks and he grabs his phone. Then he switches the song over to 'Flash' also by Perfume and I immediately start nodding my head to the beat. "You can't."

"I *can*. You're just being mean." I sit up, pushing him. "You know what I mean. I can sit still if I need to."

"No, you still can't." He laughs. "The times you've got in trouble for bouncing your leg or tapping your pen..."

I roll my eyes at him. "You're talking primary school again? I'm better than that now."

"No, I'm talking maths class during our final exam. Just a few weeks ago."

"Meh." I shrug, taking a sip from my bottle of fizzy. "I needed to focus."

"I know. I'm not disagreeing with that. You're just not able to sit still. And that's why you know all the moves to Perfume songs."

Should I tell him that part of the reason is because the girls are cute, or should I just leave him with the innocent idea that it's just their songs that make me want to listen to them all the time? I decide to just leave it, this time.

"Hey, are you and Fleur good again?" Troy looks at me.

"Yeah, we're good." I nod. "It's just... I don't know. It's sometimes scary."

"I got that part." He looks out over the canal. "But, you know, this is different. Fleur is different from all those other girls. You know that."

"Why?" I don't disagree with him, I'm just curious why he thinks that.

"Because she loves videogames." Troy grins. "She can probably kick your butt at them."

"She has." I grin too.

"Well, that's a huge difference already. She loves them, at the same level as you do. She's good at them too. She gets along with us, the guild, you know, the people you hang out with most."

"She seems to get along with you too." I eye him, not ready to stop giving him crap over him giving Fleur my address.

"That's a plus." He winks. "That way I can tell her all the things you don't want me to tell her. Like your weaknesses."

"My weaknesses?"

"Yep." He holds up the bag with all the candy I was able to hide from my mum. "Candy, sweets. Especially the ones with sugar on the outside."

"Hey." I grab the bag. "She already knows that, she also loves them." I feel my cheeks heat up.

"Oh." He lets out a laugh. "Reason two that Fleur isn't like other girls. She makes you laugh and smile much more. When you think of her, you get that look in your eyes."

"What look?" I close my eyes, rubbing my hands over my face, like the blush will go away like that.

"That look as if you're imagining her being right there with you." He shakes his head. Then he holds up three fingers. "Three. You want to spend every moment you can with her. Four. She surprises you, in the good ways."

"Okay. Okay. Enough. I think my cheeks have had enough warmth now." I wave my hands at him. When I've calmed down, I look at him. "Do you really think she's really that special?"

Troy nods. "When you're with her, you're still you. You don't try to be different."

"I always feel like I'm being weird when I'm with her." I always feel awkward because I've got no idea if what I do is right or not.

"Yeah, but that's the good type of weird. You're awkward, strange, all those things that happen because you want to impress her. You don't put on a persona. You don't try to be extra butch or extra femme for her. You don't try to fit whatever stereotype you think she'd like. You're just you."

"What? I'm not like that." I've never tried to be like that with other girls.

"You are. And I'm telling you this as a friend who has known you for far too long." He pulls out some grass at the edge of the blanket. "If the girl you like is butch, you try to be more femme. If the girl is too cutesy and femme, you try to be more butch."

"I'm not—"

"You are." Troy interrupts me, looking serious now. "But with Fleur... You're a gamer. You're a gamer first."

"What? How does that even make sense?"

"It does." He grins again. "You're just you. You're a gamer, you talk with her because you both love games. You fell for her because you met her in a videogame. Not at some party, not online on some lesbian dating app. Not anywhere where you go all awkward and self-conscious because you don't know how to act. You met her somewhere where you're just you. And Fleur may be really cute and sexy and all the things you like, but you always treat her like she's just another gamer, like you."

"You've put a lot of thought into this... Into *my* relationship." I raise an eyebrow at him.

Troy shrugs. "Hey, she's our healer. She's really good. I don't want to lose her. My involvement is purely for the good of the guild, for our game progression. Nothing more." The tone of his voice is like he's trying to sound innocent.

I snort, quickly wiping the sip of water I was taking from my chin. "You're horrible and such a gossip."

"Yeah, and you were about to push away the girl who really likes you for who you are and not some other reason." His voice is softer, his eyes serious but also sweet.

"I guess..." I was scared. I was scared that if I looked up that she'd be gone, and I *really* like her.

Troy is right. I like Fleur more than any girl I've liked in the past. I love her. And, even though this sounds really stupid, because we're both not even out of secondary school, but I feel like we may actually be able to make this work...

I love Fleur and I want her to know that.

I love her.

"You're doing it again." Troy laughs, pushing at my shoulder. "Ugh. I should never have started about Fleur."

"No." I shake my head, letting out a breath. "You're right. I keep throwing up these excuses of why I shouldn't do this, why I'm too scared. But she makes me happy. Being with her, talking to her, it makes me happy."

"Okay…" Troy rolls his eyes. "Now, can you call her or something? That way I don't have to keep looking at that sappy-blushing face of yours for the next three hours."

"You're..." I sigh. "Fine. I'm just going to check if she's having fun." Just going to check. Just making sure. That's normal, right?

I pick up my phone, dialling Fleur's number.

My heart is already beating like crazy, just thinking about hearing her voice.

I'm totally lost, aren't I?

Totally.

27
Fleur

Elite = Usually refers to 'elite mobs', monsters that are stronger than the ones around them. Some of them have names to differentiate them while other games or other types of mobs may use visual clues on the mob itself or the mob portrait, when you select to attack them. Think of them like adults or something like that… When you think you've dealt with all the mobs, the normal people, you then have to deal with the elites… Like confronting your parents about something…

My phone starts ringing and Alex' name appears on the screen.

"Is that her?" Hannah leans over. "Oh! It is!" She tries to grab my phone but I quickly pick it up.

"I'm going to take this." I hit the green button and step away from the table. "Hi." I still can't help the smile when I talk to her.

"Hey." There is already a smile in Alex' voice. "How are you doing?"

"I'm..." I look back at the table, Hannah and Sydney are staring at me. "I'm okay. How are you?"

"I'm good." I hear Yukio bark in the background and then Alex laughs loudly. "Sorry, sorry. Troy is playing with Yukio. They're being silly."

"I'm glad you're having fun." I'm happy for her, but I'm not sure I sound that convinced, my night is not going as easily as hers seems to be going.

"Hey, what's wrong?" Alex sounds more serious now.

"Nothing. Just..." I sigh, shooting a glance back at the table. Hannah and Sydney are no longer looking my way and I wander off a little more, leaning against a wall so I'm out of the routes people walk and away from most of the noise.

"Hey, you can tell me. You know that." Her voice is softer and even Yukio stops barking in the background.

"It's just... I don't know..." How do I tell her? How do I tell her that I don't know how to define myself, who I am. And that Hannah and Sydney have made it obvious how little I know about this whole not-being-straight thing. "How did you know you were a lesbian?"

"What?" That question seems to surprise her. "Hmmm. I guess I just knew. I've never really liked boys, in the sexual or relationship way."

"Yeah, but, like... how did you know you weren't something else? Like... how did you know to call yourself a 'lesbian' and not something else?" I'm starting to confuse even myself.

"I'm a girl, I like girls. That sort of made lesbian fit me the best." She's quiet for a moment. "Is someone being difficult?"

"The girls... they asked me if I was a lesbian because I called you my girlfriend. And... I don't know. I like boys, I like you. I..."

I know that liking boys and girls is usually called bisexuality, but I don't know... It doesn't feel that right.

"Now you're wondering what you should call yourself?"

"I guess. It feels right to have like... an answer, but also... Ugh." This is hard.

"You don't need to have an answer. It was easy for me, but it's not the same for everyone."

"Yeah..."

"You want to know what I think?" Somehow I feel there is a smile in her voice now.

"What?"

"I think that you like me. I think that you want to tell that to other people. And, to me, that's enough. I don't care what you call yourself, but I do care that you like me and that you really want others to know about it too."

"Thanks." I smile a little too. "Did you tell anyone?"

"I don't think there is a whole lot of 'telling' anyone going on with my friends." Alex lets out a little laugh. "Both with my sexuality when I was younger, or with me liking you..."

"There was no secret that she liked you." Troy yells and I can hear him very clearly. "Or that she was attracted to girls when she was younger."

"I don't think I want to know that story." I shake my head and Alex laughs.

"Don't listen to him. He's got weird ideas sometimes." She's quiet for a moment. "I mean it, though. I don't care what you identify as, that's not up to me, that's up to you."

"Yeah, but... apart from like... I dunno, the stuff I learned in class a few years ago, I have like... no idea." Why would I? It's not like I really questioned my sexuality before. Not that... Not that I hadn't been attracted to girls before, but I always assumed

238

it was because they were pretty. Alex is the first girl I actually like in more than just a 'hey, she's kinda pretty from afar' way, I want her, in like, many ways.

Alex doesn't answer immediately, but when she does, she sounds serious. "Bisexuality, pansexuality, omnisexuality, queer... There are many words you can use. And those aren't the only ones, really. But it needs to fit you and who you are."

I close my eyes for a moment, imagining Alex on her back in the grass, in the evening sun, having this conversation with me. "What's the difference between bisexual and pansexual?" The rest... I don't even know how many more identities there are.

"Bisexual, both, is basically homosexuality and heterosexuality combined. You're attracted to those with genders like yours, homosexuality, and people with genders other than yours, heterosexuality. Pansexual, all, means that you like people of all genders. Usually, the difference between the two comes from the importance of gender and gender expression in the person you like."

"You sound so smart." How does she know so much?

"I just..." Is she blushing? "These things have been a part of my life for a long time. I..." She trails off.

"What is it?" Something in her voice makes me worry a little.

"I guess I should just tell you this." She takes a deep breath. "I've dated a feminine non-binary person in the past. To me, femininity is attractive. I like *girls*, women. People who look feminine and mostly identify as women. So, even though I identify as lesbian, I've been attracted to people not of my gender specifically, like feminine non-binary people, in the past. Your identity is what you feel it is, not what others make it. Does that make sense?"

For a moment I have to think about Alex having dated other people, which... *bleh*. I don't like to think about that right now. But then, after pushing that aside, I nod. "Yeah. That makes sense. That makes some sense in all of this stuff." I look around the outside area. Two boys have joined Hannah and Sydney at the table, so they'll be entertained a while longer.

"Your identity is *your* choice. I can't tell you, but I can help you figure it out."

"Thanks. You may have to." Because I'm getting too lost in all of this. I just don't know.

"I'd be happy to." Alex sounds so confident. "Now, I know that you're at a party, and you're supposedly there with friends..."

"Yeah. They're... enjoying themselves." I shake my head. "But you should get back to Troy, or I'll never hear the end of how I kept your attention away all evening." I feel a lot calmer now, a lot more easy. Alex is right. There's no rush, there isn't anything that means that I have to choose *right now*, I can figure things out as we go.

"I guess so." She smiles. "I'll talk to you... tomorrow probably?"

"Yeah. I'll talk to you tomorrow. And I totally want a pic of you and Yukio in the evening sun. You probably look really cute, and I can't take the pic myself right now. I kind of want to see you like that."

"Wha... You... Hm... Hn..."

Troy bursts out laughing. "You did it, Fleur. You broke the Alex. Congrats!"

I can't help the smile that's making my cheeks ache. "I guess that's a yes. Talk to you tomorrow. Have fun."

"You too. Talk to you tomorrow." Alex' voice is soft, her voice low, and I can imagine the blush spreading over her cheeks, down her neck, and the way she looks away, her eyes vulnerable.

"Kisses." I blurt it out right before I hit the button to disconnect the call. I put my hands over my face, almost letting out a squeal. That was... *so* embarrassing! But I totally couldn't not do it!

When I've pulled myself together again, I go back over to the table.

Hannah looks up, smiling. "You really do look in love. I guess that was a good chat with your girlfriend?"

"Girlfriend?" One of the boys, way too slick for my taste, but exactly what Hannah likes, looks at me. "You have a girlfriend? I thought you were straight."

"She was." Hannah shrugs. "But now apparently she likes boys and girls." She rolls her eyes, but I still appreciate her sticking up for me, even a little.

"Cool. Is she hot?" The boy's eyes go over me in a way I do not appreciate.

"She's taken. I'm taken. So that's none of your business." I sit down and the boy looks a little confused, blinking. Why do I have the feeling that he did not expect me to talk back to him like that?

"Go Fleur." Sydney laughs and wraps her arm around my shoulder. "Well, at least you've not lost your tongue. You're going to need it anyway, you know... When you... You know."

"Sydney!" I pull back a little. "Really?" I shake my head. "We just kissed, we've not even... That's not even..." I feel my cheeks heat up, my head going all wonky.

"I'm kidding, I'm kidding." Sydney laughs more. "But that reaction. That was too adorable."

I shake my head. This is a weird evening. Like, totally strange. But I guess that by the way Hannah and Sydney are talking and teasing, maybe they accept me more easily than I thought they would.

Now, I guess there are more people who I should tell, like my parents…

⬚W⬚ ⬚A⬚ ⬚S⬚ ⬚D⬚

When I wake up the next morning, I already know that this isn't going to be a good day. My parents are having a loud argument in the living room and I think I just heard my name...

I check my phone and see that I've got a few messages from Alex but also from Sydney.

That's strange. I open the first one, it's from an hour ago... 'I'm sorry. I let slip to my parents that you have a girlfriend. I'm so sorry.' And then a second one. 'I think they may have told your parents.' And another one. 'They definitely told your parents. I'm so sorry.'

Just as I'm reading them, another message from Sydney comes in. 'I'm so so sorry. I should have kept my mouth shut.'

I take a deep breath, that may explain the argument downstairs. 'I just woke up. What happened?'

Sydney's message is quick. 'Oh, good. I was talking to my parents over breakfast, and they kept asking questions about you, and I let slip that you have a girlfriend. That... I'm sorry.' And another message. 'I was just telling them how you were so happy and then the word girlfriend slipped out and I messed up.'

Not that I'm surprised, by Sydney's slip up or our parents' reactions. 'I guess it's fine. They had to find out at some point.'

'Yeah, but it shouldn't have been from my parents, you know...'

'Yeah. Thanks for the head's up though. Did they say anything else, your parents?'

I can almost imagine the face she's making, the way she'll try to weigh up what to tell me and what not to tell me, depending on how her parents reacted exactly. But I guess it wasn't a good reaction overall, from them calling my parents and Sydney apologising. She'll be all slumped over, which her parents keep telling her off for, her eyes downcast and she'll probably be biting the edge of her thumb.

'They questioned if your parents were raising you too 'liberal' and if they should have a serious discussion with them.' And there is the bit that I know she isn't saying, her parents are questioning if I'm still such a 'good friend' for Sydney. And even though I hate the way our parents keep pushing this friendship thing on us, I also care for her. We've been sort-of-friends for so long that we can't help but care, we're like part-time triplets in how much our lives have been intertwined.

'Well, I guess I should get downstairs. Face the wrath of the parents.'

'Good luck. I'm really sorry.'

'It's okay. It'll be fine.' I put the phone down, quickly getting dressed before I even dare to look at Alex' messages. I'm going to need her courage right now.

Alex sent me a picture of her and Yukio on a blanket, on her one side is a canal and on the other side green fields as far as the eye can see. She looks beautiful, even in her simple tank top and shorts, her hair blowing in the wind. I take a couple of deep breaths, imprinting the image in my mind. This is the girl. This is my girlfriend.

And I love her.

I love her.

In the big 'she means the world to me' and the 'I don't want to ever be without her' way.

I love Alex.

And that realisation stops me, makes me sit down on my bed again, staring at my phone.

I don't just like Alex, I'm not just attracted to her, I *love* her.

And my parents are downstairs, discussing my relationship, my sexuality, and my ability to ever be able to see her again.

And suddenly, I'm so not ready to face them... Not at all.

28
Alex

Kiting = Attacking a mob and then either constantly stepping back and getting out of range of their attacks so that you can kill them without getting too much damage yourself, or, generally in the case of tanks, pulling a whole group of mobs and making them walk across the field while the DPS try to kill them off. Sometimes I feel like I'm always the one kiting people in real life, I say something, they disagree and then I have to keep sidestepping their (verbal) attacks while trying to get my own words across. It can be really exhausting, but I'm not one to give up fighting easily.

I can't believe this. I really can't believe this. I stare at the screen of my phone. Why would this happen?

On my screen is a message from Fleur, well, more precisely, from her mum... 'We don't want you to talk to our daughter right now. We don't feel that this is appropriate behaviour for a sixteen-year-old to be involved in. Good day.'

I keep staring at it but the message doesn't change. It doesn't make a difference. I'm sitting in the middle of my bedroom and don't know what to do now. Things were going so well... and now... *Argh.*

I squeeze my lips together, closing my eyes, willing the tears to stay away. I don't want to cry, not now.

I want to talk to Fleur. I want her back. She sounded so happy last night, and now... I can't imagine how confused or in pain she is right now.

I pull myself up on my bed, keeping my phone close by. *No.* I'm not letting this happen. I'm not letting her parents get between us, not when we've finally got this far. Not now. They don't get to make this choice for her.

The way down the stairs seems long, but I can't move too quickly, I'm too numb to move very fast.

I need to... I need to... someone. I need to find someone.

When I look into the living room, there isn't anyone there. So I go to the kitchen, where Mum is filling her lunchbox with sandwiches, she probably has to leave for her shift soon.

"Morning." She smiles as she looks my way, but then her face falls. "What's wrong?"

"Fleur... She..." I hold out my phone, the message visible, as I let out a sob. This hurts so much. "Just... Just look at it." I can barely get the words out of my mouth, I just... I don't know how to deal with this. How I can get Fleur back when her parents don't want me to see her.

Mum's eyes go over the screen, a frown appearing. "When... When did this happen?"

"Just received it." I was getting ready to come downstairs for a snack and looked at my phone when it buzzed at me, all happy that Fleur had woken up and seen my picture.

"Just now?"

"Yes."

Mum nods. "Did they… Did they know yet?"

I shake my head. "I don't want to lose her."

"That won't happen." Mum straightens her back, takes my phone, hitting a button and then puts it to her ear.

I grasp for her. She can't do this. *No way.*

Mum shakes her head, walking away from me, just a step out of my reach. Then her eyes light up. "Yes, hello. No, this isn't Alex. I'm her mum."

I can only stare at Mum. If there had ever been any doubt who I got my impulsivity from... Yeah, no more. Thinking through actions, especially when we're emotional, isn't our strong suit.

"Yes. Yeah, I read the message." I can hear Fleur's mum yell at her from the other side of the line but I can't hear the exact words, and I'm pretty sure I'm glad that I can't. "Inappropriate, you say? I'm pretty sure you've met my daughter, you've talked to her. And while she has a little wild side to her, inappropriate is not a word I would use for the type of relationship that they have." Mum's a psychiatrist, so she's used to dealing with people who are being difficult. "No, no. Yes, I understand. But *what* exactly do you feel is inappropriate?" Mum frowns more. "Right… And, had Alex been a boy, would you have had the same issues?" She raises an eyebrow. Trick question. "No. Like I thought. As a mum and a psychiatrist who deals a lot with teens, I would advise you to sit down with your daughter and ask her about what it is that's going on. Or, if you prefer to have someone with expertise come along, I'd be happy to join you. No? Okay." Mum raises an eyebrow at me now, but her eyes harden. "Sure, I'll talk to my daughter. Although, I'm not exactly sure what I would have to talk to her about. Do you want me to tell her that the girl who's made her so happy these last couple of weeks can't see her because her parents are bigots? Or, that her holding hands with another girl is considered dirty or too 'pornographic' for her mere seventeen years of age?"

My mouth falls open. Mum is really getting into this, isn't she? I present to you, the evidence of why I don't want to get into arguments with my mum.

"Oh. You don't want me to say those words? Bigots? Homophobia? How about meddling? Or stunting the personal growth of your child?"

Okay… I can't take this anymore. This is just upsetting me more.

I leave the kitchen, walk to the back, and out into the garden.

Yeah, I'm a coward. But I don't want to have to deal with that. I don't want mum to make things even worse than they already are right now. Like, how can this make things better?

Yukio comes up to me, wagging his tail. I kneel down, wrapping my arms around him. "Yeah, at least you're not going to ruin anything, are you?"

Yukio lets out a bark and rushes off, bringing me back a ball.

I take the ball, throwing it up into the air a few times, driving Yukio crazy, before I throw it to the other side of the garden.

His little legs carry him over there as quickly as he can. With all his speed, he rushes right past the ball the first time, twisting his body trying to grab it when he realises what has gone wrong. He skids to a stop, hopping back over to the ball, grabbing it, and rushing back over to me. He lets the ball go just a small distance away, letting the thing roll the last part on its own.

He waits, looking at me expectantly. Yukio lets out a couple of happy barks, stepping from side-to-side.

I pick up the ball, throwing it again. We play this game for a while, until I hear Mum's footsteps behind me. I look back up at her, her face is serious. Do I even want to know now?

"Alex..." She sits down next to me. "I'm Sorry." She shakes her head. Yukio comes over and she runs her hand through his fur. "I'm sorry about getting angry when this happens. I can't stand it when..." She sighs. "Sorry."

"I know..." I lean back a little, taking a deep breath. Mum can't stand it when parents dictate things like kids' sexuality or gender, and that this is hurting me won't help. "How bad is it?" What did she do?

"I don't know." There is something to her voice and when I look up, there is a small smile in her eyes.

"Why?"

"Right after you left, Fleur's dad actually took over the phone. He said that they were only trying to protect their daughter. Like I wasn't doing the same thing. And he said that he agreed somewhat with me. But that he had to think about protecting his daughter first and that if she was 'something like that' they didn't know how to protect her anymore. Which I agreed with. I guess it was a shock for them to find out that their daughter wasn't just into boys. Especially when they hear it from someone who isn't their daughter." Mum sighs. "I'm sorry. I have no idea what's going to happen now. They may be totally fine, or they may refuse to let her see you again. Really sorry."

"It's my birthday party next week. I really want her to come." I can feel the tears try to come out again. "I just want to see her again. I..."

"I know." Mum puts her hand on my arm. "And I'll try to see what I can do to make things better. But right now, I can't promise anything."

I nod. "Yeah…"

Mum holds out my phone. "You'll probably want this back. And do I need to have a conversation with you about proper phone use, selfies and sexting and things like that?"

"No. Thanks." I shake my head. "Why?" Sexting, really?

"Fleur's parents said something about a photo?"

"This one?" I unlock the phone, pulling up the pics from yesterday evening. "I sent her this, she asked for it." It's the pic with me and Yukio, and there isn't anything sexual about it. It's just me, smiling a little.

"Right." She nods. "Cute picture though. But yeah, not something to get their panties all in a twist over." Mum sighs again, then she stands up. "I'm off to work in half an hour or so. If you want to talk or anything, still, I'm here. Your dad is at the university library, working on his research. I can ask him to come home if you want to?"

I shake my head. "No. Thanks. I'll be fine. If stuff gets really…" I shrug not even sure what I'm trying to say. "I can always call Cerise or Troy."

"Right. You don't need your poor elderly parents to look after you anymore." She smiles and winks.

"Thank you for offering, though." I smile a little too. "I guess I just have to wait right now. Just… wait." My throat closes up. It's all going so fast, but at the same time… it's all going so slowly. So much more slowly than I wished. But I know that people don't just change their minds because some random stranger yelled at them to not be nasty to their daughter, not even when the person in question has like… multiple degrees in psychiatry and stuff.

"Yep. Oh, and if you could walk Yukio this afternoon and after dinner? I'm not sure your dad will be home for them." She squeezes my shoulder.

"I will." I throw the ball again and Yukio runs after it.

"It will work out, somehow. Fleur's a great girl, and this will work out." Mum's voice sounds reassuring, but I'm not as convinced as she is. Which may be my own pessimism though...

I stare over to the back of the garden, but not really seeing anything. I wish for it to work out well, yes. But there is no guarantee, no proof. And that's what makes this all so hard.

That's what scares me.

W A S D

I stare at my phone, the screen black, quiet.

I will for Fleur to call me, for the phone to light up, I need to hear her voice. She promised that she'd try to call me around ten today, because I'm about to go off with my mum and Cerise and her mum to go shopping for this weekend.

Then my phone starts vibrating and Fleur's name pops up. I immediately pick up. "Hi!"

"Hey." I can hear her smile, but then she falls quiet.

"Any news?" It's been two days since Mum blew up at Fleur's parents, and even though we've talked a few times, it's never been for long. Definitely not long enough for me anyway. Fleur's mum is still all freaked out, though her dad seems to be in a better mood.

"Dad said yes." She doesn't sound happy. "Mum is... still being difficult." Fleur sighs. "How do I explain that I just... I don't know... How do I explain that..."

"You're no different than you were?"

Fleur sighs again. "I wish that was it... Somehow, she's got it into her head that we're doing like... all sorts of sex stuff together. Like, no matter how many times I've told her that we've only kissed. She keeps like randomly mentioning things about how 'sexuality is all about sex' and that I'm too young for that."

"Yeah." Welcome to the world of not being straight... Everything is about sex and body parts and the how and the details, no matter what age you are.

"She doesn't even know that..." I smile at her frustrated sigh. "Honestly... She has these really weird ideas about the stuff I'm supposedly doing with you or even what I talk about with Jade. Because you're 'all about the sex' and Jade's family is 'too liberal' or something like that. When all we ever really talk about is videogames, and we may hold hands or kiss, but that's it. And with Jade, I just... I talk school and makeup and clothes and..." She sighs. "It's the friends she *does* approve of who she should really take a closer look at." I finally hear a small smile in her voice. "When I talked to Hannah and Sydney and said that I had something to share with them, but not out in the open, they both assumed that I was pregnant. Like... That was their first thought, and not without reason..." She trails off. I don't want to imagine what she's thinking of, especially since it would involve imagining Fleur with a boy. "Like... I don't know what my mum imagines goes on with boys. Like, she imagines that there's no sex involved there or something. Which is stupid, but still…"

"It's double. When it's about boys, nobody cares how much you're doing it. But when it's with a girl, with *me*, suddenly the sex part is all they talk about." It's not like I've not heard this before, it's all too familiar.

"Yeah..." She lets out a little laugh. "I sometimes just... I want to tell her that it doesn't really matter even if I *do* have sex with you, you can't get me pregnant anyway. But I don't think it would go over very well with her."

I let out a laugh too. "No, I don't think that's a good idea." I see Cerise and her mum come up the driveway. "I've gotta go. Do you think you'll survive?"

"I'll survive." She sounds a little calmer now.

"Do you think you can come to the party?" I'm so wishing that she answers affirmatively that I nearly jump out of my skin when the bell goes.

"I'm going to make it happen. Heck, I'll bribe my dad to bring me or something. I don't know. I have to be there." Her voice lowers. "I have to see you again."

My throat closes up a little. "Me too." I nod. "Me too. I'll... I'll get your favourite candy."

"Thanks." She laughs a little again. "Though, I'm not sure how you're going to get it past your mum."

"Don't worry. It'll work." I take a breath as I hear Cerise's footsteps coming up the stairs. "I'll talk to you soon."

"Talk to you soon. Kisses." She does it again, throwing that at me right as she disconnects the line.

Now I'm left here, my cheeks on fire, my mouth open on a gasp, as Cerise steps into my bedroom and looks at me with a raised eyebrow.

"Ready to go?" Cerise grins. "We have drinks, candy, chips and other really bad stuff to buy for our party."

I blink. "Yeah, ready." I stand up, putting my phone in my bag.

I'm ready now, strengthened by the knowledge that Fleur will do everything to be there with us this weekend. We just have to get through this...

It will work out. It will. I have to believe that.

I have to believe that or I'll fall apart.

29
Fleur

Rez/Res = Resurrect = When someone dies, healers (and sometimes other classes too) can resurrect them, bring them back to life. When this happens out in the open, people will often call out 'Res please' with their location in X and Y coordinates. Rez is just a bastardised version of the word. Resurrection, when you're dead and come back to life. Or, in the real world, when you're down so far that you feel like you've come back to life when something good happens. Like I feel right now, like how I feel now I'll be seeing Alex again.

I carefully put the box in the back of our car, letting out a deep breath. These are the final things that I'll need for the weekend. I've already got my computer case and one of my two monitors loaded into the car, and the box has the keyboard, mouse, headset, cables and Alex and Cerise's gifts.

I look at the front of the house, Mum is standing in the doorway, frowning, but Dad steps in for a kiss and she relaxes a little.

Mum is still not happy about me going, she really wants to—I don't know—something. She insists that she needs to talk to Alex again, and maybe even Alex' parents, before she'll let me go there again, or lets Alex come over to our place.

But she couldn't stop me from seeing Alex this weekend, because it's a party with a group of people, all girls, and we're going to play videogames and watch films. Apart from Alex being there, there was no reason for her not to let me go.

She told me that I was under no circumstances allowed to drink alcohol, and that I had to call her if something happened that I didn't like.

She acts like this is all new and like I've never been to a party before. I've been to parties at Jade's that were sleepovers and even mixed gender, and the same goes for parties at Hannah's and Sydney's. So, all her arguments of why I shouldn't have been allowed to go this time were invalid.

Not even the fact that Alex, my girlfriend, was going to be there was really an excuse not to let me go. I've stayed over at a party at Hannah's where my then-boyfriend also stayed over, I've been to sleepover parties at ex-boyfriends' places. Stuff like that.

So, arguing that I couldn't go because of Alex didn't go over very well, not with me or my dad, who turned out to be more of a supporter than I thought he'd be.

"See you tomorrow!" I wave at Mum while I open the car door. It's really hot, even for ten in the morning, the inside of the car is almost boiling.

"Stay safe!" Mum waves back.

"I will." I get in the car and close the door, the window is wide open or I'll fry in here.

Dad gets in behind the wheel. "Everything and everyone strapped in?"

"Yes, Dad." I want to smile, but I'm still too tense.

"Let's go." He starts the car, waves at Mum one last time, and then we drive off.

I lean back, watching the house disappear from view, and I can finally take a real breath.

I'm going. I'm on my way. I text Alex the good news immediately.

"Don't gloat too much." Dad's voice is short. "It's not becoming of you."

I nod, immediately back to earth, immediately back to knowing that this nearly didn't happen. It wasn't until two days ago, Thursday evening, that I finally got the okay to go.

I was getting desperate, but when I sat down with Mum and Dad, suddenly Dad told me that I was allowed to go, as long as they could call Alex' mum before then to make sure that everything would be safe and as long as I promised to behave. Not sure what they really thought what would happen by telling me to 'behave', but that's fine...

"Remember, be on your best behaviour. Don't break things, make sure you take your medication on time and don't drink alcohol."

"I know, Dad. I promise." This is not my first party.

"I just want to make sure that you do. And I want to make sure that you know that I'm still not convinced that all this business with Alex is such a good idea."

"I know." They made that pretty clear. It's not like they've allowed me to forget that me not being straight is a big deal to them. Such a *huge* deal.

"When you get back, we're going to have a real talk about this. No hyper-emotional outbursts, no yelling. We're going to sit down and have a grownup talk about all of this 'liking girls' stuff." He keeps looking forward.

"It's not 'stuff', I *do* like girls."

"You're too—"

"I'm *not* too young. You do *know* that Sydney's older sister had a kid at sixteen. Nobody talked about *her* being too young to even hold hands with a boy." I immediately close my mouth and look out the window. I'm not supposed to snap at him, he's bringing me to the party I really want to get to. He's the only one sort-of on my side.

"She isn't our daughter. And she too was too young to have sex."

"Yeah, but her interest in boys wasn't questioned. And I'm not having sex with Alex." Again with this sex thing.

"Yet..." His voice is edging on frustrated.

I almost say something that I'll know I'll regret, like pointing out that he didn't get this worked up over me spending alone time with boys in the past, or that I'm not a virgin anymore. I don't think I want to point *that* out to him right now. "Yet. And I'm not planning to, *yet*." Sex is a little too... still a little outside of things I want to do with Alex, still on the list of things that are just scary. I want to hold and kiss her, I'm happy with that for now.

"Don't do anything you'll regret."

"I won't. I promise. Can we put some music on?" I don't want to have this conversation anymore.

I want to think about seeing Alex again, about being near her, holding her. That's what I want to think about. Not my dad scolding me over things that aren't even happening.

Alex opens the door to Cerise's house, widely grinning. She immediately takes my computer case from me, freeing up my arms.

"So happy that you came! Come on in!" She starts walking to the back and I already hear a lot of other people talking.

Alex puts the case on a big table where multiple computers are already set up, ranging from a laptop to a huge case with big see-through panels that makes me a little green with envy. I put my bag with clothes and other things on the floor next to the table.

Alex takes my hand and pulls me along to some open doors which lead to the garden out back. A group of girls are sitting around a picnic table and on some comfy chairs, enjoying the sun.

They're happily talking, arms moving and everything, though they quiet when they see us.

Alex makes an exaggerated bow. "Everyone, this is Fleur. Fleur, you know Cerise."

"Hi." Cerise smiles and waves. "Glad that you could make it."

"The others are, Izzy, Sara, Emma, Sofia, Layla and Zoey. You've talked to Zoey before, she's also in the guild, and I think you've met Izzy on one of the raids." Alex points at the other girls sitting around.

"Hi." I wave at them, a little intimidated with the number of people here. I hadn't realised there would be so many.

Everyone waves back and I'm hoping I'll remember all their names before the end of tomorrow.

"Okay." Alex tugs on my arm. "We should get the rest of your computer from the car too. Let's not make your dad wait." She grins.

"I'll help." Cerise stands up. "Parents tend to like me." I can understand that, she's got the whole 'sensible friend' vibe going on, and she looks grownup-ish, more than just the two years older than me that she really is. Cerise winks as she walks in front of us back to the car.

I eye Dad, who is still standing at the back of the car, waiting for me to pick up the rest of my things. "Dad, this is Alex." I point at Alex, and Dad starts frowning a little. "And this is Cerise. She's the other girl who is celebrating her birthday this weekend."

While Dad frowned as he looked at Alex, he relaxes more when he nods at Cerise. She's right, adults trust her immediately. "Nice to get to know you girls. I hope you'll have a lovely party." He eyes the back of the car. "I think there are a couple more things you're going to need today?"

He hands me my monitor, which I immediately give to Alex, then I grab my box with the extras, which I hand to Cerise, and finally I get my sleeping bag and airbed.

"Thanks, Dad." I lean to him, bumping my shoulder into his.

"Be safe." He nods at me, he looks a little less worried now though.

"I will. I promise."

"I'm picking you up tomorrow at five, right?" He starts walking to the driver's door and I follow him.

"Yes, around that time." I nod. Though I'm hoping he'll be a little late, but I'm not saying that out loud.

"Good." He gets in and I step back, waiting. "See you tomorrow." He waves and starts the car, driving off.

I watch the car drive out of the street, I can't actually wave with my hands so full, but I do it in my head, which should be good enough.

Somewhere behind me, Alex lets out a squeal and I jump, only to then laugh as I look her way. "What?"

"No parents." She grins, turning around and carrying the monitor inside with her.

Right. No parents.

Just a bunch of girls playing videogames all night.

Yeah, that sounds pretty good.

I grin as I follow them into the house.

This is going to be awesome!

W A S D

"Have you seen the pics of Izzy that got featured in one of those fan magazines?" Cerise grins, her dark eyes filled with joy and a little mischief.

We're sitting outside in the garden. The sun is too nice to not sit in and nobody has really felt like connecting all the computers up yet.

Cerise pulls up a photo on her phone and shows it around.

My mouth falls open when she shows it to me. In the picture is someone dressed up like a perfect replica of Victorique from the *Gosick* anime. All frilly layers, fabric flowers, long blond hair and everything.

I look at the modestly dressed girl in a T-shirt and shorts on the other side of the picnic table bench. "That's you?" I look at the picture Cerise is showing again. Not really able to connect the two. "Really?"

Izzy blushes, looking down at her hands. "Yeah."

"What? That's so cool and brave. Do you have more pictures?" I slide over to her.

I haven't met someone who's this good at making cosplay before. I've dabbled in it, making a few pieces that look like something from an anime, but I've never got this good at it. I've never been able to pull together the whole look for it.

Izzy eyes Cerise for a moment, but then pulls out her phone, her cheeks still a little pink but her eyes sparkling. "Sure. I've got a couple of them." She shows me some pictures. She's made so many cosplay outfits, and every one is even more detailed than the previous.

"You're really good. These are so well done." I keep looking as she scans through the pictures. "How much time do they take?"

"Weeks, months sometimes. But a lot of that is waiting for materials though." Izzy grins. "I often work on multiple projects at the same time. I like to keep busy."

"I can imagine. *Wow.*" This is skill. "That's..." Dedication, a lot of work, a much higher level than I'd ever reach.

"You should show Fleur the one you made of your Destruction of Elysium character." Alex grins from the other side of the picnic table.

"You really did that?" I'm fangirling, aren't I?

Izzy nods. "I went to a gaming convention. They had a stall for DoE. So I went as FrIzzyBang, my mage. They were impressed."

"Yeah. Though too bad she can't play with us so often anymore." Cerise play-pouts. "She was a really good mage."

"Hey, you know I love playing with you guys." She smiles at Cerise sweetly. "But it just wasn't doable anymore to raid every week with you guys." Izzy shrugs a little. "Classes, exams and then having to make the cosplays for the convention. And a job to pay for all of that. I just didn't have the time." She frowns, sighing. "Doesn't mean I don't miss you guys. It's been much too long since we've all played together. Really."

Alex and Cerise nod. Then Alex eyes the kitchen table. "Let's do it. Let's play."

"What? Now?" Izzy looks up. "Are you sure?"

"Yeah. I'm ready to go kick some monster butt." Alex' eyes sparkle.

"Let's do it." I grin.

Playing together, getting to know new people. I'm all for it.

Now that I'm here, surrounded by all these girls who also all love videogames, Alex at my side. I finally feel calm. I finally feel like everything is right again, even for a short while.

Everything is almost right now.

30
Alex

Battlefront = Instanced PvP area where teams compete against each other to fulfil the objective. This comes in different types like 'capture the flag' where you have to get hold of the other team's flag, 'resource race' where your team has to collect points or resources the first, or 'death match' where your objective is to eliminate the other team before your team is eliminated. I don't do them very often because I don't like to do them with random strangers, but I do love playing them.

I've already connected my computer to the system here, since I arrived yesterday to help set things up. But I quickly help Fleur connect her computer too.

As I'm staring at her keyboard, I can't help but be a little envious. I guess that with her having a part-time job and everything, she has the money to buy cooler things than me. Hmmm… I feel like I should fix that.

After we've connected Fleur's computer, I quickly boot my own and on the other side of the table, Izzy and Cerise are all ready to start.

Cerise leans over to Izzy. "Are you sure you're up-to-date, that you've got all the latest patches?"

"Of course." Izzy laughs. "Did you think I'd come here and not update the game beforehand?"

Cerise opens her mouth again.

"Or make sure I've got enough days on my subscription left to actually play," Izzy deadpans. "This isn't my first party you know. I've known you two long enough to know these kinds of things." Her eyes flit over to me as I'm about to make a comment. "And yes, I'm even pretty decently geared. But with the lack of time lately, I only got my last piece of gear last night." She leans back on her chair, stretching a little.

"Well, they're all valid questions." I raise my eyebrow at Izzy, who just grins.

"Right…"

I've known Izzy for a couple of years now, and even though she's pretty underdressed in her shorts and a T-shirt right now, she usually almost always wears dresses. The first time I met her outside of a videogame it was kind of… surprising. She can be a little rough and I expected her to be a little tomboy-ish. So when she showed up with her hair very neatly curled, in a pastel green poofy dress, and wearing really delicate heels, I was very surprised.

But, apparently, hanging out and playing videogames doesn't warrant a dress. Or it's the heat, which I can also understand.

I boot DoE, logging on, and selecting my character. As I'm put into the world, I remember what Cerise and I were doing this morning. We were doing some PVP, hoping to get some sort of advantage over the other players tonight.

I eye Cerise over the top of our computers and grin.

Cerise grins back at me. "What, no thank you?"

As I open my in-game mailbox, I find an extra set of weapons for my tank. I'm not exactly sure when she got them, but they are exactly what I need.

We're all in the game now, but a party of four isn't big enough to do anything without having to get a random extra player. "Hey, Zoey. Can you come kick some butt?"

Zoey looks up, raising her eyebrow. "Kick some butt?" She stands up. "Do you even have to ask?" She quickly comes over to the table, sitting down at her computer on Cerise's other side. We all wait as she boots her computer and logs onto the game. "Okay, what do you need me to play as?" She looks at me.

"Ehm, a rogue would be a good idea. We've already got Fleur as our healer, Izzy and Cerise as our mages and I'm going to be the one who gets hit all the time."

Zoey grins. "Sounds good to me."

I invite everyone into a party and then I sign us up to a battlefront.

We're queued for a 'capture the flag' type of battlefront. This means that you have two teams in one instanced zone. Our team has to capture the flag from the other team and bring it back to our base, while the other team also has to grab ours. We have to retrieve their flag back to our base five times. It's always one of the most fun types of battlefronts. Although, we're only playing small teams right now. So this can get really intense, or not intense at all.

"We all know what we're doing, right?" I look over the others.

"Yeah, yeah." Izzy rolls her eyes. "Just make sure you grab that damn flag. I don't want to have to be the one carrying it around the whole field again."

"Harsh." I grin. Though it's not like that hasn't happened before.

"I don't know if your girlfriend is ready to heal flimsy little me from one side of the field to the other." Izzy eyes Fleur now, who's looking a little surprised.

I can't help the smile, the pride inside me, as I look at Fleur for a moment. "Oh, you'd be surprised."

Fleur colours and she looks at me, her mouth opening before she smiles. "Don't make promises I can't keep."

I reach out to her, touching her arm for a moment. "I wouldn't say it if I didn't trust that you'd be able to pull it off." Fleur has proven to be quite the healer these last few weeks.

"Oh, is that a dare?" Izzy's voice turns teasing. "You want to try it out?"

"Oh, no." Zoey groans, probably remembering the last time we did this at a previous party. We got our backs handed to us by the other team.

I look between Izzy and Fleur, ready to step in if Izzy pushes her too much, but Fleur thinks for just a moment before she nods.

"Sure, let's do this. You and me. Alex, Cerise and..." She thinks for a moment. "Zoey, you try to kill anyone who attacks us."

"What? You're serious?" Cerise leans forward. "You're almost as bad as Alex." She shoots me a glare like this is all my fault now.

"You have no idea." I grin.

A screen pops up and I accept the invitation for the battlefront. We're all transported to the instance and a twenty second timer starts counting down.

"Are we really doing this?" Izzy stretches her arms over her head, rolling her neck, before she puts her hands on the keys.

"Yes." Fleur looks so focused. "Do not underestimate my skills." She looks up and grins at me. "Ready?"

"Ready." I nod.

The starting area boundary lifts and we all race to the other end of the field. I keep my eyes on Izzy and Fleur, on where they are, and try to kick everyone who gets in their way.

It's fun and interesting, though other players don't die very fast from just my attacks, since tanks are built for defence, not offence. But I can just keep trying. I can keep others busy as Fleur and Izzy rush to get to the flag.

Cerise is the first to fall and is forced to respawn at the starting area, having to run all the way back to where we are.

"Got it." Izzy cheers. "Okay, now the way back."

This is the difficult part. Getting the flag back to our side. Since the flag will be very visible, so that everyone can either try to kill the carrier, when they're on the other team, or protect them, when they're on your own team.

Next to me, Fleur is clicking furiously, her screen moving quickly and this is the first time I actually see her hands during playing. She looks... *Wow*. It's so fast. Even for a healer, she really keeps busy and on top of things.

I nearly get killed myself, just from getting distracted by what she's doing. Luckily, I'm able to get away from the other player quickly. Then I follow Fleur and Izzy to our side, trying to get all the pets to automatically target me instead of them. The pets usually attack people based on aggro, not on actual player input. So at least I can try to get them to target me and I also throw some 'area of effect' spells to slow enemy players down.

We reach our home base where our own flag is still standing, but the other team is close behind us.

At the last moment, an enemy rogue comes out of the shadows and kills Izzy. Without thinking I step in and grab the flag, going the last bit of the way as Fleur starts healing me.

'Red team captured the blue flag'

The message shows up in the middle of our screens.

First win!

But we don't get to enjoy it for very long as the blue team now grabs our flag and makes a run for it.

"Go, go, go." I start running after them, watching the others follow me as we start hunting the blue flag carrier down now.

I love this. I love the energy and excitement of the capture, the chase, the working together with friends.

This is why I love getting people from the guild together for parties. Just seeing everyone's excitement as we all play together.

This is what guilds are made for. This playing together.

This is the best.

W A S D

After two rounds in the battlefront, the last girls have also arrived and we're now a party of twelve.

Most of us play DoE, which is how we got to know each other. But I don't know how many matches we'll still play this weekend. Something about there also being multiple game consoles, and that other games are much faster.

Some of us are first going to play a few of rounds of *Mario Kart* and I saw Izzy come by with a game of *Twister* for outside.

Fleur taps me on my shoulder, leaning in. "I'm going outside. I heard Izzy and Zoey talk about a combination of Twister and something with a hose?"

I blink, nearly missing a corner in the Rainbow Road stage. "Sure. I'll be right there." I need to focus. I'm in second place, Emma is in front of me and I've nearly caught up with her. But the idea of Fleur outside, playing Twister and slipping all over the place... It's kind of distracting.

Just as I'm almost at the finish line, I get hit by something and spin round in my place, the others now passing me by at high speed. *Argh.* Of course, that always happens. This is why I never get first place on *Mario Kart.*

Emma looks back at me, grinning. "Almost."

"Yeah, yeah." I roll my eyes at her as I shake my head. "Anyone else wanna play?"

"Me." Sara stands up, taking the controller I hold out to her. "Thanks. Gotta kick Emma's butt for the previous round." She sits back down again on the pillow right next to Emma.

I stand up, stretching before I go outside, standing in the doorway as I look out over the garden.

The Twister is already set up and Izzy and Zoey are doing something with soap and a hose. Their favourite way to play Twister is a little... it includes obstacles and a lot of sliding around.

It's fun. But also the reason I made sure to bring extra shirts and shorts so that I'd have something dry to wear after playing instead of having to sit around in wet clothes. Because this is pretty standard fare for a guild meeting.

Although, I'm not sure how much giggling it will involve when it's just girls playing. The best fun usually happens when the guys also try to play with us. Some of them do not play according to most of the standard rules. But I guess that as long as nobody gets hurt or is put in awkward positions, that everything is going to be okay.

I sit down next to Fleur, who is drinking a glass of water with an adorable red straw and cute heart-shaped ice cubes in it. "They still setting up?"

"Yeah." She grins. "I didn't realise that the reason you told me to bring extra clothes would be because of a game like Twister."

"You wouldn't have believed me if I told you why." I lean against her. "Can I have a sip?"

"Sure." She slides the glass over a little, and I take a sip through the straw. The water is nice and cold, exactly what I need on a hot day like today.

"Thanks."

"You're welcome." She looks at me, her lips so close to mine.

I lean in, but, of course, Izzy chooses that moment to sit down at the other side of the table.

"Okay. Tell me. How long has this been going on?" Her eyes glitter with excitement. "I'm *so* not used to seeing Alex like this."

"Ehm." I shrug. "A few weeks."

"Really? I've been *so* missing out on things. Seriously." She sighs. "Higher Vocational Education sucks sometimes with how much time it takes up. And I'm hurt that Cerise didn't tell me about this."

"You can't be everywhere at the same time." I take another sip from Fleur's glass.

"True." Izzy nods, thinking. "I know that Alex is a lesbian. We all know that." She winks at me. "But you…" She leans to Fleur. "First girl or not?"

"Izzy…" I sigh, turning to Fleur, hoping she doesn't take this the wrong way. "You don't have to answer her. She's being nosey."

"Alex is the first." Fleur's voice is soft, sweet. "I didn't expect to fall for a girl. But it happened."

"Cool. That's cool." Izzy smiles as she stands up again. "Well, I'm going to change into something that's allowed to get dirty, and so should you two. Come on. Let the fun begin."

I stand up too. "You haven't had anything alcoholic yet, have you?" I level a look at Izzy.

"No." Izzy's smile widens. "Just having fun. I'm totally sober. Maybe a little excited, but you know me." She winks and basically skips off into the house.

Izzy is a little odd, but she's sweet and she's the biggest fangirl of anyone she meets. I know that things haven't always been easy for her, but I can't help but admire how she's been able to move forward and still be upbeat most of the time.

"You playing too?" I look at Fleur.

"Sure." She nods, grinning. "I didn't bring those clothes with me for nothing."

"I bet." I wink, but as soon as I do it a blush spreads up my neck to my cheeks. *Yikes.* Okay…

It's totally the sun making me act like a fool.

The sun, I tell you!

Really!

31
Fleur

Level Cap = The maximum level you can reach in a game. This depends on the game you're playing, but you generally hit it when you've finished the quests from the main quest line. Some games will have some extra quests after you hit the level cap, to introduce you to the final dungeons or other content, but when you hit the level cap, you can't collect any more levelling XP. After this, you start collecting better gear and sometimes secondary types of experience points. That is, until an expansion or something comes out. Like in a relationship, when you tell the other person you love them and when you're in a relationship is the first level cap, until the 'living together' or 'getting married' or such expansions becomes available. Then you'll be able to reach a new level cap. You get to enjoy even more content.

Izzy's comment keeps going through my head as I quickly get changed into other clothes in the bathroom. With these clothes it doesn't matter if they get all wet and dirty, sort of.

I grin. Sure, 'sort of'. I mostly chose them because they're easy to clean and I still look kind of cute in them.

When I get back to the garden, Izzy is already sitting on the steps, wearing a really cute frilly bikini top and a different pair of shorts. I wish I'd thought of that myself. If I'd known the change of clothes was because of a messy game of Twister, I would have done the same, instead of choosing clothes that could handle something like climbing trees, hey, you never know.

It's really hot, the middle of summer, so showing off in a cute bikini and shorts to my girlfriend would have been totally normal. Maybe next time, probably next time.

"Hey." I sit down next to Izzy, time for me to be nosey. "How long have you known Alex?"

"A few years." Izzy grins. "We met through Cerise in a different game."

I nod, thinking how to phrase this. "Have you ever met any of her previous girlfriends?"

Izzy shakes her head, her eyes softening. "No. They never seemed interested in doing something like this. You know, a gaming weekend, playing videogames all day. And..." She looks at the door, when I follow her eyes, I don't see anyone there. Though, I guess she's more checking whether Alex is showing up yet. "Alex' relationships never lasted long. Usually because the girls didn't like the amount of time Alex spent playing videogames."

"No problem like that with me." I smile.

"I know. Heck. You're a great healer. I get why Alex fell for you." She winks at me and I can't help but smile.

"Thanks?" I look around. "Hey. Ehhh. Do you like boys and girls, or boys, or girls, or... Sorry, just... I don't know." Why am I even asking her this?

"I'm pansexual." Izzy shrugs like it's the most obvious answer in the world. "I fall for someone as a person before their gender. I don't really care, just as long as the person is kind and makes me happy." There is something in her voice when she says the last words, something sad, but I'm not sure if I should ask about it. "You? You said that Alex is your first girl crush?"

"Yeah. I don't know." I sigh. "I've been thinking about it, but I don't know if there really is a difference for me between me being bisexual or pansexual. When I first met Alex, I thought she was a boy, with her screen name and character and all." I pull a face, still not liking the memory. Maybe I'll be able to laugh at it at some point, but not yet. "So maybe it doesn't matter as much to me as I thought at first, or not. I don't know." This is confusing. Pansexual feels more 'right', but I don't know if I'd want to explain the difference between the two every time I talk to someone who doesn't know… Is it egotistical to think like that? To choose one over the other just because it's 'easier'?

Izzy nods, thoughtful. "Well, it's up to you. Nobody but you will be able to answer that question. And on that note." She jumps up, smiling. "Let's get the game started. Alex probably got distracted by the games inside." She reaches out to me.

I look at the doors again. Yeah, I guess that's likely with Alex because she is taking her sweet time getting changed. "Sure." I take Izzy's hand and she pulls me up too.

"You turn on the tap, I'm getting more of the bubbles." Izzy points at the wall where the hose is connected.

Oh, this is going to be so much fun. So dirty, and so fun.

I can totally see myself becoming friends with Izzy and some of the other girls.

Their idea of having a good time is exactly what I like too.

Alex and Izzy are the last ones standing on the mat. They're both totally wet and covered in bubbles. But they're not giving up, not at all.

Zoey just fell and had to get off the mat, so she's sitting down next to me.

"Wanna bet how long these two last?" She leans closer.

"No, thanks." I grin. Alex and Izzy are both just as good and I don't think I can predict who'd win out of the two of them.

"You should have said that Alex would have won anyway, you're her girlfriend." Zoey looks at me, smiling.

"I don't think that would have been fair on either of them. And I don't think I should bet on her just because she's my girlfriend, that could get me in big trouble. Plus..." I level a look at Zoey. "You've got an unfair advantage because you've seen them play before. I have no idea how good either of them really is." I lean back more, trying to get the sun to dry my clothes at least a little before the next round.

"I know a way to end this really quickly." Zoey starts grinning and I'm not sure I want to know what she's thinking of.

"No..." I reach out to her, but she jumps up and stands behind me.

"Oh! No! Fleur! What did you *do*?" She puts on a very surprised voice and looks at me with an evil glint in her eyes.

Then I hear an 'oof' and a loud thud coming from the mat.

When I look back over to Alex and Izzy, they're both on the floor, glaring our way.

"Done." Zoey gives me a thumbs up. "I'm going to get some drinks. I'm getting thirsty, aren't you?" And she skips off. Way too happy about what she just did.

"Zoey!" Izzy groans as she untangles herself from Alex. "She's evil. That was not fair." She sits up, glaring at the door Zoey disappeared through. "I was winning."

"But I won." Alex grins, she's on her back on the mat. "That was intense."

Izzy looks behind her and rolls her eyes. "Whatever. I'll get you next time." She pushes herself up, stretching. "I guess Zoey is right. Need me to get you two something to drink? Water?" She looks at us.

"I'd like that, thanks." I nod at her.

"Yes, please. I think I've got soap in my mouth." Alex pulls a face.

"Serves you right for tripping me." Izzy laughs, then she also goes back into the house.

I stand up and walk over to Alex, sitting down next to her. "You're way better at this than I expected."

Alex winks, sliding her fingers over my arm, leaving behind goosebumps even though it's seriously hot. "That's what you get when you're really clumsy, you get used to having to be extra strong and flexible to not get in trouble."

"Is that your excuse? Not that you were trying to show off?" I lean closer to her, raising one eyebrow.

Alex' eyes go to my lips immediately, licking hers. "Maybe..." She winks again, but her voice has dropped.

"Maybe?" I lean in even closer. "What do you mean, maybe?"

Alex' hand slides behind my head, pulling me so close that our lips almost meet. "I mean that I *might* have been showing off to my cute girlfriend."

I can't help my grin, then I press our lips together. She's soft, sweaty and indeed tastes a little like soap. I put my hands to both sides of her body and keep kissing her, each kiss longer than the previous one.

Alex slips her arms around me. She holds me, keeps me. It feels good being here. It feels good being in her arms. It's like this is the place where I belong. It relaxes me.

I pull back a little, looking down at Alex, at the way she's gazing up at me. I don't think I'll ever get tired of this, kissing her, holding her. This feels right.

Alex reaches up, running her thumb over my lower lip. "What are you thinking of?"

I open my mouth, trying to reply to her. But the words won't come. Something is stuck in my chest, my throat, behind my lips. I swallow hard. Not sure where the words that are stuck are coming from right now, but they feel so true.

"Hmmm?" Alex starts to frown a little, worry appearing in her eyes. "What's wrong?"

I shake my head. There's nothing *wrong*. That's kind of the point. I open my mouth again. "I love you. Like, really *love*-love you." My voice shakes, my whole body starts to shake. I'm so scared. I'm so scared that…

Alex nods, relaxing a little, her eyes softening. "I love you too." She pulls me closer, pulls me so we're squashed together, her arms tightly around me as I hide my face against her neck.

I can't believe I just said it. I can't believe it. I'm not sure where I suddenly got the courage from to tell her that I love her.

"I love you so much," Alex whispers the words, her voice lower, her grip around me tighter now.

"I love you too." I also tighten my grip around her. This is heady, this feeling, this is so much more than I thought would happen.

We're quiet for a while, just staying together, being together.

"When did you realise it? When did you..." Alex' voice is unsure.

"I don't know." I can barely hear myself, let alone if Alex can hear me. "I don't know when I realised it. I think I... I think it may have been from the start. I think I may have always loved you. I just didn't know how to say it yet."

When I met Alex in Destruction of Elysium she was just someone who I got along with immediately. She was someone who really just made me feel at home. And when I met her at the guild meet, I don't know, I may have imagined her as a boy, but that didn't have anything to do with my feelings for her. It just had to do with me never having imagined myself with a girl before. So when I found out what she really looked like, I was surprised. I had to change my idea of Alex. But nowhere in there... Nowhere in there did I stop liking her. It never mattered. Alex is Alex and she's always been the Alex I fell in love with.

"I guess this is the best birthday gift anyone could ever give me." Alex lets out a laugh. "Thank you."

"You haven't even seen my birthday gift yet." I laugh, sliding off her to her side, still looking at her. "No, thank *you*. You're amazing." I lean in and give her a quick kiss on her cheek, but then pull a face. She really is covered in soap, she may have licked it from her lips, but the rest of her is definitely covered in soap.

Alex laughs, sitting up. "I'm pretty sure Izzy was supposed to bring us something to drink."

My cheeks heat up. If Izzy came back with drinks, she would have seen what just happened. And I'm pretty sure she didn't want to interrupt us if she had seen us.

Alex stands up, reaching out to me. I take her hand, letting her pull me up too. But once I stand, she doesn't let go of my hand. "Let's get that drink ourselves."

I nod, following Alex as she pulls me along, still a little dazed and a lot of happy.

When we get to the back door, the whole room is quiet. The girls are staring at us, all grinning. They must have been waiting for us to come in, they must know.

Cerise stands up, her arms wide. "Congratulations!"

All the girls start cheering.

My cheeks heat up even more, and I don't know how to answer, overwhelmed by everyone's response. We were girlfriends before, but that was before I… Yeah. *Before.*

Alex' grip on my hand tightens. I look her way and see the redness on her cheeks too. Seeing her blush like that is rare but it's always just as special as that first time I got to see it.

I pull her close, wrapping my arms around her, and keep her tight.

Yes. Yes, this is right.

This is where I'm supposed to be.

32
Alex

Endgame = Game content that you get to play when you reach the level cap and the end of the main quest line. This generally involves special dungeons, raids and battlefronts. This is also where most of the new content in patches gets added. I guess it's a little like curling up on the couch or hanging out with the person you love after you get into a relationship. It's the fun stuff that starts when all the things leading up to it, all the initial growing, has finished.

I can't believe it. I can't believe what just happened. I keep my arms around Fleur, keeping her close.

I never expected Fleur to say the words 'I love you', at least, not yet. I didn't expect her to be ready to take that next step already. I thought that she might still have been too scared, too unsure. Although, she did look a little scared when she said it, very nervous.

And then all the other girls, you know, cheering us on like that. It's… It's all a little overwhelming. It feels so good to get the support from the people who mean the most to me, who've always been there with me.

But that doesn't mean that my heart isn't beating like crazy, that I'm not super happy about it all. I'm nervous, but I'm also really, really happy.

As soon as the cheers have died down, I slowly let go of Fleur. But I can't keep my eyes off her, I can't stop looking at her.

I reach out, running my fingers over her cheek. She's so beautiful, so amazing. I want to kiss her again, but I'm not sure I should do that, you know, in front of everyone, with all of them staring at us.

Then Fleur steps closer, angling her head a little. An invitation.

I close the last distance between us, my lips on hers, hers on mine. With every breath I take I can smell her, I can feel her, her warmth, her love.

My heart is still beating like it's trying to break out of my chest and joining Fleur's inside her body. This isn't our first kiss, but it feels like the first one in a special way. It's the first one after everyone knows about our love.

Then Fleur steps back again, her eyes shining, a big grin on her face. She takes a couple of breaths. "I'm pretty sure we were talking about getting something to drink."

"Yes, I'm pretty sure that we were." I start pulling her backwards to Cerise's kitchen. Giving us a little bit of privacy. Fleeing the room.

I'm not ready to face everyone right now. I feel a little raw, sensitive, overstimulated. There is so much going through my head, my heart. So many sensations, that I just need a little alone time with Fleur now.

The girls shout after us, laughing, but they leave us alone, letting us be for now.

As soon as we reach the kitchen, I take Fleur in my arms again, holding her tight. I'm almost scared that when I let her go, this will be all over.

It's real, but it doesn't feel real yet.

And I don't mind, I don't mind living in this dream for a while longer.

W A S D

I'm curled up on the couch, my head on Fleur's shoulder.

We're all watching some romantic comedy. I'm not even sure what it's called. But I like being here in this spot, I like sitting here with Fleur. It feels so special to finally be able to do this, to finally be able to spend time together, being able to touch. I like this. This is good, this is right.

Just a few weeks ago, we met in Destruction of Elysium. It's really only been just a handful of weeks, but everything has changed in that time. At least, it feels that way.

When our party in DoE got grouped up with Fleur to do that dungeon, it was just… it was just another run. It was just another round in a dungeon we'd done tens of times.

But it went so well, so easily. It was almost like she knew what I was going to do before I even did it. That's when things changed. That's when I realised that I found someone who understood me, even if it was just within the game.

When we talked, we had fun. We just had so much fun those first days, and it gave me the courage to ask her to join us at our next guild meeting.

When I met her, I saw the look in her eyes, I saw the way that she looked at me. And I thought that everything was over, that our connection was broken. That it wouldn't work out at all. I was so scared.

But Fleur was the one who came up to me, she was the one who gave me courage again, who showed me that there may actually be a chance for the two of us. That didn't stop my fear, my anxiety, the not-so-fun parts of my past, from getting us into a lot of trouble.

Only, when Fleur showed up at my house, and she told me that she was interested in me, most of that fear disappeared. So I guess this is right, I guess this really is like coming home in someone's heart.

Fleur's tightens her arm around my shoulder and I look up at her. She's smiling, her eyes shining. "Are you enjoying yourself?" She whispers, teasing.

"Yes. Very much." I keep my voice low too.

Fleur raises her eyebrow at me, not looking very convinced.

"I'm really enjoying being with you." I'm not even sure she can really hear me.

Fleur's cheeks start to colour, and she swallows. "Oh."

I can't help smiling at her, she's… a little innocent sometimes, so it's easy to catch her off guard, but that's also the cute part about her.

This is shaping up to be the best birthday party and the best weekend of my life, ever.

W A S D

I check the time again. I really don't want to be late, but I just can't make the bus go any faster than it's going right now.

One of the bridges on our way out of the city had been open because so many people were out and about on yachts and boats because of the beautiful weather. It took *sooo* long, there were so many boats. And it made me so nervous, which was stupid, but I guess that it couldn't be helped.

Today is the two-month anniversary of meeting Fleur in real life. I can't believe it's already been two months now, so many things have happened.

We're going to celebrate by going out for dinner and then I'm staying over at her place. Fleur's parents have finally allowed it. They talked with my parents and then also with Fleur. And they realised that while they maybe don't understand everything, this wasn't something which would just go away by ignoring it, and them being against our relationship was more about me being a girl than about Fleur dating anyone at all.

I guess it's easy for me to be frustrated about something like this, but that's because my parents were much more open. For them, my sexuality was something that they'd known for years and they'd accepted it a long time ago. They may not be able to understand being attracted to someone of the same gender, but they understood love, and to them that was the most important part.

But Fleur's parents care about what other people think much more than my parents do, and they don't know how to not let that matter as much to them. Many of their issues were about their own fears. Their fears of Fleur being bullied, of people excluding her, of people treating their family differently now that Fleur has a girlfriend. But they've agreed to try and let such things not interfere with Fleur and me meeting up, and us going on dates and things like that. It took a while, but we've got here now.

So, we're about to do just that. Meeting up, going out for dinner somewhere and then I get to go back home with her. I suppress another squee as I think about all the time we'll have together.

I know that Fleur already set up an airbed for me to sleep on tonight, because that's where I'll have to sleep, on the floor but right next to her bed. Which is annoying, but if it means I get to spend the weekend at Fleur's, I'll take it, I'll take anything.

The bus turns onto the square and my eyes immediately search for Fleur. It doesn't take long for me to spot her.

The sight of her takes my breath away, as she does every time. She's wearing a light summer dress with big yellow flowers on it, cute sandals and a really broad-brimmed hat with a big yellow bow on it. She has to keep holding the hat because the wind keeps pulling on it, trying to blow it away.

She grins when she spots the bus. She walks like the wind is carrying her, the dress billowing around her legs, until she almost trips and stumbles for a moment before she's back on her feet.

A laugh bubbles up inside me, and I keep looking at her as the bus slows down. Then Fleur spots me and waves enthusiastically. I wave back at her, pulling my bag over my shoulder and get off the bus.

Fleur takes me into her arms and spins us around, her laughter so infectious that I keep laughing with her. "Hey."

"Hey." I tighten my arms around her too, savouring the moment.

"I missed you." Fleur's voice is softer, lower, this time. "I missed this."

I nod, my heart both bursting with happiness and filled with anxiety about having to leave again on Sunday. "I missed you too."

I never imagined I'd feel like this, this anxious sensation about seeing someone. But I guess this is what happens when you're in love, when you wish you could just be with the person you love all the time.

Fleur pulls back a little, looking at me with a soft smile. "Can I kiss you?"

I nod, not able to find my voice for a moment.

She leans in and the next moment her lips are on mine. Soft kisses, little more than pecks against my lips, make my heart go into overdrive. Then the kisses get longer and longer, lingering, the tip of her tongue sliding along my lips. I press in closer too, deepening the kiss until we both have to pull back, out of breath, laughing.

I keep holding her hand, tightening my grip and she squeezes back. "So, what did you have planned?"

Fleur's eyes sparkle. "Dinner at a place where they have the best spareribs you can find in this tiny city. And, after that, we're going back to my place." Her cheeks colour. "I don't really have more planned than that."

"No worries. I think we'll figure something out." I wink and Fleur grins.

"I bet we will." She grabs hold of her hat again before it blows away, then she tugs on my hand. "Let's go."

I watch her from the back as she pulls me along, mesmerised by the happiness that just seems to surround her, by the way she makes everything around her look lighter, makes everything so much more bright.

My heart won't slow down, at all. How did I find a girl like this? How did I find such a beautiful and happy girl?

She makes me the happiest girl alive, and that's exciting and scary at the same time.

I love her, so much.

The September evening is warm and we're in the back garden of Fleur's place, looking up at the slowly darkening sky above us. Fleur's parents have gone off to a party somewhere and left us here on our own.

I weave my fingers through Fleur's, holding on.

"What is your biggest dream when it comes to your future?" Fleur's voice sounds like she's thinking really hard.

I turn my head a little, but she's got her eyes closed, though she's still smiling a little. "My biggest dream?"

"Yeah. What would you love to do? What would be the best thing ever?" She looks my way for a moment, but then stares back up at the sky. I can't read her eyes, her look. I can't figure out where this is going.

"My biggest dream, eh?" I also look back up at the sky, at the wisp of cloud passing by. "Finish secondary school. Get into the University of Applied Sciences I want. Maybe even live together with the girl of my dreams." I can't help but smile now. "Why?"

"I was talking with Jade earlier, she asked me this. I don't know why, but it kept playing through my head." She lets out a breath and squeezes my hand a little.

"What did you answer?" It sounds like this is more important to her than she's letting on.

Fleur is quiet for a moment and I turn to her again, leaning up on my arm, a little worried now. That wasn't a bad question, right? She asked me the same. "Fleur?"

She opens her eyes, they're watery, then she runs her teeth over her lower lip. "I always thought I would end up like my mum. Find some boy at a party, date, marry, babies. Stuff like that."

A knot forms in my stomach. I don't know if this is good or not. "And now?"

"Now…" Her voice wavers, then she meets my eyes, her lip quivering. She reaches up, sliding her fingers along my cheek, putting her hand to the side of my jaw. "Now, I want those things with you. I know it's fast. And crazy, we're not even out of school. But, lying here, I just know it. I always want to be at your side. I want all of *that* with you. Do all those things, grow old."

I swallow hard, my own vision going blurry. Then I lean closer, putting my lips to hers. Kissing her until I can feel her smile again. I slowly pull back again, looking down at her. "I want that too. I want you at my side. I want to do everything together with you."

"I love you." Fleur's voice is still thick with the tears that now slide down her cheeks, broken free from her eyes.

"I love you too." I kiss her again. "And I bet you'll look amazing in a wedding dress."

"What?" Fleur lets out a surprised laugh.

"Imagine it. A summer afternoon. A big field filled with white and yellow and pink flowers. You're wearing one of those wedding dresses with a corset at the top and lots of layers of skirt. The skirt flows to the side in the breeze. Your hair is loose." I play with a strand of her hair through my fingers. "And the wind is playing with it too. You're standing with your back to the sun, I have to look up at you as you're surrounded by so much light that you look like you've just stepped out of a fairy-tale."

Fleur lets out another laugh, grinning. "And you're wearing one of those slim dresses, hugging your whole body, but it flares out a little at the bottom so you can still walk and dance. Your hair all tied up, dotted with pearls."

I feel my face heat up. Imagining myself like that is quite different from what I normally wear, but I can also imagine it looking really good. "Why is my hair tied up?"

Fleur pushes herself up a little. "Because it means I can look at your beautiful neck, and kiss it." She does exactly that. Her lips moving over my neck, shooting sparks all through my body, taking my breath away.

Then I wrap my arms around her, pulling her on top of me as I let myself fall back.

I keep laughing, happiness filling me so much. This is so good. This feeling of constantly being surrounded by magic.

This, right here, being with Fleur, having her at my side. This is exactly right.

"I love you." I kiss her bare shoulder. "I love you so much."

Being with Fleur, it's like paradise.

Fleur is my own Elysium, my own magical place of happiness.

My Elysium.

Epilogue
Fleur

Elysium = Greek mythological version of paradise. It's the afterlife meant for heroes chosen by the gods. It's a beautiful place where the weather is always good, the food is plenty and life is easy. It's paradise. While in real life, this place does not exist, I do feel like this when I'm with Alex, and for me, that's just as important.

I'm nervous, I keep running my hands over my skirt, trying to dry them off. Alex' mum puts her hand on my arm, squeezing a little. I look up at her and she smiles at me. I'm not even sure why I'm actually this nervous, it's not like something could go wrong now. All the work is already behind us.

Today, Alex is graduating secondary school. I'm at her graduation ceremony. Like... for real. I'm sitting here, in a room full of people I don't know. Although, Troy is graduating too today, but, apart from him, I have no idea who is who.

For each person graduating, one of the teachers says something about them, and I've had to listen to a lot of anecdotes about people I don't know and don't really care to know. Or is that just nerves?

Then Alex' name shows up on the screen, together with an old picture of her. My mouth drops open. It's a picture of Alex when she was younger, probably right when she first started secondary school, and she's wearing a really cute pastel nightdress and as she's smiling you can see she's got braces on her teeth.

As Alex walks onto the stage, she looks at the picture and her mouth falls open before she looks at her parents, glaring.

"I can't believe you," she mouths at her mum, who just grins.

Then one of the teachers stands up, going over to the microphone. She smiles at Alex before she starts talking. "I've been Alex' maths and algebra teacher for almost her whole secondary school career. Which doesn't happen often, I have to say. Few people take the number of advanced classes she's taken and it's been a real treat to have her in my classes each year." She looks at Alex again. "I know that not all teachers felt like that when they had Alex in their classes, and I know that things haven't always been easy for Alex either. She can be... active. She has some trouble sitting still, especially when she's bored, and she isn't always able to stay quiet. But she's always been the first to understand new concepts when I explained them. She's always ranked top of my classes with her grades and I've seen the side of her that I hope she'll keep showing when she goes on to university." She turns to Alex, holding out a folder. "Alex."

Alex steps over, looking a little uncomfortable, but then she takes the folder.

"I wish you all the best. I know that you're going to study computer science, and that you'll be leaving this beautiful city behind as you go on your own path. Congratulations, and I wish you all the best." The teacher shakes Alex' hand and the whole room starts clapping.

Alex nods to the room and then quickly walks off the stage down the side, coming over to where we're sitting. When she looks at me, she's still tense and taking shallow breaths, but when I take her hand and she sits down next to me, she smiles again.

"Congratulations," I whisper to her, as the next person has walked on stage.

"Thanks." She bumps her shoulder into my arm.

Alex' mum reaches past me and squeezes Alex' shoulder a little. "Congrats."

Alex nods, smiling more. Her breathing evens out, she's finally relaxing again. When she looks back at me, her eyes are sparkling and she starts grinning. "No more exams," she whispers. "Summer break has finally started."

My final exam of the year was yesterday morning and I immediately went over to Alex' place in the afternoon.

Alex has been finished with everything for two weeks already, her final exams were earlier than mine since they were the final school exams and those always end earlier. But it also means that while I've been studying like crazy for the last two weeks, she's already been playing DoE every day. So unfair.

Sitting here, holding Alex' hand, I realise that a year has passed. Alex just graduated secondary school and I'll be starting my final year soon. Just one more year left.

Last year, when summer break started, a whole year before Alex' graduation seemed so long. But now, just one year until I'll be graduating myself, it's short and very scary.

Alex will be at college and I'll still be at home, studying my butt off to make sure I graduate with grades as good as Alex.

Because that's going to be my challenge, trying to do better than Alex. Having seen her grades, I know I'm really going to have to step up my game. I have a scarily smart girlfriend.

But, first, we get to celebrate Alex' graduation and then play videogames all summer. Relaxation and fun.

All together with my amazing girlfriend.

Win!

⬜W⬜A⬜S⬜D⬜

"Welcome home." Alex gives me a quick kiss on my cheek before she takes the box I'm holding and pushes something in front of the door to keep it propped open.

I follow her down the hallway into the living room, where Troy is sitting in front of the TV playing a game. I wave at him and he waves back before he goes back to his game.

"Ah! I can't believe this is real now." Alex' voice is going so fast. She turns around and wraps her arms around me. "I can't believe that you're moving in here, with us, with me." She lets out another squeal.

"I know." I wrap my arms around her too. "This is unreal." I tighten my grip around her and then let her go. We've been planning this all year, but it still feels strange to move in here myself.

"Welcome." Cerise yawns as she comes out of her bedroom. "I thought that you weren't coming until later?"

"It *is* later." Alex shakes her head at Cerise. "Maybe you shouldn't have stayed up until five this morning."

"Zoey and Izzy wanted to do one last run." Cerise yawns and stretches. "Couldn't leave them on their own."

Mum and Dad also come into the house with boxes. "Hi, everyone." Dad greets them with a smile, then his eyes fall on me. "You helping? They're your boxes."

"I know. I know." I follow him back out the door.

I'm going to be studying biochemistry at the same university as Alex, Cerise and Troy are attending. And we're all going to be staying in the same house.

The three of them already moved in here last year when Alex and Troy came to study in this city, but their fourth housemate, Rick, also a Destruction of Elysium player but from a different guild, was already in his last year. So he moved out last week, and now I'm moving in. It's like a dream, being able to live together with Alex, and of course also Cerise and Troy, and going on to further education.

I feel like this is going to be one crazy experience, filled with games, parties and loads of fun.

When we've moved my last boxes, and of course my computer, into the house, my parents stay for some coffee. But when they finally leave, you can almost feel everyone relax. We're on our own, no more adulty-adults around.

"Okay. Sooo..." Alex takes my hand, grinning. "Excuse us, we're going to unpack in Fleur's room." She has a sparkle in her eyes that makes my whole body buzz.

"Sure. *Unpack* ahead." Cerise shakes her head, smiling. "Just remember that the walls and floors are a little thin. Okay?"

"Noted." Alex laughs, pulling me along up the stairs. Cerise's room is downstairs, but the other three bedrooms are all upstairs.

We walk past Alex' door to my new room. She opens the door and lets me step inside first. This is my new room, this is the start of my new life.

The room is bare, though some of my boxes are already stacked against one of the walls.

Then Alex closes the door behind me and I feel her arms snake around my waist, pressing her body against mine. "Finally alone. Finally our own place." She brushes her lips against the back of my neck and I shiver, excitement rushing through me.

I turn around in her embrace, making her step back until her back is against the door, then I push closer still. "I'm sure that you have *no idea* what we could do with all this time and space in front of us, our own space."

"No idea at all." Alex grins, one of her hands sliding up my back, while the other one slips under my shirt, her hand on my bare skin.

I grin back. Then I kiss her, hard. My need for her so strong. I need to feel her, I need to touch her.

I know that we'll have all the time in the world together. But right now, being close to her, touching her skin, it feels like the most important thing in the world.

I need her. Now and forever.

Alex is my one place of safety, my one paradise.

My Elysium.

This chapter was originally posted as chapter 9.5, so there is some character progression between then and here, but nothing that's not obvious after you've finished the book.

Halloween
Fleur

Halloween = One of those holidays that somehow all online videogame worlds share even though only very few countries in our world celebrate it. It often comes with outfits, special items and... shapeshifting.

"Are you sure?" I turn around in front of the small mirror hanging on Alex' closet door. "I'm not..."

Alex steps behind me, looking over my shoulder, meeting my eyes in the mirror. "Yeah. Definitely sure."

I roll my eyes at her, but then turn around again, shaking my head. Today is the Halloween meet with the guild. We're all supposed to dress up and Alex and I may have had the worst idea yet.

"At least you have it easy." I look her way, and she checks herself out in the mirror too, then shrugs, grinning.

"Can't help it that mine is easier to pull off." She twirls around a little. She pulls up her knee and stretches out one of her arms, making a victory pose from DoE, and I look away, butterflies in my stomach.

For the last couple of days, we've worked hard to make these costumes. Not only are we going as our game characters, but we're going as genderswapped versions of our game characters.

This year, as one of the rare Halloween buffs in DoE, you would be randomly assigned one of the races for half an hour, even some cool non-playable races were in the mix. Somehow, as we were talking about that late at night, we got the idea that it would be cool to genderswap our characters. Especially since I originally mistook Alex for a guy because she plays a male character. So, sort of as a play on the buff but also on how we met.

We worked our brains and bodies to the limit. First to find references of the gear we'd want to wear, and then we actually had to put the gear together.

Luckily, I'm a caster, a healer. So even though I had to sew some clothes together, it wasn't too complicated, just time-consuming.

But then I had to make some pieces of foam and other stuff to make my shoulders wider and make me a little broader than I really am because the male version of my race is bulkier than the female version I normally play. It was very fun, especially when I kept trying things on. In one of the earlier creations my shoulder pads would slide to the front or the back, not exactly where you want shoulders to be.

Alex, on the other hand, had to make quite a few structural plate-like pieces that she would still be able to move around in.

Female tank gear isn't exactly the most practical, but we were able to find a gear set that was both not too complicated to make and would be wearable in the late October weather. Making it was fun. But to now see her wear it, that's a different type of feeling of fun.

I push at my shoulders, making sure they're in place. Then I pull on the shirt, trying to make myself look like a male dryad. While uncommon in actual Greek mythology, there seem to have been a handful of references to them actually existing. Anyway, DoE did choose to include them, which made our idea possible in the first place.

I'm mostly lucky that dryads are slim, not like the more mountain bound race that Alex plays. Some of the races, especially ones more connected to earth or mountains, are huge, and I don't think I'd have been able to pull that off.

Alex puts her hand on my shoulder. "You'll be fine. Really." She turns me to her, plucking at my hair a bit. We've pulled it up a little, shortening my hair to a more masculine style. "Just one more spray of hairspray and you're ready to go." She steps back and my eyes are drawn to her long legs.

She's wearing heels, which she doesn't do often, and with the fishnet tights and the short gladiator-type skirt, her legs look even longer than normal.

She turns to me, raising her eyebrows. "What?"

"Nothing." My cheeks heat up.

"Right." She steps closer, putting her hand over my face as she sprays. Then she steps back. "Looks good."

"Thanks." I take a deep breath, almost bursting out coughing from the lingering hairspray. "You need help with yours?"

"Yeah. I need to put my hair up, and then we have to put the final shoulder layer on, with the cape." She turns and I step closer, putting my hand on her waist. Alex leans into the touch, relaxing for a moment.

"You look great." I'm so close I can almost kiss her neck.

"Thank you." Alex' voice is a little lower than normal. Then she steps out of my reach and collects all her hair in one hand, pulling it out of the way. "Can you hold it like this, and then we need to put the cape and the shoulders on."

"Will do." I take her hair in my hand, keeping it up.

Alex wraps the cape around herself, attaching it to her top as I hold the back of it with my other hand to make it easier. This way I get a beautiful view of her slim neck. I have a thing for necks, at least Alex', and it doesn't help that it's one of her sensitive spots.

"Fleur." Alex sounds amused, though a little impatient.

"Yeah." I blink.

"Can you grab my shoulders, I think they're behind you." She laughs a little.

I look around and find the top set of the shoulders. They help the cape stay in place better, and they look cool. I guess the second reason is why they used it in the game anyway, but for us, it made making the cosplay easier by distributing the weight of the cape more evenly.

"Here." I lean the back of them on the back of Alex' shoulders and she attaches a couple of things before she moves it forward and closes it at the front.

I carefully let her hair down, smoothing it over the back. "There you go."

Alex grins as she turns to me. "Good. Ready to go!"

She grabs her sword and shield, also made in the last few days, and jumps up, doing another one of the in-game poses. Only, of course, she pokes the sword right into the ceiling and the tip breaks off... She looks a little flustered as she quickly assesses the damage.

"Shoot." She frowns.

I feel bad for her, but I can't help my laugh bubbling up. It looked pretty cool, until she hit the ceiling.

Alex eyes me, also smiling a little. "Figures." She lets out a shaky breath, holding the piece of the tip that broke off. "You know what. Never mind." She still looks a little troubled, but then puts the tip on her desk. She straightens her shoulders and then hands me my staff

As I take it from her she wraps her hand around mine for a moment, holding it.

Butterflies seem to try to jet out of my stomach, especially with the way Alex looks at me, but then she smiles and lets go.

"Time to leave, before we break even more of the cosplay." There is a laugh in her voice as she leaves her room.

WASD

Alex' mum drops us off at Cerise's house, promising to pick us up at the end of the night and urging us to not do too many stupid things. But even as she says it, I can see that she doesn't really believe we're capable of that. And, with Alex' behaviour from earlier, I also don't think that we can promise her anything.

We're both laughing as Alex' mum drives off. Of course, right after Alex' mum gave us the warning, Alex promptly dropped her shield and I nearly poked Alex' eye out with my staff as I was trying to pick it up. Yeah, we may be a slight danger to ourselves and others when we're excited. Only a *slight* danger, though.

The door opens and Cerise stands in the doorway, dressed in some cat-like outfit, and her eyes go wide as she looks at the both of us.

"Wow." She comes over, walking around us for a moment. "That is..."

Troy follows her moments after. "I thought you two would never make it."

"Slight issues with equipment," Alex grumbles as she looks my way and I burst out laughing again. Pretty sure we did that ourselves.

"Right." Troy eyes me, raising his eyebrows. "And I do hope she didn't break you?"

"No." I grin, following Cerise and Troy into the house. "Not yet."

"*Oi.*" Alex sounds a little offended behind me. "Don't jinx it."

"So, you're what...?" Cerise turns to us as she walks through the kitchen to the garage at the back. "Healer and tank, but..."

"I'm BeauFleur." I drop my voice a little.

"And I'm... still AlexTheDestroyer." Alex laughs. "Just female."

"I can definitely see that." Aaron comes over from the back. "I didn't think you'd actually do it."

"What? Why not?" Alex shrugs.

"Because it's so much work?" He looks her over, and then me. "Looks really cool though."

"You should thank Fleur for that. She's the one who helped with the sewing. I just did the plated stuff and the *fitting.*" Alex turns to me, sliding her fingers over my hand and I entwine our hands.

"Thanks. It was fun to do." I feel my cheeks heat up.

"Okay. Time to get to the rest of the party." Troy starts walking to the back, where I can hear the sounds of more people.

We follow them and it almost feels like there are more people now than there were at the meet this summer. But that may just be a feeling, since everyone is dressed up in a huge range of different outfits and that makes it a little crowded.

"You want something to drink?" Alex pulls me to a table at the side. The table is filled with cups with weirdly coloured drinks and for a moment I'm worried that this night may end up a little more chaotic than planned.

Though, luckily, I see plates in front of all the cups and one of them says 'water'. So, maybe not that bad.

W A S D

I log back out of my account, my heart still going a mile an hour.

Cerise has set up a couple of big screens and some computers and we've been taking turns participating in Halloween themed PVP content. The instances aren't that long, so we log in a few people at a time and play a round. This has been going on all evening and my team just had our fourth win.

I stretch as I look around. I need a drink, and maybe a few moments of calm, because my brain is doing the zoning-out thing that I know happens right before I crash from exhaustion.

I make my way over to the table with drinks and candy and grab a couple of sour candies before taking a cup with green water. Then I turn, watching Alex kick butt in the instance. She's so focused, so set on winning, and I like watching her like that.

That intensity, that focus, it's so different from the bubbly and a little bit clumsy Alex who I normally see. When she's focused on the game like that, she's a totally different person.

"She's gonna win, isn't she?" Troy steps next to me.

"Yeah. They're gonna win, and their score will overtake ours." I sigh. We've been keeping score of each team's wins and points in the game, and right now, my team is on top, but just looking at this round. I know that Alex' team are going to score higher and overtake us. As we're watching, Alex kills two enemy players. "They're gonna win."

It only takes a couple more minutes before their round is over and as Alex gets out of her chair, Cerise writes the points on the board and my prediction came true. Her team is on top now.

Alex grins as she comes over. "That was a good round."

"They should have just let me in the team with you," Troy grumbles.

"That wouldn't have been fun." Alex winks. "Putting me, Fleur, you and Cerise, all on the same team. It wouldn't have been fair on the others." Alex reaches out, taking my hand. "I need some fresh air."

I nod, following her as she makes her way to one of the doors at the side. When we get to the door she wraps her cape around her, pulling it tight before she gets through the door. I shiver as I step through the door too, closing it behind us. It's cold outside, but the fresh air is nice.

"Can I have a sip?" Alex looks at the cup I'm holding.

"Sure." I hand her the cup as I step a little closer, away from the door but nearer to Alex' warmth.

Alex takes a few gulps from the cup, then lowers it and looks at me. "You cold?"

I nod a little, wrapping my arms around me.

"Come here." She holds her cape open.

"But I'm cold already, that's gonna be cold for you." I don't step in just yet.

"It will be warmer in a bit, the two of us under here together." She moves the cape more, stepping closer and wrapping it around me.

I slide my arms around her waist, her body heat is nice and the cape keeps us both warm at the same time.

"You know…" Alex' voice is low, close to my ear. "When I wear heels, I'm at the perfect height."

"The perfect height for what?" I look up at her, but as I move, I realise that her lips are very close. Her breath now on my cheek.

Alex puts one hand under my chin, turning me more, her eyes now on my lips. She comes closer, her dark red lips tempting as they near mine. "The perfect height for a kiss."

Emmy Engberts has been writing for years, she writes under different pen names, depending on the topic and type of story. As Rosa Swann, she was involved in the surge of the mpreg sub-genre in gay romance, and most of her work under that pen name are still gay romance. As Skylar Heart she publishes straight romance with characters who deal with difficult subjects, but still end up finding someone to love.

As Emmy, she writes Young Adult fiction with diverse characters who won't apologise for being different and who celebrate their differences.

She is Dutch and has lived in the Netherlands for almost all her life apart from when she studied English and Creative Writing at the University of Chichester in England. This really inspired her to make writing her career and has been working towards that goal ever since.

Emmy currently lives in Groningen with her partner and two cats, and if she's not writing, you can find her playing videogames or working on one of her many creative projects.

www.emmyengberts.com